The Trampling of the Lilies

Rafael Sabatini

The Trampling of the Lilies

The present edition is a reproduction of previous publication of this classic work. Minor typographical errors may have been corrected without note; however, for an authentic reading experience the spelling, punctuation, and capitalization have been retained from the original text.

ISBN: 978-1-63637-530-4

CONTENTS

PART I

THE OLD RULE

These are they
Who ride on the court gale, control its tides;

* * *

Whose frown abases and whose smile exalts.
They shine like any rainbow—and, perchance,
Their colours are as transient.

Old Play

CHAPTER I

MONSIEUR THE SECRETARY

It was spring at Bellecour—the spring of 1789, a short three months before the fall of the Bastille came to give the nobles pause, and make them realise that these new philosophies, which so long they have derided, were by no means the idle vapours they had deemed them.

By the brook, plashing its glittering course through the park of Bellecour, wandered La Boulaye, his long, lean, figure clad with a sombreness that was out of harmony in that sunlit, vernal landscape. But the sad-hued coat belied that morning a heart that sang within his breast as joyously as any linnet of the woods through which he strayed. That he was garbed in black was but the outward indication of his clerkly office, for he was secretary to the most noble the Marquis de Fresnoy de Bellecour, and so clothed in the livery of the ink by which he lived. His face was pale and lean and thoughtful, but within his great, intelligent eyes there shone a light of new-born happiness. Under his arm he carried a volume of the new philosophies which Rousseau had lately given to the world, and which was contributing so vastly to the mighty change that was impending. But within his soul there dwelt in that hour no such musty subject as the metaphysical dreams of old Rousseau. His mood inclined little to the "Discourses upon the Origin of Inequality" which his elbow hugged to his side. Rather was it a mood of song and joy and things of light, and his mind was running on a string of rhymes which mentally he offered up to his divinity. A high-born lady was she, daughter to his lordly employer, the most noble Marquis of Bellecour. And he a secretary, a clerk! Aye, but a clerk with a great soul, a secretary with a great belief in the things to come, which in that musty tome beneath his arm were dimly prophesied.

And as he roamed beside the brook, his feet treading the elastic, velvety turf, and crushing heedlessly late primrose and stray violet, his blood quickened by the soft spring breeze, fragrant with hawthorn and the smell of the moist brown earth, La Boulaye's happiness gathered strength from the joy that on that day of spring seemed to invest all Nature. An old-world song stole from his firm lips-at first timidly, like a thing abashed in new surroundings, then in bolder tones that echoed faintly through the trees

"Si le roi m'avait donne
Paris, sa grande ville,
Et qui'il me fallut quitter
L'amour de ma mie,
Je dirais au roi Louis
Reprenez votre Paris.
J'aime mieux ma mie, O gai!
J'aime mieux ma mie!"

How mercurial a thing is a lover's heart! Here was one whose habits were of solemnity and gloomy thought turned, so joyous that he could sing aloud, alone in the midst of sunny Nature, for no better reason than that Suzanne de Bellecour had yesternight smiled as—for some two minutes by the clock—she had stood speaking with him.

"Presumptuous that I am," said he to the rivulet, to contradict himself the next moment. "But no; the times are changing. Soon we shall be equals all, as the good God made us, and—"

He paused, and smiled pensively. And as again the memory of her yesternight's kindness rose before him, his smile broadened; it became a laugh that went ringing down the glade, scaring a noisy thrush into silence and sending it flying in affright across the scintillant waters of the brook. Then that hearty laugh broke sharply off, as, behind him, the sweetest voice in all the world demanded the reason of this mad-sounding mirth.

La Boulaye's breath seemed in that instant to forsake him and he grew paler than Nature and the writer's desk had fashioned him. Awkwardly he turned and made her a deep bow.

"Mademoiselle! You—you see that you surprised me!" he faltered, like a fool. For how should he, whose only comrades had been books, have learnt to bear himself in the company of a woman, particularly when she belonged to the ranks of those whom—despite Rousseau and his other dear philosophers—he had been for years in the habit of accounting his betters?

"Why, then, I am glad, Monsieur, that I surprised you in so gay a humour—for, my faith, it is a rare enough thing."

"True, lady," said he foolishly, yet politely agreeing with her, "it is a rare thing." And he sighed—"Helas!"

At that the laughter leapt from her young lips, and turned him hot and cold as he stood awkwardly before her.

"I see that we shall have you sad at the thought of how rare is happiness, you that but a moment back were—or so it seemed—so joyous. Or is it that my coming has overcast the sky of your good humour?" she demanded archly.

3

He blushed like a school-girl, and strenuously protested that it was not so. In his haste he fell headlong into the sin of hastiness—as was but natural—and said perhaps too much.

"Your coming, Mademoiselle?" he echoed. "Nay but even had I been sad, your coming must have dispelled my melancholy as the coming of the sun dispels the mist upon the mountains."

"A poet?" She mocked him playfully, with a toss of black curls and a distracting glance of eyes blue as the heavens above them. "A poet, Monsieur, and I never suspected it, for all that I held you a great scholar. My father says you are."

"Are we not all poets at some season of our lives?" quoth he, for growing accustomed to her presence—ravished by it, indeed—his courage was returning fast and urging him beyond the limits of discretion.

"And in what season may this rhyming fancy touch us?" she asked. "Enlighten me, Monsieur."

He smiled, responsive to her merry mood, and his courage ever swelling under the suasion of it, he answered her in a fearless, daring fashion that was oddly unlike his wont. But then, he was that day a man transformed.

"It comes, Mademoiselle, upon some spring morning such as this—for is not spring the mating season, and have not poets sung of it, inspired and conquered by it? It comes in the April of life, when in our hearts we bear the first fragrant bud of what shall anon blossom into a glorious summer bloom red as is Love's livery and perfumed beyond all else that God has set on earth for man's delight and thankfulness."

The intensity with which he spoke, and the essence of the speech itself, left her a moment dumb with wonder and with an incomprehensible consternation, born of some intuition not yet understood.

"And so, Monsieur, the Secretary," said she at last, a nervous laugh quivering in her first words, "from all this wondrous verbiage I am to take it that you love?"

"Aye, that I love, dear lady," he cried, his eyes so intent upon her that her glance grew timid and fell before them. And then, a second later, she could have screamed aloud in apprehension, for the book of Jean Jacques Rousseau lay tumbled in the grass where he had flung it, even as he flung himself upon his knees before her. "You may take it indeed that I love—that I love you, Mademoiselle."

The audacious words being spoken, his courage oozed away and anti-climax, followed. He paled and trembled, yet he knelt on until she should bid him rise, and furtively he watched her face. He

4

saw it darken; he saw the brows knit; he noted the quickening breath, and in all these signs he read his doom before she uttered it.

"Monsieur, monsieur," she answered him, and sad was her tone, "to what lengths do you urge this springtime folly? Have you forgotten so your station—yes, and mine—that because I talk with you and laugh with you, and am kind to you, you must presume to speak to me in this fashion? What answer shall I make you, Monsieur—for I am not so cruel that I can answer you as you deserve."

An odd thing indeed was La Boulaye's courage. An instant ago he had felt a very coward, and had quivered, appalled by the audacity of his own words. Now that she assailed him thus, and taxed him with that same audacity, the blood of anger rushed to his face—anger of the quality that has its source in shame. In a second he was on his feet before her, towering to the full of his lean height. The words came from him in a hot stream, which for reckless passion by far outvied his erstwhile amatory address.

"My station?" he cried, throwing wide his arms. "What fault lies in my station? I am a secretary, a scholar, and so, by academic right, a gentleman. Nay, Mademoiselle, never laugh; do not mock me yet. In what do you find me less a man than any of the vapid caperers that fill your father's salon? Is not my shape as good? Are not my arms as strong, my hands as deft, my wits as keen, and my soul as true? Aye," he pursued with another wild wave of his long arms, "my attributes have all these virtues, and yet you scorn me— you scorn me because of my station, so you say!"

How she had angered him! All the pent-up gall of years against the supercilia of the class from which she sprang surged in that moment to his lips. He bethought him now of the thousand humiliations his proud spirit had suffered at their hands when he noted the disdain with which they addressed him, speaking to him— because he was compelled to carve his living with a quill—as though he were less than mire. It was not so much against her scorn of him that he voiced his bitter grievance, but against the entire noblesse of France, which denied him the right to carry a high head because he had not been born of Madame la Duchesse, Madame la Marquise, or Madame la Comtesse. All the great thoughts of a wondrous transformation, which had been sown in him by the revolutionary philosophers he had devoured with such appreciation, welled up now, and such scraps of that infinity of thought as could find utterance he cast before the woman who had scorned him for his station. Presumptuous he had accounted himself—but only until she had found him so. By that the presumption, it seemed, had been lifted from him, and he held that what he had said to her of the love

5

he bore her was no more than by virtue of his manhood he had the right to say.

She drew back before him, and shrank in some measure of fear, for he looked very fierce. Moreover, he had said things which professed him a revolutionist, and the revolutionists, whilst being a class which she had been taught to despise and scorn, dealt, she knew, in a violence which it might be ill to excite.

"Monsieur," she faltered, and with her hand she clutched at her riding-habit of green velvet, as if preparing to depart, "you are not yourself. I am beyond measure desolated that you should have so spoken to me. We have been good friends, M. La Boulaye. Let us forget this scene. Shall we?" Her tones grew seductively conciliatory.

La Boulaye half turned from her, and his smouldering eye fell upon "The Discourses" lying on the grass. He stooped and picked up the volume. The act might have seemed symbolical. For a moment he had cast aside his creed to woo a woman, and now that she had denied him he returned to Rousseau, and gathered up the tome almost in penitence at his momentary defection.

"I am quite myself, Mademoiselle," he answered quietly. His cheeks were flushed, but beyond that, his excitement seemed to have withered. "It is you who yesternight, for one brief moment and again to-day—were not yourself, and to that you owe it that I have spoken to you as I have done."

Between these two it would seem as the humour of the one waned, that of the other waxed. Her glance kindled anew at his last words.

"I?" she echoed. "I was not myself? What are you saying, Monsieur the Secretary?"

"Last night, and again just now, you were so kind, you—you smiled so sweetly—"

"Mon Dieu!" she exclaimed, angrily interrupting him. "See what you are for all your high-sounding vaunts of yourself and your attributes! A woman may not smile upon you, may not say one kind word to you, but you must imagine you have made a conquest. Ma foi, you and yours do not deserve to be treated as anything but vassals. When we show you a kindness, see how you abuse it. We extend to you our little finger and you instantly lay claim to the whole arm. Because last night I permitted myself to exchange a jest with you, because I chance to be kind to you again to-day, you repay me with insults!"

"Stop!" he cried, rousing himself once more. "That is too much to say, Mademoiselle. To tell a woman that you love her is never to insult her. To be loved is never to be slighted. Upon the meanest of His creatures it is enjoined to love the same God whom the King loves, and there is no insult to God in professing love for Him. Would you make a woman more than that?"

"Monsieur, you put questions I have no mind to answer; you suggest a discussion I have no inclination to pursue. For you and me let it suffice that I account myself affronted by your words, your tone, and your manner. You drive me to say these things; by your insistence you compel me to be harsh. We will end this matter here and now, Monsieur, and I will ask you to understand that I never wish it reopened, else shall I be forced to seek protection at the hands of my father or my brother."

"You may seek it now, Suzanne," quoth a voice from the thicket at her back, a voice which came to startle both of them though in different ways. Before they had recovered from their surprise the Marquis de Bellecour stood before them. He was a tall man of some fifty years of age, but so powerful of frame and so scrupulous in dress that he might have conveyed an impression of more youth. His face, though handsome in a high-bred way, was puffed and of an unhealthy yellow. But the eyes were as keen as the mouth was voluptuous, and in his carefully dressed black hair there were few strands of grey.

He came slowly forward, and his lowering glance wandered from his daughter to his secretary in inquiry. At last—

"Well?" he demanded. "What is the matter?"

"It is nothing, Monsieur," his daughter answered him. "A trifling affair 'twixt M. la Boulaye and me, with which I will not trouble you."

"It is not nothing, my lord," cried La Boulaye, his voice vibrating oddly. "It is that I love your daughter and that I have told her of it." He was in a very daring mood that morning.

The Marquis glanced at him in dull amazement. Then a flush crept into his sallow cheeks and mounted to his brow. An inarticulate grunt came from his thick lips.

"Canaille!" he exclaimed, through set teeth. "Can you have presumed so far?"

He carried a riding-switch, and he seemed to grasp it now in a manner peculiarly menacing. But La Boulaye was nothing daunted. Lost he already accounted himself, and on the strength of the logic that if a man must hang, a sheep as well as a lamb may be the cause of it, he took what chances the time afforded him to pile up his debt.

"There is neither insolence nor presumption in what I have done," he answered, giving back the Marquis look for look and scowl for scowl. "You deem it so because I am the secretary to the Marquis de Bellecour and she is the daughter of that same Marquis. But these are no more than the fortuitous circumstances in which

7

we chance to find ourselves. That she is a woman must take rank before the fact that she is your daughter, and that I am a man must take rank before the fact that I am your secretary. Not, then, as your secretary speaking to your daughter have I told this lady that I love her, but as a man speaking to a woman. To utter that should be—nay, is—the right of every man; to hear it should be honouring to every woman worthy of the name. In a primitive condition—"

"A thousand devils!" blazed the Marquis, unable longer to contain himself. "Am I to have my ears offended by this braying? Miserable scum, you shall be taught what is due to your betters."

His whip cracked suddenly, and the lash leapt serpentlike into the air, to descend and coil itself about La Boulaye's head and face. A cry broke from the young man, as much of pain as of surprise, and as the lash was drawn back, he clapped his hands to his seared face. But again he felt it, cutting him now across the hand with which he had masked himself. With a maddened roar he sprang upon his aggressor. In height he was the equal of the Marquis, but in weight he seemed to be scarce more than the half of his opponent's. Yet a nervous strength dwelt unsuspected in those lean arms and steely wrists.

Mademoiselle stood by looking on, with parted lips and eyes that were intent and anxious. She saw that figure, spare and lithe as a greyhound, leap suddenly upon her father, and the next instant the whip was in the secretary's hands, and he sprang back from the nobleman, who stood white and quivering with rage, and perhaps, too, with some dismay.

"That I do not break it across your back, M. le Marquis, said the young man," as he snapped the whip on his knee, "you may thank your years." With that he flung the two pieces wide into the sunlit waters of the brook. "But I will have satisfaction, Monsieur. I will take payment for this." And he pointed to the weal that disfigured his face.

"Satisfaction?" roared the Marquis, hoarse in his passion. "Would you demand satisfaction of me, animal?"

"No," answered the young man, with a wry smile. "Your years again protect you. But you have a son, and if by to-morrow it should come to pass that you have a son no more, you may account yourself, through this"—and again he pointed to the weal—"his murderer."

"Do you mean that you would seek to cross swords with the Vicomte?" gasped the nobleman, in an unbelief so great that it gained the ascendency over his anger.

"That is what I mean, Monsieur. In practice he has often done so. He shall do so for once in actual earnest."

8

"Fool!" was the contemptuous answer, more coldly delivered now, for the Marquis was getting himself in hand. "If you come near Bellecour again, if you are so much as found within the grounds of the park, I'll have you beaten to death by my grooms for your presumption. Keep you the memory of that promise in mind, Sir Secretary, and let it warn you to avoid Bellecour, as you would a plague-house. Come, Suzanne," he said, turning abruptly to his daughter, "Enough of this delightful morning have we already wasted on this canaille."

With that he offered her his wrist, and so, without so much as another glance at La Boulaye, she took her departure.

The secretary remained where they had left him, pale of face—saving the fortuitous crimson mark which the whip had cut—and very sick at heart. The heat of the moment being spent, he had leisure to contemplate his plight. A scorned lover, a beaten man, a dismissed secretary! He looked sorrowfully upon his volume of "The Discourses," and for the first time a doubt crossed his mind touching the wisdom of old Jean Jacques. Was there would there ever be any remedy for such a condition of things as now prevailed?

Already the trees had hidden the Marquis and his daughter from La Boulaye's sight. The young revolutionist felt weary and lonely—dear God, how lonely! neither kith nor kin had he, and of late all the interest of his life—saving always that absorbed by Jean Jacques—had lain in watching Suzanne de Bellecour, and in loving her silently and distantly. Now that little crumb of comfort was to be his no more, he was to go away from Bellecour, away from the sight of her for all time. And he loved her, loved her, loved her!

He tossed his arms to Heaven with a great sigh that was a sob almost, then he passed his hands over his face, and as they came in contact with the swollen ridge that scored it, love faded from his mind, and vindictiveness came to fill its room.

"But for this," he cried aloud. "I shall take payment—aye, as there is a God!"

Then turning, and with "The Discourses" held tightly to his side, he moved slowly away, following the course of the gleaming waters.

9

CHAPTER II

LORDS OF LIFE AND DEATH

One friend did La Boulaye count in the village of Bellecour. This was old Duhamel, the schoolmaster, an eccentric pedant and a fellow-worshipper of the immortal Jean Jacques. It was to him that La Boulaye now repaired intent upon seeking counsel touching a future that wore that morning a singularly gloomy outlook.

He found Duhamel's door open, and he stepped across the threshold into the chief room of the house. But there he paused, and hesitated. The chamber was crowded with people in holiday attire, and the centre of attraction was a well-set-up peasant with a happy, sun-tanned face, whose golden locks were covered by a huge round hat decked with a score of gaily-coloured ribbons.

At sight of him La Boulaye remembered that it was Charlot's wedding-day. Popular amongst the women by virtue of his comeliness, and respected by the men by virtue of his strength, Charlot Tardivet was a general favourite of the countryside, and here, in the room of old Duhamel, the schoolmaster, was half the village gathered to do him honour upon his wedding morn. It was like Duhamel, who, in fatherliness towards the villagers, went near out-rivalling M. le Cure, to throw open his house for the assembling of Charlot's friends, and La Boulaye was touched by this fresh sign of kindliness from a man whose good heart he had not lacked occasion to observe and appreciate. But it came to the secretary that there was no place for him in this happy assemblage. His advent would, probably, but serve to cast a gloom upon them, considering the conditions under which he came, with the signs of violence upon his face to remind them of the lords of life and death who dwelt at the Chateau up yonder. And such a reminder must fall upon them as does the reminder of some overhanging evil clutch suddenly at our hearts in happy moments of forgetfulness. To let them be happy that day, to leave their feasts free of a death's head, La Boulaye would have withdrawn had he not already been too late. Duhamel had espied him, and the little, wizened old man came hurrying forward, his horn-rimmed spectacles perched on the very end of his nose, his keen little eyes beaming with delight and welcome.

"Ah, Caron, you are very choicely come," he cried, holding out both hands to La Boulaye. "You shall embrace our happy Hercules yonder, and wish him joy of the wedded life he has the audacity to exploit." Then, as he espied the crimson ridge across the secretary's countenance, "Mon Dieu!" he exclaimed, "what have you done to yourself, Caron?"

"Pish! It is nothing," answered La Boulaye hurriedly, and would have had the subject dismissed, but that one of the onlooking peasants swore by the memory of some long-dead saint that it was the cut of a whip. Duhamel's eyes kindled and his parchment-like skin was puckered into a hundred evil wrinkles.

"Who did it, Caron?" he demanded.

"Since you insist, old master," answered the secretary, still endeavouring to make light of it, "learn that is the lord Marquis's signature to his order of my dismissal from his service."

"The dog!" ejaculated the school-master.

"Sh! let it be. Perhaps I braved him overmuch. I will tell you of it when these good folks have gone. Do not let us cast a gloom over their happiness, old master. And now to embrace this good Charlot."

Though inwardly burning with curiosity and boiling with indignation, Duhamel permitted himself to be guided by La Boulaye, and for the moment allowed the matter to rest. La Boulaye himself laughingly set aside the many questions with which they pressed him. He drank the health of the bride-elect—who was not yet of the party—and he pledged the happiness of the pair. He embraced Charlot, and even went so far as to urge upon him, out of his own scanty store, a louis d'or with which to buy Marie a trinket in memory of him.

Then presently came one with the announcement that M. le Cure was waiting, and in answer to that reminder that there was a ceremony to be gone through, Charlot and his friends flung out of the house in joyous confusion, and went their way with laughter and jest to the little church of St. Ildefonse.

"We will follow presently—M. la Boulaye and I—Charlot," Duhamel had said, as the sturdy bridegroom was departing. "We shall be there to shake Madame by the hand and wish her joy of you."

When at last they were alone in the schoolmaster's room, the old man turned to La Boulaye, the very embodiment of a note of interrogation. The secretary told him all that had passed. He reddened slightly when it came to speaking of his love for Mlle. de Bellecour, but he realised that if he would have guidance he must withhold nothing from his friend.

Duhamel's face grew dark as the young man spoke, and his eyes became sad and very thoughtful.

"Alas!" he sighed, when La Boulaye had ended. "What shall I say to you, my friend? The time is not yet for such as we—you and

11

I—to speak of love for a daughter of the Seigneurie. It is coming, I doubt it not. All things have their climax, and France is tending swiftly to the climax of her serfdom. Very soon we shall have the crisis, this fire that is already smouldering, will leap into a great blaze, that shall lick the old regime as completely from the face of history as though it had never been. A new condition of things will spring up, of that I am convinced. Does not history afford us many instances? And what is history but the repetition of events under similar circumstances with different peoples. It will come in France, and it will come soon, for it is very direly needed."

"I know, I know, old master," broke in La Boulaye; "but how shall all this help me? For all that I have the welfare of France at heart, it weighs little with me at the moment by comparison with my own affairs. What am I to do, Duhamel? How am I to take payment for this?" And he pressed his finger to his seared cheek.

"Wait," said the old man impressively. "That is the moral you might have drawn from what I have said. Be patient. I promise you your patience shall not be overtaxed. To-day they say that you presume; that you are not one of them—although, by my soul, you have as good an air as any nobleman in France." And he eyed the lean height of the secretary with a glance of such pride as a father might take in a well-grown son.

Elegant of figure, La Boulaye was no less elegant in dress, for all that, from head to foot—saving the silver buckles on his shoes and the unpretentious lace at throat and wrists—he was dressed in the black that his office demanded. His countenance, too, though cast in a mould of thoughtfulness that bordered on the melancholy, bore a lofty stamp that might have passed for birth and breeding, and this was enhanced by the careful dressing of his black unpowdered hair, gathered into a club by a broad ribbon of black silk.

"But what shall waiting avail me?" cried the young man, with some impatience. "What am I to do in the meantime?"

"Go to Amiens," said the other. "You have learning, you have eloquence, you have a presence and an excellent address. For success no better attributes could be yours." He approached the secretary, and instinctively lowered his voice. "We have a little club there—a sort of succursal to the Jacobins. We are numerous, but we have no very shining member yet. Come with me, and I will nominate you. Beginning thus, I promise you that you shall presently become a man of prominence in Picardy. Anon we may send you to Paris to represent us in the States-General. Then, when the change comes, who shall say to what heights it may not be yours to leap?"

12

"I will think of it," answered La Boulaye cordially, "and not a doubt of it but that I will come. I did not know that you had gone so far—"

"Sh! You know now. Let that suffice. It is not good to talk of these things just yet."

"But in the meantime," La Boulaye persisted, "what of this?" And again he pointed to his cheek.

"Why, let it heal, boy."

"I promised the Marquis that I would demand satisfaction of his son, and I am tempted to do so and risk the consequences."

"I am afraid the consequences will be the only satisfaction that you will get. In fact, they will be anticipations rather than consequences, for they'll never let you near the boy."

"I know not that," he answered. "The lad is more generous than his sire, and if I were to send him word that I have been affronted, he might consent to meet me. For the rest, I could kill him blindfolded," he added, with a shrug.

"Bloodthirsty animal!" rejoined Duhamel. "Unnatural tutor! Do you forget that you were the boy's preceptor?"

With that Duhamel carried the argument into new fields, and showed La Boulaye that to avenge upon the young Vicomte the insults received at the hands of the old Marquis was hardly a worthy method of taking vengeance. At last he won him to his way, and it was settled that on the morrow La Boulaye should journey with him to Amiens.

"But, Caron, we are forgetting our friend Charlot and his bride," he broke off suddenly. "Come, boy; the ceremony will be at an end by this."

He took La Boulaye by the arm, and led him out and down the street to the open space opposite St. Ildefonse. The wedding-party was streaming out through the door of the little church into the warm sunshine of that April morning. In the churchyard they formed into a procession of happy be-ribboned and nosegayed men and women—the young preceding, the old following, the bridal couple. Two by two they came, and the air rang with their laughter and joyous chatter. Then another sound arose, and if the secretary and the pedagogue could have guessed of what that beating of hoofs was to be the prelude, they had scarce smiled so easily as they watched the approaching cortege.

From a side street there now emerged a gaily apparelled cavalcade. At its head rode the Marquis de Bellecour, the Vicomte, and a half-dozen other gentlemen, followed by, perhaps, a dozen lacqueys. It was a hunting party that was making its way across the village to the open country beyond. The bridal procession crossing

13

their path caused them to draw rein, and to wait until it should have passed—which argued a very condescending humour, for it would not have been out of keeping with their habits to have ridden headlong through it. Their presence cast a restraint upon the peasants. The jests were silenced, the laughter hushed, and like a flight of pigeons under the eye of the hawk, they scurried past the Seigneurie, and some of them prayed God that they might be suffered to pass indeed.

Bellecour eyed them in cold disdain, until presently Charlot and his bride were abreast of him. Then his eye seemed to take life and his sallow face to kindle into expression. He leant lightly from the saddle.

"Stay!" he commanded coldly, and as they came to a halt, daring not to disobey him—"approach, girl," he added.

Charlot's brows grew black. He looked up at the Marquis, but if his glance was sullen and threatening, it was also not free from fear. Marie obeyed, with eyes downcast and a heightened colour. If she conjectured at all why they had been stopped, it was but to conclude that M. le Marquis was about to offer her some mark of appreciation. Uneasiness, in her dear innocence, she knew none.

"What is your name, child?" inquired the Marquis more gently.

"It was Marie Michelin, Monseigneur," she made answer timidly. "But it has just been changed to Marie Tardivet."

"You have just been wed, eh?"

"We are on our way from church, Monseigneur."

"C'est ca," he murmured, as if to himself, and his eyes taking such stock of her as made Charlot burn to tear him from his horse. Then, in a kindly, fatherly voice, he added: "My felicitations, Marie; may you be a happy wife and a happier mother."

"Merci, Monseigneur," she murmured, with crimson cheeks, whilst Charlot breathed once more, and from his heart gave thanks to Heaven, believing the interview at an end. But he went too fast.

"Do you know, Marie, that you are a very comely child?" quoth the Marquis, in tones which made the bridegroom's blood run cold.

Some in that noble company nudged one another, and one there was who burst into a loud guffaw.

"Charlot has often told me so," she laughed, all unsuspicious.

The Marquis moved on his horse that he might bend lower. With his forefinger he uptilted her chin, and now, as she met his glance thus at close quarters, an unaccountable fear took possession of her, and the colour died out of her plump cheeks.

"Yes," said Bellecour, with a smile, "this Tardivet has good taste. My congratulations, to him. We must find you a wedding gift, little woman," he continued more briskly. "It is an ancient and honoured custom that is falling somewhat into neglect. Go up to the Chateau with Blaise and Jean there. This good Tardivet must curb his impatience until to-morrow."

He turned in his saddle, and beckoning the two servants he had named, he bade Marie to mount behind Blaise.

She drew back now, her cheeks white as those of the dead. With a wild terror in her eyes she turned to Charlot, who stood the very picture of anguish and impotent rage. In the cortege, where but a few moments ago all had been laughter, a sob or two sounded now from some of the women.

"By my faith," laughed Bellecour contemptuously eyeing their dejection, "you have more the air of a burial than a bridal party."

"Mercy my lord!" cried the agonised voice of Charlot, as, distraught with grief, he flung himself before the Marquis.

"Who seeks to harm you, fool?" was Bellecour's half-derisive rejoinder.

"Do not take her from me, my lord," the young man pleaded piteously.

"She shall return to-morrow, booby," answered the noble. "Out of the way!"

But Charlot was obstinate. The Marquis might be claiming no more than by ancient law was the due of the Seigneur, but Charlot was by no means minded to submit in craven acquiescence to that brutal, barbarous law.

"My lord," he cried, "you shall not take her. She is my wife. She belongs to me. You shall not take her!"

He caught hold of the Marquis's bridle with such a strength and angry will that the horse was forced to back before him.

"Insolent clod!" exclaimed Bellecour, with an angry laugh and a sharp, downward blow of the butt of his whip upon the peasant's head. Charlot's hand grew nerveless and released the bridle as he sank stunned to the ground. Bellecour touched his horse with the spur and rode over the prostrate fellow with no more concern than had he been a dog's carcase. "Blaise, see to the girl," he called over his shoulder, adding to his company: "Come, messieurs, we have wasted time enough."

Not a hand was raised to stay him, not a word of protest uttered, as the nobles rode by, laughing, and chatting among themselves, with the utmost unconcern of the tragedy that was being enacted.

Like a flock of frightened sheep the peasants stood huddled together and watched them go. In the same inaction—for all that not

15

a little grief was blent with the terror on their countenances—they stood by and allowed Blaise to lift the half-swooning girl to the withers of his horse. No reply had they to the coarse jest with which he and his fellow-servant rode off. But La Boulaye, who, from the point where he and Duhamel had halted, had observed the whole scene from its inception, turned now a livid face upon his companion.

"Shall such things be?" he cried passionately. "Merciful God! Are we men, Duhamel, and do we permit such things to take place?"

The old pedagogue shrugged his shoulders in despair. His face was heavily scored by sorrow.

"Helas!" he sighed. "Are they not masters of all that they may take? The Marquis goes no further than is by ancient law allowed his class. It is the law needs altering, my friend, and then the men will alter. Meanwhile, behold them—lords of life and death."

"Lords of hell are they!" blazed the young revolutionist. "That is where they belong, whence they are come, and whither they shall return. Poltroons!" he cried, shaking his fist at the group of cowed peasants that surrounded the prostrate Charlot "Sheep! Worthless clods! The nobles do well to despise you, for, by my faith, you invite nothing but contempt, you that will suffer rape and murder to be done under your eyes, and never do more than look scared encouragement upon your ravishers!"

"Blame not these poor wretches, Caron," sighed the old man. "They dare not raise a hand."

"Then, pardieu! here, at least, is one who does dare," he cried furiously, as from the breast pocket of his coat he drew a pistol.

Blaise, with the girl across the withers of his horse, was approaching them, followed by Jean.

"What would you do?" cried the old man fearfully, setting a restraining hand upon La Boulaye's sleeve. But Caron shook himself free.

"This," was all he answered, and simultaneously, he levelled his pistol and fired at Blaise.

Shot through the head, the servant collapsed forward; then, as the horse reared and started off at a gallop, he toppled sideways and fell. The girl went down with him and lay in the road whilst he was dragged along, his head bumping horribly on the stones as faster and faster went the frightened horse.

With a shout that may have been either anger or dismay Jean reined in his horse, and sat for a second hesitating whether to begin by recovering the girl, or avenging his comrade. But his doubts were solved for him by La Boulaye, who took a deliberate aim at him.

"Begone!" cried the secretary, "unless you prefer to go by the road I've sent your fellow." And being a discreet youth, Jean made off in silence by the street down which poor Blaise had been dragged.

"Carom" cried Duhamel, in a frenzy of apprehension. "I tremble for you, my son. Fly from Bellecour at once—now, this very instant. Go to my friends at Amiens; they will—"

But Caron had already left his side to repair to the spot where Marie was lying. The peasantry followed him, though leisurely, in their timid hesitation. They were asking themselves whether, even so remotely as by tending the girl, they dared participate in the violence La Boulaye had committed. That a swift vengeance would be the Seigneur's answer they were well assured, and a great fear possessed them that in that vengeance those of the Chateau might lack discrimination. Charlot was amongst them, and on his feet, but still too dazed to have a clear knowledge of the circumstances. Presently, however, his faculties awakening and taking in the situation, he staggered forward, and came lurching towards La Boulaye, who was assisting the frightened Marie to rise. With a great sob the girl flung herself into her husband's arms.

"Charlot, mon Charlot!" she cried, and added a moment later: "It was he—this brave gentleman—who rescued me."

"Monsieur," said Charlot, "I shall remember it to my dying day."

He would have said more, but the peasants, stirred by fear, now roused themselves and plucked at his coat.

"Get you gone, Charlot, Get you gone quickly," they advised him. "And if you are wise you will leave Bellecour without delay. It is not safe for you here."

"It is not safe for any of us," exclaimed one. "I have no mind to be caught when the Seigneur returns. There will be a vengeance. Ah Dieu! what a vengeance!"

The warning acted magically. There were hurried leave-takings, and then, like a parcel of scuttling rabbits, they made for their burrows to hide from the huntsman that would not be long in coming. And ere the last of them was out of sight there arose a stamping of hoofs and a chorus of angry voices. Down tine street thundered the Marquis's cavalcade, brought back by the servant who had escaped and who had ridden after them. Some anger there was—particularly in the heart of the Lord of Bellecour—but greater than their anger was their excitement at the prospect of a man-hunt, with which the chase on which they had been originally bent made but a poor comparison.

"There he is, Monseigneur" cried Jean, as he pointed to La Boulaye. "And yonder are the girl and her husband."

"Ah! The secretary again, eh?" laughed the nobleman, grimly, as he came nearer. "Ma foi, life must have grown wearisome to him. Secure the woman, Jean."

Caron stood before him, pale in his impotent rage, which was directed as much against the peasants who had fled as against the nobles who approached. Had these clods but stood there, and defended themselves and their manhood with sticks and stones and such weapons as came to their hands, they might have taken pride in being trampled beneath the hoofs of the Seigneurie. Thus, at least, might they have proved themselves men. But to fly thus—some fifty of them from the approach of less than a score—was to confess unworthiness of a better fate than that of which their seigneurs rendered themselves the instruments.

Himself he could do no more than the single shot in his pistol would allow. That much, however, he would do, and like him whose resources are reduced, and yet who desires to spend the little that he has to best advantage, he levelled the weapon boldly at the advancing Marquis, and pulled the trigger. But Bellecour was an old campaigner, and by an old campaigner's trick he saved himself at the last moment. At sight of that levelled barrel he pulled his horse suddenly on to its haunches, and received the charge in the animal's belly. With a shriek of pain the horse sought to recover its feet, then tumbled forward hurling the Marquis from the saddle. La Boulaye had an inspiration to fling himself upon the old roue and seek with his hands to kill him before they made an end of himself. But ere he could move to execute his design a horseman was almost on top of him. He received a stunning blow on the head. The daylight faded in his eyes, he felt a sensation of sinking, and a reverberating darkness engulfed him.

CHAPTER III

THE WORD OF BELLECOUR

When La Boulaye recovered consciousness he was lying on his back in the middle of the courtyard of the Chateau de Bellecour. From a great stone balcony above, a little group, of which Mademoiselle de Bellecour was the centre, observed the scene about the captive, who was being resuscitated that he might fittingly experience the Seigneur's vengeance.

She had returned from the morning's affair in the park with a conscience not altogether easy. To have stood by whilst her father had struck Caron, and moreover, to have done so without any sense of horror, or even of regret, was a matter in which she asked herself whether she had done well. Certainly La Boulaye had presumed unpardonably in speaking to her as he had spoken, and for his presumption it was fitting that he should be punished. Had she interfered she must have seemed to sympathise, and thus the lesson might have suffered in salutariness. And yet Caron La Boulaye was a man of most excellent exterior, and, when passion had roused him out of his restraint and awkwardness, of most ardent and eloquent address. The very sombreness that—be it from his mournful garments or from a mind of thoughtful habit—seemed to envelop him was but an additional note of poetry in a personality which struck her now as eminently poetical. In the seclusion of her own chamber, as she recalled the burning words and the fall of her father's whip upon the young man's pale face, she even permitted herself to sigh. Had he but been of her own station, he had been such a man as she would have taken pride in being wooed by. As it was—she halted there and laughed disdainfully, yet with never so faint a note of regret. It was absurd! She was Mademoiselle de Bellecour, and he her father's secretary; educated, if you will—aye, and beyond his station—but a vassal withal, and very humbly born. Yes, it was absurd, she told herself again: the eagle may not mate with the sparrow.

And when presently she had come from her chamber, she had been greeted with the story of a rebellion in the village, and an attempted assassination of her father. The ringleader, she was told, had been brought to the Chateau, and he was even then in the courtyard and about to be hanged by the Marquis. Curious to behold this unfortunate, she had stepped out on to the balcony where already an idle group had formed. Inexpressible had been her shock upon seeing him that lay below, his white face upturned to the heavens, his eyes closed.

"Is he dead?" she asked, when presently she had overcome her feelings.

"Not yet Mademoiselle," answered the graceful Chevalier de Jacquelin, toying with his solitaire. "Your father is bringing him to life that he may send him back to death."

And then she heard her father's voice behind her. The Marquis had stepped out on to the balcony to ascertain whether La Boulaye had yet regained consciousness.

"He seems to be even now recovering," said someone.

"Ah, you are there, Suzanne," cried Bellecour. "You see your friend the secretary there. He has chosen to present himself in a new role to-day. From being my servant, it seems that he would constitute himself my murderer."

However unfilial it might be, she could not stifle a certain sympathy for this young man. She imagined that his rebellion, whatever shape it had assumed, had been provoked by that weal upon his face; and it seemed to her then that he had been less than a man had he not attempted to exact some reparation for the hurt the whip had inflicted at once upon his body and his soul.

"But what is it that he has done, Monsieur?" she asked, seeking more than the scant information which so far she had received.

"Enough, at least, to justify my hanging him," answered Bellecour grimly. "He sought to withstand my authority; he incited the peasants of Bellecour to withstand it; he has killed Blaise, and he would have killed me but that I preferred to let him kill my horse."

"In what way did he seek to withstand your authority!" she persisted.

He stared at her, half surprised, half angry.

"What doers the manner of it signify?" he asked impatiently. "Is not the fact enough? Is it not enough that Blaise is dead, and that I have had a narrow escape, at his hands?"

"Insolent hound that he is!" put in Madame la Marquise—a fleshly lady monstrously coiffed. "If we allow such men as thus to live in France our days are numbered."

"They say that you are going to hang him," said Suzanne, heedless of her mother's words, and there was the faintest note of horror in her voice.

"They are mistaken. I am not."

"You are not?" cried the Marquise. "But what, then, do you intend to do?"

20

"To keep my word, madame," he answered her. "I promised that canaille that if he ever came within the grounds of Bellecour I would have him flogged to death. That is what I propose."

"Father," gasped Suzanne, in horror, a horror that was echoed by the other three or four ladies present. But the Marquise only laughed.

"He will be; richly served," she approved, with a sage nod of her pumpkin-like head-dress—"most richly served."

A great pity arose now in the heart of Mademoiselle, as her father went below that he might carry out his barbarous design. She was deaf to the dainty trifles which the most elegant Chevalier de Jacquelin was murmuring into her ear. She stood, a tall, queenly figure, at the balcony's parapet and watched the preparations that were being made.

She heard her father's harshly-voiced commands. She saw them literally tear the clothes from the unfortunate secretary's back, and lash him—naked to the waist—to the pump that stood by the horse-trough at the far end of the yard. His body was now hidden from her sight, but his head appeared surmounting the pillar of the pump, his chin seeming to rest upon its summit, and his face was towards her. At his side stood a powerful knave armed with a stout, leather-thonged whip.

"How many strokes, Monseigneur?" she heard the man inquire.

"How many?" echoed the Marquise. "Do I know how many it will take to make an end of him? Beat him to death, man. Allons! Set about it."

She saw the man uncoil his lash and step forward. In that instant Caron's eyes were raised, and they met hers across the intervening space. He smiled a valedictory smile that seemed to make her heart stand still. She and her mother were now the only women on the balcony. The others had made haste to withdraw as soon as La Boulaye had been pilloried. The Marquise remained because she seemed to find entertainment in the spectacle. Suzanne remained because horror rooted her to the spot—horror and a great pity for this unfortunate who had looked so strong and brave that morning, when he had had the audacity to tell her that he loved her.

The lash sang through the air, quivered, hummed, and cut with a sickening crackle into the young man's flesh.

The hideous sound roused her. She shuddered from head to foot, and turning she put her hands to her face and rushed within, followed by the Marquise's derisive laughter.

"Mon Dieu! It is horrible! Horrible!" she cried as she sank into the nearest chair, and clapped her hands to her ears. But she could not shut it out. Still she heard the humming of the whip and the cruel sound of the falling blows. Mechanically she counted them, unconsciously almost, and at twenty she heard them cease. Was it over? Was he dead, this poor unfortunate? Moved by a curiosity that was greater than her loathing, she rose and went to the threshold of the balcony.

"Is it ended?" she asked.

"Ended?" echoed Monsieur de Jacquelin, with a shrug. "It is scarce begun, it seems. The executioner is pausing for breath, that is all. The fellow has not uttered a sound. He is as obstinate as a mule."

"As enduring as a Spartan," more generously put in the Vicomte, her brother. "Look at him, Suzanne."

Almost involuntarily she obeyed, and moved forward a step that she might behold him. A face, deathly pale, she saw, which in the sunshine glistened with the sweat of agony that bedewed it; but the lips were tightly closed and the countenance grimly expressionless. Even as she looked she heard her father command the man to lay on anew. Then, as before, his eyes met hers; but this time no smile did she see investing them.

Again the whip cracked and fell. She drew back, but his glance seemed to haunt her even when she no longer saw his face. A sudden resolution moved her, and in a frenzy of anger and compassion she flung out of the room. A moment later she burst like a beautiful virago into the courtyard.

"Stop!" she commanded shrilly, causing both her father and the executioner to turn, and the latter pausing in his hideous work. But a glance from the Marquis bade him resume, and resume he did, as though there had been no interruption.

"What is this?" demanded Bellecour, half amused, half vexed, whilst a sudden new light leapt to the eyes of La Boulaye, which but a moment back had been so full of agony.

But Mademoiselle never paused to answer her father. Seeing the executioner proceeding, despite her call to cease, she sprang upon him, caught him by the arms and wrested the whip from hands that dared not resist her.

"Did I not bid you stop?" she blazed, her face white, her eyes on fire; and raising the whip she brought it down upon his head and shoulders, not once but half-a-dozen times in quick succession, until he fled, howling, to the other side of the horse trough for shelter. "It stings you, does it" she cried, whilst the Marquis, from angered that at first he had been, now burst into a laugh at her fury and at this turning of tables upon the executioner. She made shift to pursue the fellow to his place of refuge, but coming of a sudden

22

upon the ghastly sight presented by La Boulaye's lacerated back, she drew back in horror. Then, mastering herself—for girl though she was, her courage was of a high order—she turned to her father.

"Give this man to me, Monsieur," she begged.

"To you!" he exclaimed. "What will you do with him?"

"I will see that you are rid of him," she promised. "What more can you desire? You have tortured him enough."

"Maybe. But am I to blame that he dies so hard?"

She answered him with renewed insistence, and unexpectedly she received an ally in M. des Cadoux—an elderly gentleman who had been observing the flogging with disapproval, and who had followed her into the courtyard.

"He is too brave a man to die like this, Bellecour," put in the newcomer. "I doubt if he can survive the punishment he has already received. Yet I would ask you, in the name of courage, to give him the slender chance he may have."

"I promised him he should be flogged to death—" began the Marquis, when Des Cadoux and Mademoiselle jointly interrupted him to renew their intercessions.

"But, sangdieu," the Marquis protested "you seem to forget that he has killed one of my servants."

"Why, then, you should have hanged him out of hand, not tortured him thus," answered Des Cadoux shortly.

For a moment it almost seemed as if the pair of them would have fallen a-quarrelling. Their words grew more heated, and then, while they were still wrangling, the executioner came forward to solve matters with the news that the secretary had expired. To Bellecour this proved a very welcome conclusion.

"Most opportunely!" he laughed "Had the rascal lived another minute I think we had quarrelled, Cadoux." He turned to the servant, "You are certain that it is so?" he asked.

"Look, Monsieur," said the fellow, as he pointed with his whip to the pilloried figure of La Boulaye. The Marquis looked, and saw that the secretary had collapsed, and hung limp in his bonds, his head fallen back upon his shoulders and his eyes closed.

With a shrug and a short laugh Bellecour turned to his daughter.

"You may take the carrion, if you want to. But I think you can do no more than order it to be flung into a ditch and buried there."

But she had no mind to be advised by him. She had the young man's body cut down from the pump, and she bade a couple of servants convey it to the house of Master Duhamel, she for remembered that La Boulaye and the old pedagogue were friends.

"An odd thing is a woman's heart," grumbled the Marquis, who begrudged La Boulaye even his last act of mercy. "She may care never a fig for a man, and yet, if he has but told her that he loves her, be he never so mean and she never so exalted, he seems thereby to establish some measure of claim to her."

CHAPTER IV

THE DISCIPLES OF ROUSSEAU

The Marquis of Bellecour would, perhaps have philosophised less complacently had he known that the secretary was far from dead, and that what the executioner had, genuinely enough, mistaken for death was no more than a passing swoon. Under ordinary circumstances he might not have been satisfied to have taken the fellow's word; he would himself have ascertained the truth of the statement by a close inspection of the victim. But, as we have seen, the news came as so desirable a solution to the altercation that was waxing 'twixt himself and Des Cadoux that he was more than glad to avail himself of it.

The discovery that Caron lived was made while they were cutting him down from his pillory, and just as the Marquis was turning to go within. A flutter of the eyelids and a gasp for breath announced the fact, and the executioner was on the point of crying out his discovery when Mademoiselle's eyes flashed him a glance of warning, and her voice whispered feverishly:

"Hush! There are ten louis for each of you if you but keep silent and carry him to Master Duhamel as I told you."

The secretary opened his eyes but saw nothing, and a low moan escaped him. She shot a fearful glance at the retreating figure of her father, whilst Gilles—the executioner—hissed sharply into his ear:

"Mille diables! be still, man. You are dead."

Thus did he escape, and thus was he borne—a limp, agonised, and bleeding mass, to the house of Duhamel. The old schoolmaster received them with tears in his eyes—nor were they altogether tears of sorrow, for all that poor Caron's mangled condition grieved him sorely; they were in a measure tears of thankfulness; for Duhamel had not dared hope to see the young man alive again.

At the pedagogue's door stood a berline, and within his house there was a visitor. This was a slight young man of medium stature, who had not the appearance of more than twenty-five years of age, for all that, as a matter of fact, he was just over thirty. He was dressed with so scrupulous a neatness as to convey, in spite of the dark colour of his garments, an impression almost of foppishness. There was an amplitude about his cravat, an air of extreme care about the dressing of his wig and the powdering of it, and a shining brightness about his buttons and the buckles of his shoes which seemed to proclaim the dandy, just as the sombreness of the colour chosen seemed to deny it. In his singularly pale countenance a similar contradiction was observable. The weak, kindly eyes almost appeared to give the lie to the astute prominence of his cheekbones; the sensitiveness of the mouth seemed neutralised by the thinness of the lips, whilst the oddly tip-tilted nose made a mock of the austerity of the brow.

He was perfectly at ease in his surroundings, and as La Boulaye was carried into the schoolmaster's study and laid on a couch, he came forward and peered curiously at the secretary's figure, voicing an inquiry concerning him.

"It is the young man of whom I was telling you, Maximilien," answered Duhamel. "I give thanks to God that they have not killed him outright. It is a mercy I had not expected from those wolves, and one which, on my soul, I cannot understand."

"Monsieur," said Gilles, "will understand it better perhaps if I tell you that the Marquis believes him to be dead. He was cut down for dead, and when we discovered that he still lived it was Mademoiselle who prevailed upon us to save him. She is paying us to keep the secret, but not a fortune would tempt me if I thought the Seigneur were ever likely to hear of it. He must be got away from Bellecour; indeed, he must be got out of Picardy at once, Monsieur. And you must promise me that this shall be done or we will carry him back to the Chateau and tell the Marquis that he has suddenly revived. I must insist, Monsieur; for if ever it should transpire that he was not dead the Seigneur would hang us."

The stranger's weak eyes seemed to kindle in anger, and his lips curled until they exaggerated the already preposterous tilt of his nose.

"He would hang you, eh?" said he. "Ma foi, Duhamel, we shall change all this very soon, I promise you."

"God knows it needs changing," growled Duhamel. "It seems that it was only in the Old Testament that Heaven interfered with human iniquity. Why it does not rain fire and brimstone on the Chateau de Bellecour passes the understanding of a good Christian. I'll swear that in neither Sodom nor Gomorrah was villainy more rampant."

The stranger plucked at his sleeve to remind him of the presence of the servants from the Chateau. Duhamel turned to them.

"I will keep him concealed here until he is able to get about," he assured them. "Then I shall find him the means to leave the province."

But Gilles shook his head, and his companion grunted an echo of his disapproval.

"That will not serve, master," he answered sullenly. "What if the Seigneur should have word of his presence here? It is over-dangerous. Someone may see him. No, no, Either he leaves Bellecour this very night, and you swear that he shall, or else we carry him back to the Chateau."

"But how can I swear this?" cried Duhamel impatiently.

"Why, easily enough," put in the stranger. "Let me take him in my berline. I can leave him at Amiens or at Beauvais, or any one of the convenient places that I pass. Or I can even carry him on to Paris with me."

"You are very good, Maximilien," answered the old man, to which the other returned a gesture of deprecation.

In this fashion, then, was the matter settled to the satisfaction of the Seigneur's retainers, and upon having received Duhamel's solemn promise that Caron should be carried out of Bellecour, and, for that matter, out of Picardy, before the night was spent, they withdrew.

Within the schoolmaster's study he whom Duhamel called Maximilien strode to and fro, his hands clasped behind his back, his head bent, his chin thrust forward, denouncing the seigneurial system, of whose atrocity he had received that evening instances enough—for he had heard the whole story of La Boulaye's rebellion against the power of Bellecour and the causes that had led to it.

"We will mend all this, I promise you, Duhamel," he was repeating. "But not until we have united to shield the weak from oppression, to restrain the arrogant and to secure to each the possession of what belongs to him; not until all men are free and started upon equal terms in the race of life; not until we shall have set up rules of justice and of peace, to which all—rich and poor, noble and simple alike—shall be obliged to conform. Thus only can we repair the evil done by the caprice of fortune, which causes the one to be born into silk and the other into fustian. We must subject the weak and the mighty alike to mutual duties, collecting our forces into the supreme power to govern us all impartially by the same laws, to protect alike all members of the community, to repel our common foes and preserve us in never-ending concord. How many crimes, murders, wars, miseries, horrors shall thus be spared us, Duhamel? And it will come; it will come soon, never fear."

Caron stirred on the couch where Duhamel was tending him, and raised his head to glance at the man who was voicing the doctrines that for years had dwelt in his heart.

"Dear Jean Jacques," he murmured.

The stranger turned sharply and stepped to the young man's side.

"You have read the master?" he inquired, with a sudden, new-born interest in the secretary.

"Read him?" cried Carom forgetting for the moment the sore condition of his body in the delight of discovering one who was bound to him by such bonds of sympathy as old Rousseau established.

"Read him, Monsieur? There is scarce a line in all his 'Discourses' that I do not know by heart, and that I do not treasure, vaguely hoping and praying that some day such a state as he dreamt of may find itself established, and may sweep aside these corrupt, tyrannical conditions."

Maximilien's eyes kindled.

"Boy," he answered impressively, "Your hopes are on the eve of fruition, your prayers are about to be heard. Yes—even though it should entail trampling the Lilies of France into the very dust.

"Who are you, Monsieur?" asked La Boulaye, eyeing this prophet with growing interest.

"Robespierre is my name," was the answer, and to La Boulaye it conveyed no enlightenment, for the name of Maximilien Marie Isidore de Robespierre, which within so very short a time was to mean so much in France, as yet meant nothing.

La Boulaye inclined his head as if acknowledging an introduction, then turned his attention to Duhamel who was offering him a cup of wine. He drank gratefully, and the invigorating effects were almost instantaneous.

"Now let us see to your hurts," said the schoolmaster, who had taken some linen and a pot of unguents from a cupboard. La Boulaye sat up, and what time Duhamel was busy dressing his lacerated back, the young man talked with Robespierre.

"You are going to Paris, you say, Monsieur?"

"Yes, to the States-General," answered Maximilien.

"As a deputy?" inquired Caron, with ever-heightening interest.

"As a deputy, Monsieur. My friends of Arras have elected me to the Third Estate of Artois."

"Dieu! How I envy you!" exclaimed La Boulaye, to cry out a moment later in the pain to which Duhamel's well-intentioned operations were subjecting him. "I would it might be mine," he added presently, "to take a hand in legislation, and the mending of it; for as it stands at present it is inferior far to the lawless anarchy of the aborigines. Among them, at least, the conditions are more normal, they offer better balance between faculty and execution; they are by far more propitious to happiness and order than is this

28

broken wreck of civilisation that we call France. It is to equality alone," he continued, warming to his subject, "that Nature has attached the preservation of our social faculties, and all legislation that aims at being efficient should be directed to the establishment of equality. As it is, the rich will always prefer their own fortune to that of the State, whilst the poor will never love—nor can love—a condition of laws that leaves them in misery."

Robespierre eyed the young man in some surprise. His delivery was impassioned, and although in what he said there was perhaps nothing that was fresh to the lawyer of Arras, yet the manner in which he said it was impressive to a degree.

"But Duhamel," he cried to the schoolmaster, "you did not tell me this young patriot was an orator."

"Nor am I, Monsieur," smiled La Boulaye. "I am but the mouthpiece of the great Rousseau. I have so assimilated his thoughts that they come from me as spontaneously as if they were my own, and often I go so far as to delude myself into believing that they are."

No better recommendation than this could he have had to the attention of Robespierre, who was himself much in the same case, imbued with and inspired by those doctrines, so ideal in theory, but, alas! so difficult, so impossible in practice. For fully an hour they sat and talked, and each improved in his liking of the other, until at last, bethinking him of the flight of time, Robespierre announced that he must start.

"You will take him to Paris with you, Maximilien?" quoth the old pedagogue.

"Ma foi, yes; and if with such gifts as Nature appears to have given him, and such cultivation of them as, through the teachings of Rousseau, he has effected, I do not make something of him, why, then, I am unworthy of the confidence my good friends of Arras repose in me."

They made their adieux, and the schoolmaster, opening his door, peered out. The street was deserted save for de Robespierre's berline and his impatient postillion. Between them Duhamel and Maximilien assisted Caron to the door of the carriage. The moving subjected him to an excruciating agony, but he caught his nether lip in his teeth, and never allowed them to suspect it. As they raised him into the berline, however, he toppled forward, fainting. Duhamel hastened indoors for a cordial, and brought also some pillows with which to promote the young man's comfort on the journey that was before him—or, rather, to lessen the discomfort which the jolting was likely to occasion him.

Caron recovered before they started, and with tears in his eyes he thanked old Duhamel and voiced a hope that they might meet again ere long.

Then Robespierre jumped nimbly into the berline. The door closed, the postillion's whip cracked briskly, and they set out upon a journey which to La Boulaye was to be as the passing from one life to another.

PART II

THE NEW RULE

Allons! Marchons!
Qu'un sang impur
Abreuve nos sillons!
La Marseillaise.

CHAPTER V

THE SHEEP TURNED WOLVES

There were roars of anger and screams of terror in the night, and above the Chateau de Bellecour the inky blackness of the heavens was broken by a dull red glow, which the distant wayfarer might have mistaken for the roseate tint of dawn, were it possible for the dawn to restrict itself to so narrow an area.

Ever and anon a tongue of flame would lick up into the night towards that russet patch of sky, betraying the cause of it and proclaiming that incendiaries were at work. Above the ominous din that told of the business afoot there came now and again the crack of a musket, and dominating all other sounds was the sullen roar of the revolted peasants, the risen serfs, the rebellious vassals of the Siegneur de Bellecour.

For time has sped and has much altered in the speeding. Four years have gone by since the night on which the lacerated Caron la Boulaye was smuggled out of Bellecour in Robespierre's berline and in that four years much of the things that were prophesied have come to pass —aye, and much more besides that was undreamt of at the outset by the revolutionaries. A gruesome engine that they facetiously called the National Razor—invented and designed some years ago by one Dr. Guillotin—is but an item in the changes that have been, yet an item that in its way has become a very factor. It stands not over-high, yet the shadow of it has fallen athwart the whole length and breadth of France, and in that shadow the tyrants have trembled, shaken to the very souls of them by the rude hand of fear; in that shadow the spurned and downtrodden children of the soil have taken heart of grace. The bonds of servile cowardice that for centuries had trammelled them have been shaken off like cobwebs, and they that were as sheep are now become the wolves that prey on those that preyed on them for generations.

There is, in the whole of France, no corner so remote but that, sooner or later, this great upheaval has penetrated to it. Louis XVI.—or Louis Capet, as he is now more generally spoken of—has been arraigned, condemned and executed. The aristocrats are in full emigratory flight across the frontiers—those that have not been rent by the vassals they had brought to bay, the people they had outraged. The Lilies of France lie trampled under foot in the shambles they have made of that fair land, whilst overhead the

32

tricolour—that symbol of the new trinity, Liberty, Equality, Fraternity—is flaunted in the breeze.

A few of the more proud and obstinate—so proud and obstinate as to find it a thing incredible that the order should indeed change and the old regime pass away—still remain, and by their vain endeavours to lord it in their castles provoke such scenes as that enacted at Bellecour in February of '93 (by the style of slaves) or Pluviose of the year One of the French Republic, as it shall presently come to be known in the annals of the Revolution.

Bellecour, the most arrogant of arrogants, had stood firm, and desperately contrived through all these months of revolution to maintain his dominion in his corner of Picardy. But even he was beginning to realise that the end was at hand, and he made his preparations to emigrate. Too proud, however, to permit his emigration to savour of a flight, he carried the leisureliness of his going to dangerous extremes. And now, on the eve of departure, he must needs pause to give a fete at once of farewell and in honour of his daughter's betrothal to the Vicomte Anatole d'Ombreval. This very betrothal at so unpropitious a season was partly no more than contrived by the Marquis that he might mark his ignoring and his serene contempt of the upheaval and the new rule which it had brought.

All that was left of the noblesse in Picardy had flocked that day to the Chateau de Bellecour, and the company there assembled numbered perhaps some thirty gallants and some twenty ladies. A banquet there had been, which in the main was a gloomy function, for the King's death was too recent a matter to be utterly lost sight of. Later, however, as the generous supply of wine did its work and so far thawed the ice of apprehension that bound their souls as to dispose them to enjoy, at least, the present hour in forgetfulness, there was a better humour in the air. This developed, and so far indeed did it go that in the evening a Pavane was suggested, and, the musicians being found, it was held in the great salon of the Chateau.

It was then that the first alarm had penetrated to their midst. It had found them a recklessly merry crew, good to behold in their silks and satins, powder and patches, gold lace and red heels, moving with waving fans, or hand on sword, and laced beaver under elbow, through the stately figures of the gavotte.

Scared, white-faced lackeys had brought the news, dashing wildly in upon that courtly assembly. The peasants had risen and were marching on Bellecour.

Some of his sudden rage the Marquis vented by striking the servants' spokesman in the face.

"Dare you bring me such a message?" he cried furiously.

"But, my lord, what are we to do?" gasped the frightened lackey.

"Do, fool?" returned Bellecour. "Why, close the gates and bid them return home as they value their lives. For if they give me trouble I'll hang a round dozen of them."

Still was there that same big talk of hanging men. Still did it seem that the Marquis of Bellecour accounted himself the same lord of life and death that he and his forbears had been for generations. But there were others who thought differently. The music had ceased abruptly, and a little knot of gentlemen now gathered about the host, and urged him to take some measures of precaution. In particular they desired to ensure the safety of the ladies who were being thrown into a great state of alarm, so that of some of these were the screams that were heard in that night of terror. Bellecour's temper was fast gaining, and as he lost control of himself the inherent brutality of his character came uppermost.

"Mesdames," he cried rudely, "this screeching will profit us nothing. Even if we must die, let us die becomingly, not shrieking like butchered geese."

A dozen men raised their voices angrily against him in defence of the women he had slighted. But he waved them impatiently away.

"Is this an hour in which to fall a-quarrelling among ourselves?" he exclaimed. "Or do you think it one in which a man can stop to choose his words? Sang-dieu! That screaming is a more serious matter than at first may seem. If these rebellious dogs should chance to hear it, it will be but so much encouragement to them. A fearless front, a cold contempt, are weapons unrivalled if you would prevail against these mutinous cravens."

But his guests were insistent that something more than fearless fronts and cold contempts should be set up as barriers between themselves and the advancing peasantry. And in the end Bellecour impatiently quitted the room to give orders for the barricading of the gates and the defending of the Chateau, leaving behind him in the salon the very wildest of confusions.

From the windows the peasantry could now be seen, by the light of their torches, marching up the long avenue that fronted the Chateau, and headed by a single drum on which the bearer did no more than beat the step. They were a fierce, unkempt band, rudely armed—some with scythes, some with sickles, some with hedge-knives, and some with hangers; whilst here and there was one who carried a gun, and perhaps a bayonet as well. Nor were there men only in the rebellious ranks. There were an almost equal number of women in crimson caps, their bosoms bare, their heads dishevelled, their garments filthy and in rags—for the tooth of poverty had bitten deeply into them during the past months.

As they swung along to the rhythmical thud of the drum, their voices were raised in a fearful chorus that must have made one think of the choirs of hell, and the song they sang was the song of Rouget de l'Isle, which all France had been singing these twelve months past:

> *"Aux armes, citoyens!*
> *Formez vos bataillons.*
> *Allons, marchons!*
> *Qu'un sang inpur*
> *Abreuve nos sillons!"*

Ever swelling as they drew nearer came the sound of that terrible hymn to the ears of the elegant, bejewelled, bepowdered company in the Chateau. The gates were reached and found barred. An angry roar went up to Heaven, followed by a hail of blows upon the stout, ironbound oak, and an imperious call to open.

In the courtyard below the Marquis had posted the handful of servants that remained faithful—for reasons that Heaven alone may discern—to the fortunes of the house. He had armed them with carbines and supplied them with ammunition. He had left them orders to hold off the mob from the outer gates as long as possible; but should these be carried, they were to fall back into the Chateau itself, and make fast the doors. Meanwhile, he was haranguing the gentlemen—some thirty of them, as we have seen—in the salon and urging them to arm themselves so that they might render assistance.

His instances were met with a certain coldness, which at last was given expression by the most elegant Vicomte d'Ombreval—the man who was about to become his son-in-law.

"My dear Marquis," protested the young man, his habitually supercilious mouth looking even more supercilious than usual as he now spoke, "I beg that you will consider what you are proposing. We are your guests, we others, and you ask us to defend your gates against your own people for you! Surely, surely, sir, your first duty should have been to have ensured our safety against such mutinies on the part of the rabble of Bellecour."

The Seigneur angrily stamped his foot. In his choler he was within an ace of striking Ombreval, and might have done so had not the broad-minded and ever-reasonable old Des Cadoux interposed at that moment to make clear to the Marquis's guests a situation than which nothing could have been clearer. He put it to them that the times were changed, and that France was no longer what France had been; that allowances must be made for M. de Bellecour, who was in no better case than any other gentleman in that unhappy country! and finally, that either they must look to arming and defending themselves or they must say their prayers and submit to being butchered with the ladies.

"For ourselves," he concluded calmly, tapping his gold snuffbox and holding it out to Bellecour, for all the world with the air of one who was discussing the latest fashion in wigs, "I can understand your repugnance at coming to blows with this obscene canaille. It is doing them an honour of which they are not worthy. But we have these ladies to think of, Messieurs, and—" he paused to apply the rappee to his nostrils—"and we must exert ourselves to save them, however disagreeable the course we may be compelled to pursue. Messieurs, I am the oldest here; permit that I show you the way."

His words were not without effect; they kindled chivalry in hearts that, after all, were nothing if not prone to chivalry—according to their own lights—and presently something very near enthusiasm prevailed. But the supercilious and very noble Ombreval still grumbled.

"To ask me to fight this scum!" he ejaculated in horror "Pardi! It is too much. Ask me to beat them off with a whip like a pack of curs, and I'll do it readily. But fight them—!"

"Nothing could delight us more, Vicomte, than to see you beat them off with a whip," Des Cadoux assured him. "Arm yourself with a whip, by all means, my friend, and let us witness the prodigies you can perform with it."

"See what valour inflames the Vicomte, Suzanne," sneered a handsome woman into Mademoiselle's ear. "With what alacrity he flies to arms that he may defend you, even with his life."

"M. d'Ombreval is behaving according to his lights," answered Suzanne coldly.

"Ma foi, then his lights are unspeakably dim," was the contemptuous answer.

Mademoiselle gave no outward sign of the deep wound her pride was receiving. The girl of nineteen, who had scorned the young secretary-lover in the park of Bellecour that morning four years ago, was developed into a handsome lady of three-and-twenty.

"It would be beneath the dignity of his station to soil his hands in such a conflict as my father has suggested," she said at last.

"I wonder would it be beneath the dignity of his courage," mused the same caustic friend. "But surely not, for nothing could be beneath that."

"Madame!" exclaimed Suzanne, her cheeks reddening; for as of old, and like her father, she was quickly moved to anger. "Will it please you to remember that M. d'Ombreval is my affianced husband?"

"True," confessed the lady, no whit abashed. "But had I not been told so I had accounted him your rejected suitor, who, broken-hearted, gives no thought either to his own life or to yours."

In a pet, Mademoiselle gave her shoulder to the speaker and turned away. In spite of the words with which she had defended him, Suzanne was disappointed in her betrothed, and yet, in a way, she understood his bearing to be the natural fruit of that indomitable pride of which she had observed the outward signs, and for which, indeed as much as for the beauty of his person, she had consented to become his wife. After all, it was the outward man she knew. The marriage had been arranged, and this was but their third meeting, whilst never for an instant had they been alone together. By her mother she had been educated up to the idea that it was eminently desirable she should become the Vicomtesse d'Ombreval. At first she had endured dismay at the fact that she had never beheld the Vicomte, and because she imagined that he would be, most probably, some elderly roue, as did so often fall to the lot of maidens in her station. But upon finding him so very handsome to behold, so very noble of bearing, so lofty and disdainful that as he walked he seemed to spurn the very earth, she fell enamoured of him out of very relief, as well as because he was the most superb specimen of the other sex that it had ever been hers to observe.

And now that she had caught a glimpse of the soul that dwelt beneath that mass of outward perfections it had cost her a pang of disappointment, and the poisonous reflection cast upon his courage by that sardonic lady with whom she had talked was having its effect.

But the time was too full of other trouble to permit her to indulge her thoughts overlong upon such a matter. A volley of musketry from below came to warn them of the happenings there. The air was charged with the hideous howls of the besieging mob, and presently there was a cry from one of the ladies, as a sudden glare of light crimsoned the window-panes.

"What is that?" asked Madame de Bellecour of her husband.

"They have fired the stables," he answered, through set teeth. "I suppose they need light to guide them in their hell's work."

He strode to the glass doors opening to the balcony the same balcony from which four years ago his guests had watched the flogging of La Boulaye—and, opening them, he passed out. His appearance was greeted by a storm of execration. A sudden shot rang out, and the bullet, striking the wall immediately above him, brought down a shower of plaster on his head. It had been fired by a demoniac who sat astride the great gates waving his discharged carbine and yelling such ordures of speech as it had never been the most noble Marquis's lot to have stood listening to. Bellecour never flinched. As calmly as if nothing had happened, he leant over the parapet and called to his men below.

"Hold, there! Of what are you dreaming slumberers. Shoot me that fellow down."

Their guns had been discharged, but one of them, who had now completed his reloading, levelled the carbine and fired. The figure on the gates seemed to leap up from his sitting posture, and then with a scream he went over, back to his friends without.

The fired stables were burning gaily by now, and the cheeriest bonfire man could have desired on a dark night, and in the courtyard it was become as light as day.

The Marquis on the balcony was taking stock of his defences and making rapid calculations in his mind. He saw no reason why, so well protected by those stout oaken gates they should not—if they were but resolute—eventually beat back the mob. And then, even as his courage was rising at the thought, a deafening explosion seemed to shake the entire Chateau, and the gates—their sole buckler, upon whose shelter he had been so confidently building—crashed open, half blown away by the gunpowder keg that had been fired against it.

He had a fleeting glimpse of a stream of black fiends pouring through the dark gap and dashing with deafening yells into the crimson light of the courtyard. He saw his little handful of servants retreat precipitately within the Chateau. He heard the clang of the doors that were swung to just as the foremost of the rabble reached the threshold—With all this clearly stamped upon his mind, he turned, and springing into the salon he drew his sword.

"To the stairs, Messieurs!" he cried "To the stairs!"

And to the stairs they went. The extremity was now too great for argument. They dared not so much as look at their women-folk, lest they should be unmanned by the sight of those huddled creatures—their finery but serving to render them the more pitiable in their sickly affright. In a body the whole thirty of them swept from the room, and with Bellecour at their head and Ombreval somewhere in the rearmost rank, they made their way to the great staircase.

Here, armed with their swords and a brace of pistols to each man, whilst for a few the Marquis had even found carbines, they waited, with faces set and lips tight pressed for the end that they knew approached.

Nor was their waiting long. As the peasants had blown down the gates so now did they blow down the doors of the Chateau, and in the explosion three of Bellecour's servants—who had stood too near—were killed. Over the threshold they swarmed into the dark gulf of the great hall to the foot of the staircase. But here they were at a disadvantage. The light of the burning stables, shining through the open doorway, revealed them to the defenders, whilst they themselves looked up into the dark. There was a sudden cracking of pistols and a few louder reports from the guns, and the mob fled, screaming, back into the yard, leaving a score of dead and wounded on the polished floor of the hall.

Old M. des Cadoux laughed in the dark, as with his sword hanging from his wrist he tapped his snuff-box.

"Ma foi," said he to his neighbour, "they are discovering that it is not to be the triumphal march they had expected. A pinch of rappee, Stanislas?"

But the respite was brief. In a moment they saw the glare increase at the door, and presently a half-dozen of the rabble entered with torches, followed by some scores of their comrades. They paused at sight of that company ranged upon the stairs, as well they might, for a more incongruous sight could scarcely be imagined. Across the bodies of the slain, and revealed by the lifting powder smoke, stood that little band of thirty men, a blaze of gay colours, a sheen of silken hose, their wigs curled and powdered, their costly ruffles scintillant with jewels; calm, and supercilious, mocking to a man. There was a momentary gasp of awe, and then the spell was broken by the aristocrats themselves. A pistol spoke, and a volley followed. In the hall some stumbled forward, some hurtled backward, and some sank down in nerveless heaps. But those that remained did not again retreat. Reinforced by others, that crowded in behind, they charged boldly up the stairs, headed by a ragged, red capped giant named Souvestre—a man whom the Marquis had once irreparably wronged.

The sight of him was a revelation to Bellecour. This assault was Souvestre's work; the fellow had been inciting the people of Bellecour for the past twelve months, long indeed before the outbreak of the revolution proper, and at last he had roused them to the pitch of accompanying him upon his errand of tardy but relentless vengeance.

With a growl the Marquis raised his pistol. But Souvestre saw the movement, and with a laugh he did the like. Simultaneously there were two reports, and Bellecour's arm fell shattered to his side. Souvestre continued to advance, his smoking pistol in one hand and brandishing a huge sabre with the other. Behind him, howling and roaring like the beasts of prey they were become, surged the tenantry of Bellecour to pay the long-standing debt of hate to their seigneur.

"Here," said Des Cadoux, with a grimace, "endeth the chapter of our lives. I wonder, do they keep rappee in heaven?" He snapped down the lid of his gold snuffbox—that faithful companion and consoler of so many years—and cast it viciously at the head of one of the oncoming peasants. Then tossing back the lace from his wrist he brought his sword into guard and turned aside a murderous stroke which an assailant aimed at him.

"Animal," he snapped viciously, as he set to work, "it is the first time that my chaste blade has been crossed with such dirty steel as yours. I hope, for the honour of Cadoux, that it may not be quite the last."

Up, and ever up, swept that murderous tide. The half of those that had held the stairs lay weltering upon them as if in a last attempt to barricade with their bodies what they could no longer defend with their hands. A bare half-score remained standing, and amongst these that gallant old Cadoux, who had by now accounted for a half-dozen sans-culottes, and was hence in high glee, a man rejuvenesced. His sallies grew livelier and more barbed as the death-tide rose higher about him. His one regret was that he had been so hasty in casting his snuff box from him, for he was missing its familiar stimulus. At his side the Marquis was fighting desperately, fencing with his left arm, and in the hot excitement seeming oblivious of the pain his broken right must be occasioning.

"It is ended, old friend," he groaned at last, to Des Cadoux. "I am losing strength, and I shall be done for in a moment. The women," he almost sobbed, "mon Dieu, the women!"

Des Cadoux felt his old eyes grow moist, and the odd, fierce mirth that seemed to have hitherto infected him went out like a candle that is snuffed. But suddenly before he could make any answer, a new and unexpected sound, which dominated the din of combat, and seemed to cause all—assailants and defenders alike—to pause that they might listen, was wafted to their ears.

It was the roll of the drum. Not the mere thudding that had beaten the step for the mob, but the steady and vigorous tattoo of many sticks upon many skins.

"What is it? Who comes?" were the questions that men asked one another, as both aristocrats and sansculottes paused in their bloody labours. It was close at hand. So close at hand that they could discern the tramp of marching feet. In the infernal din of that fight upon the stairs they had not caught the sound of this approach until now that the new-comers—whoever they might be—were at the very gates of Bellecour.

From the mob in the yard there came a sudden outcry. Men sprang to the door of the Chateau and shouted to those within.

"Aux Armes," was the cry. "A nous, d nous!"

And in response to it the assailants turned tail, and dashed down the stairs, overleaping the dead bodies that were piled upon them, and many a man slipping in that shambles and ending the descent on his back. Out into the courtyard they swept: leaving that handful of gentlemen, their fine clothes disordered, splashed with blood and grimed with powder, to question one another touching this portent, this miracle that seemed wrought by Heaven for their salvation.

CHAPTER VI

THE CITIZEN COMMISSIONER

It was, after all, no miracle, unless the very timely arrival upon the scene of a regiment of the line might be accepted in the light of Heaven-directed. As a matter of fact, a rumour of the assault that was to be made that night upon the Chateau de Bellecour had travelled as far as Amiens, and there, that evening, it had reached the ears of a certain Commissioner of the National Convention, who was accompanying this regiment to the army of Dumouriez, then in Belgium.

Now it so happened that this Commissioner had meditated making a descent upon the Chateau on his own account, and he was not minded that any peasantry should forestall or baulk him in the business which he proposed to carry out there. Accordingly, he issued certain orders to the commandant, from which it resulted that a company, two hundred strong, was immediately despatched to Bellecour, to either defend or rescue it from the mob, and thereafter to await the arrival of the Commissioner himself.

This was the company that had reached Bellecour in the eleventh hour, to claim the attention of the assailants. But the peasants, as we have seen, were by no means disposed to submit to interference, and this they signified by the menacing front they showed the military, abandoning their attack upon the Chateau until they should be clear concerning the intentions of the newcomers. Of these intentions the Captain did not leave them long in doubt. A brisk word of command brought his men into a bristling line of attack, which in itself should have proved sufficient to ensure the peasantry's respect.

"Citizens" cried the officer, stepping forward, "in the name of the French Republic I charge you to withdraw and to leave us unhampered in the business we are here to discharge."

"Citizen-captain," answered the giant Souvestre, constituting himself the spokesman of his fellows, "we demand to know by what right you interfere with honest patriots of France in the act of ridding it of some of the aristocratic vermin that yet lingers on its soil?"

The officer stared at his interlocutor, amazed by the tone of the man as much as by the sudden growls that chorused it, but nowise intimidated by either the one or the other.

"I proclaimed my right when I issued my charge in the name of the Republic," he answered shortly.

"We are the Republic," Souvestre retorted, with a wave of the hand towards the ferocious crowd of men and women behind him. "We are the Nation—the sacred people of France. In our own name, Citizen-soldier, we charge you to withdraw and leave us undisturbed."

Here lay the basis of an argument into which, however, the Captain, being neither politician nor dialectician, was not minded to be drawn. He shrugged his shoulders and turned to his men.

"Present arms!" was the answer he delivered, in a voice of supreme unconcern.

"Citizen-captain, this is an outrage," screamed a voice in the mob. "If blood is shed, upon your own head be it."

"Will you withdraw?" inquired the Captain coldly.

"To me, my children," cried Souvestre, brandishing his sabre, and seeking to encourage his followers. "Down with these traitors who dishonour the uniform of France! Death to the blue-coats!"

He leapt forward towards the military, and with a sudden roar his followers, a full hundred strong sprang after him to the charge.

"Fire!" commanded the Captain, and from the front line of his company fifty sheets of flame flashed from fifty carbines.

The mob paused; for a second it wavered; then before the smoke had lifted it broke, and shrieking in terror, it fled for cover, leaving the valorous Souvestre alone, to revile them for a swarm of cowardly rats.

The Captain put his hands to his sides and laughed till the tears coursed down his cheeks. Checking his mirth at last, he called to Souvestre, who was retreating in disgust and anger.

"Hi! My friend the patriot! Are you still of the same mind or will you withdraw your people?"

"We will not withdraw," answered the giant sullenly. "You dare not fire upon free citizens of the French Republic."

"Dare I not? Do you delude yourself with that, nor think that because this time I fired over your heads I dare not fire into your ranks. I give you my word that if I have to command my men to fire a second time it shall not be mere make-believe, and I also give you my word that if at the end of a minute I have not your reply and you are not moving out of this—every rogue of you shall have a very bitter knowledge of how much I dare."

Souvestre was headstrong and angry. But what can one man, however headstrong and however angry, do against two hundred, when his own followers refuse to support him. The valour of the peasants was distinctly of that quality whose better part is

43

discretion. The thunder of that fusillade had been enough to shatter their nerve, and to Souvestre's exhortations that they should become martyrs in the noble cause, of the people against tyranny, in whatsoever guise it came, they answered with the unanswerable logic of caution.

The end was that a very few moments later saw them in full retreat, leaving the military in sole and undisputed possession of Bellecour.

The officer's first thought was for the blazing stables, and he at once ordered a detachment of his company to set about quenching the fire, a matter in which they succeeded after some two hours of arduous labour.

Meanwhile, leaving the main body bivouacked in the courtyard, he entered the Chateau with a score of men, and came upon the ten gentlemen still standing in the shambles that the grand staircase presented. With the Marquis de Bellecour the Captain had a brief and not over courteous interview. He informed the nobleman that he was acting under the orders of a Commissioner, who had heard at Amiens, that evening, of the attack that was to be made upon Bellecour. Not unnaturally the Marquis was mistrustful of the ends which that Commissioner, whoever he might be, looked to serve by so unusual an act. Far better did it sort with the methods of the National Convention and its members to leave the butchering of aristocrats to take its course. He sought information at the Captain's hands, but the officer was reticent to the point of curtness, and so, their anxiety but little relieved, since it might seem that they had but escaped from Scylla to be engulfed in Charbydis, the aristocrats at Bellecour spent the night in odious suspense. Those that were tending the wounded had perhaps the best of it, since thus their minds were occupied and saved the torture of speculation.

The proportion of slain was mercifully small: of twenty that had fallen it was found that but six were dead, the others being more or less severely hurt. Conspicuous among the men that remained, and perhaps the bravest of them all was old Des Cadoux. He had recovered his snuff-box, than which there seemed to be nothing of greater importance in the world, and he moved from group to group with here a jest and there a word of encouragement, as seemed best suited to those he addressed. Of the women, Mademoiselle de Bellecour and her sharp tongued mother, showed certainly the most undaunted fronts.

Suzanne had not seen her betrothed since the fight upon the stairs. But she was told that he was unhurt, and that he was tending a cousin of his who had been severely wounded in the head.

It was an hour or so after sunrise when he sought her out, and they stood in conversation together—a very jaded pair—looking down from one of the windows upon the stalwart blue-coats that were bivouacked in the quadrangle.

Suddenly on the still morning air came the sound of hoof-beats, and as they looked they espied a man in a cocked hat and an ample black cloak riding briskly up the avenue.

"See?" exclaimed Ombreval; "yonder at last comes the great man we are awaiting—the Commissioner of that rabble they call the National Convention. Now we shall know what fate is reserved for us."

"But what can they do?" she asked.

"It is the fashion to send people of our station to Paris," he replied, "to make a mock of us with an affair they call a trial before they murder us."

She sighed.

"Perhaps this gentleman is more merciful," was the hope she expressed.

"Merciful?" he mocked. "Ma foi, a ravenous tiger may be merciful before one of these. Had your father been wise he had ordered the few of us that remained to charge those soldiers when they entered, and to have met our end upon their bayonets. That would have been a merciful fate compared with the mercy of this so-called Commissioner is likely to extend us."

It seemed to be his way to find fault, and that warp in his character rendered him now as heroic—in words—as he had been erstwhile scornful.

Suzanne shuddered, brave girl though she was.

"Unless you can conceive thoughts of a pleasanter complexion," she said, "I should prefer your silence, M. d'Ombreval."

He laughed in his disdainful way—for he disdained all things, excepting his own person and safety—but before he could make any answer they were joined by the Marquis and his son.

In the courtyard the horseman was now dismounting, and a moment or two later they heard the fall of feet, upon the stairs. A soldier threw open the door, and holding it, announced:

"The Citizen-deputy La Boulaye, Commissioner of the National Convention to the army of General Dumouriez."

"This," mocked Ombreval, to whom the name meant nothing, "is the representative of a Government of strict equality, and he is announced with as much pomp as was ever an ambassador of his murdered Majesty's."

Then a something out of the common in the attitude of his

45

companions arrested his attention. Mademoiselle was staring with eyes full of the most ineffable amazement, her lips parted, and her cheeks whiter than the sleepless night had painted them. The Marquis was scowling in a surprise that seemed no whit less than his daughter's, his head thrust forward, and his jaw fallen. The Vicomte, too, though in a milder degree, offered a countenance that was eloquent with bewilderment. From this silent group Ombreval turned his tired eyes to the door and took stock of the two men that had entered. One of these was Captain Juste, the officer in command of the military; the other was a tall man, with a pale face, an aquiline nose, a firm jaw, and eyes that were very stern—either of habit or because they now rested upon the man who four years ago had used him so cruelly.

He stood a moment in the doorway as if enjoying the amazement which had been sown by his coming. There was no mistaking him. It was the same La Boulaye of four years ago, and yet it was not quite the same. The face had lost its boyishness, and the strenuous life he had lived had scored it with lines that gave him the semblance of a greater age than was his. The old, poetic melancholy that had dwelt in the secretary's countenance was now changed to strength and firmness. Although little known as yet to the world at large, the great ones of the Revolution held him in high esteem, and looked upon him as a power to be reckoned with in the near future. Of Robespierre—who, it was said, had discovered him and brought him to Paris—he was the protege and more than friend, a protection and friendship this which in '93 made any man almost omnipotent in France.

He was dressed in a black riding-suit, relieved only by the white neck-cloth and the tricolour sash of office about his waist. He removed his cocked hat, beneath which the hair was tied in a club with the same scrupulous care as of old.

Slowly he advanced into the salon, and his sombre eyes passed from the Marquis to Mademoiselle. As they rested upon her some of the sternness seemed to fade from their glance. He found in her a change almost as great as that which she had found in him. The lighthearted, laughing girl of nineteen, who had scorned his proffered love when he had wooed her that April morning to such disastrous purpose, was now ripened into a stately woman of three-and-twenty. He had thought his boyish passion dead and buried, and often in the years that were gone had he smiled softly to himself at the memory of his ardour, as we smile at the memory of our youthful follies. Yet now, upon beholding her again, so wondrously transformed, so tall and straight, and so superbly beautiful, he

46

experienced an odd thrill and a weakening of the stern purpose that had brought him to Bellecour.

Then his glance moved on. A moment it rested on the supercilious, high-bred countenance of the Vicomte d'Ombreval, standing with so proprietary an air beside her, then it passed to the kindly old face of Des Cadoux, and he recalled how this gentleman had sought to stay the flogging of him. An instant it hovered on the Marquis, who—haggard of face and with his arm in a sling—was observing him with an expression in which scorn and wonder were striving for the mastery; it seemed to shun the gaze of the pale-faced Vicomte, whose tutor he had been in the old days of his secretaryship, and full and stern it returned at last to settle upon the Marquis.

"Citizen Bellecour," he said, and his voice, like his face, seemed to have changed since last the Marquis had heard it, and to have grown more deep and metallic, "you may marvel, now that you behold the Commissioner who sent a company of soldiers to rescue you and your Chateau from the hands of the mob last night, what purpose I sought to serve by extending to you a protection which none of your order merits, and you least of any, in my eyes."

"The times may have wrought sad and overwhelming changes," answered the Marquis, with cold contempt, "but it has not yet so utterly abased us that we bring ourselves to speculate upon the purposes of the rabble."

A faint crimson flush crept into Caron's sallow cheeks.

"Indeed, I see how little you have changed!" he answered bitterly. "You are of those that will not learn, Citizen. The fault lies here," he added, tapping his head, "and it will remain until we remove the ones with the other. But now for the business that brings me," he proceeded, more briskly. "Four years ago, Citizen Bellecour, you laid your whip across my face in the woods out yonder, and when I spoke of seeking satisfaction action you threatened me with your grooms. I will not speak of your other brutalities on that same day. I will confine myself to that first affront."

"Be brief, sir," cried the Marquis offensively. "Since you have the force to compel us to listen to you, let me beg that you will at least display the generosity of detaining us no longer than you need."

"I will be as brief as it lies within the possibility of words," answered Caron coldly. "I am come, Citizen Bellecour, to demand of you to-day the satisfaction which four years ago you refused me."

"Of me?" cried the Marquis.

"Through the person of your son, the Vicomte, as I asked for it

47

four years ago," said Caron. "You are am old man, Citizen, and I do not fight old men."

"I am yet young enough to cut you into ribbons, you dog, if I were minded to dishonour myself by meeting you." And turning to Ombreval for sympathy, he vented a low laugh of contemptuous wonder.

"Insolence!" sneered Ombreval sympathetically, whilst Mademoiselle stood looking on with cheeks that were growing paler, for that this event would end badly for either her father or her brother she never doubted.

"Citizen Bellecour," said Caron, still very coldly, "you have heard what I propose, as have you also, Citizen-vicomte."

"For myself," began the youth "I am—"

"Silence, Armand!" his father commanded, laying a hand upon his sleeve. "Understand me, citizen-deputy, or citizen-commissioner, or citizen-blackguard or whatever you call your vile self, you are come on a fruitless journey to Bellecour. Neither I nor my son is so lost to the duty which we owe our rank as to so much as dream of acceding to your preposterous request. I think, sir, that you had been better advised to have left the mob to its work last night, if you but restrained it for this purpose."

"Is that your last word?" asked La Boulaye, still calmly weathering that storm of insults.

"My very last, sir."

"There are more ways than one of taking satisfaction for that affront, Citizen Bellecour," rejoined La Boulaye, "and if the course which I now pursue should prove more distasteful to you than that which I last suggested, the blame of it must rest with you." He turned to the bluecoat at the door. "Citizen-soldier, my whip."

There was a sudden movement among the aristocrats—a horrified recoiling—and even Bellecour was shaken out of his splendid arrogance.

"Insolent cur!" exclaimed Ombreval with withering scorn; "to what lengths is presumption driving you?"

"To the length of a horsewhip," answered La Boulaye pleasantly.

He received the whip from the hands of the soldier and he now advanced towards Bellecour, unwinding the lash as he came. Ombreval barred his way with an oath.

"By Heaven: you shall not!" he cried.

"Shall not?" echoed La Boulaye, his lips curling. "You had best stand aside—you that are steeped in musk and fierceness." And before the stern and threatening contempt of La Boulaye's glance

48

the young nobleman fell back. But his place was taken by the Vicomte de Bellecour, who advanced to confront Caron.

"Monsieur la Boulaye," he announced, "I am ready and willing to meet you." And considering the grim alternative with which the Republicans had threatened him, the old Marquis had not the courage to interfere again.

"Ah!" It was an exclamation of satisfaction from the Commissioner. "I imagined that you would change your minds. I shall await you, Citizen, in the garden in five minutes' time."

"I shall not keep you waiting, Monsieur," was the Vicomte's answer.

Very formally La Boulaye bowed and left the room accompanied by the officer and followed by the soldier.

"Mon Dieu!" gasped the Marquise, fanning herself as the door closed after the Republicans. "Open me a window or I shall stifle! How the place reeks with them. I am a calm woman, Messieurs, but, on my honour, had he addressed any of you by his odious title of 'citizen' again, I swear that I had struck him with my own hands."

There were some that laughed. But Mademoiselle was not of those.

Her eyes travelled to her brother's pale face and weakly frame, and her glance was such a glance as we bend upon the beloved dead, for in him she saw one who was going inevitably to his death.

CHAPTER VII

LA BOULAYE DISCHARGES A DEBT

Along the northern side of the Chateau ran a terrace bordered by a red sandstone balustrade, and below this the Italian garden, so called perhaps in consequence of the oddly clipped box-trees, its only feature that suggested Italy. At the far end of this garden there was a strip of even turf that might have been designed for a fencing ground, and which Caron knew of old. Thither he led Captain Juste, and there in the pale sunshine of that February morning they awaited the arrival of the Vicomte and his sponsor.

But the minutes went by and still they waited-five, ten, fifteen minutes elapsed, yet no one came. Juste was on the point of returning within to seek the reason of this delay when steps sounded on the terrace above. But they were accompanied by the rustle of a gown, and presently it was Mademoiselle who appeared before them. The two men eyed her with astonishment, which in the case of La Boulaye, was tempered by another feeling.

"Monsieur la Boulaye," said she, her glance wandering towards the Captain, "may I speak with you alone?"

Outwardly impassive the Commissioner bowed.

"Your servant, Citoyenne," said he, removing his cocked hat. "Juste, will you give us leave?"

"You will find me on the terrace when you want me, Citizen-deputy," answered the officer, and saluting, he departed.

For a moment or two after he was gone Suzanne and Caron stood confronting each other in silence. She seemed smitten with a sudden awkwardness, and she looked away from him what time he waited, hat in hand, the chill morning breeze faintly stirring a loose strand of his black hair.

"Monsieur," she faltered at last, "I am come to intercede."

At that a faint smile hovered a second on the Republican's thin lips.

"And is the noblesse of France fallen so low that it sends its women to intercede for the lives of its men? But, perhaps," he added cynically, "it had not far to fall."

Her cheeks reddened. His insult to her class acted upon her as a spur and overcame the irresoluteness that seemed to have beset her.

"To insult the fallen, sir, is worthy of the new regime, whose representative you are, Enfine! We must take it, I suppose, as we take everything else in these disordered times—with a bent head and a meek submission."

"From the little that I have seen, Citoyenne," he answered, very coldly, roused in his turn, "it rather seems that you take things on your knees and with appeals for mercy."

"Monsieur," she cried, and her eyes now met his in fearless anger, "if you persist in these gratuitous insults I shall leave you."

He laughed in rude amusement, and put on his hat. The spell that for a moment her beauty had cast over him when first she had appeared had been attenuating. It now broke suddenly, and as he covered himself his whole manner changed.

"Is this interview of my seeking?" he asked. "It is your brother I am awaiting. Name of a name, Citoyenne, do you think my patience inexhaustible? The ci-devant Vicomte promised to attend me here. It was the boast of your order that whatever sins you might be guilty of you never broke your word. Have you lost even that virtue, which served you as a cloak for untold vices? And is your brother fled into the woods whilst you, his sister, come here to intercede with me for his wretched life? Pah! In the old days you aroused my hatred by your tyrannies and your injustices; to-day you weary and disgust me by your ineffable cowardices, from that gentleman in Paris who now calls himself Orleans-Egalite downwards."

"Monsieur," she began But he was not yet done. His cheeks were flushed with a reflection of the heart within.

"Citoyenne, I have a debt to discharge, and I will discharge it in full. Intercessions are vain with me. I cannot forget. Send me your brother within ten minutes to meet me here, man to man, and he shall have—all of you shall have—the chance that lies in such an encounter. But woe unto every man at Bellecour if he should fail me. Citoyenne, you know my mind."

But she overlooked the note of dismissal in his voice.

"You speak of a debt that you must discharge," said she, with no whit less heat than he had exhibited. "You refer to the debt of vengeance which you look to discharge by murdering that boy, my brother. But do you not owe me a debt also?"

"You?" he questioned. "My faith! Unless it be a debt of scorn, I know of none."

"Aye," she returned wistfully, "you are like the rest. You have a long memory for injuries, but a short one for benefits. Had it not been for me, Monsieur, you would not be here now to demand this that you call satisfaction. Have you forgotten how I—"

"No," he broke in. "I well remember how you sought to stay them when they were flogging me in the yard there. But you came too late. You might have come before, for from the balcony above you had been watching my torture. But you waited overlong. I was cast out for dead.".

She flashed him a searching glance, as though she sought to read his thoughts, and to ascertain whether he indeed believed what he was saying.

"Cast out for dead?" she echoed. "And by whose contrivance? By mine, M. la Boulaye. When they were cutting you down they discovered that you were not dead, and but that I bribed the men to keep it secret and carry you to Duhamel's house, they had certainly informed my father and you would have been finished off."

His eyes opened wide now, and into them there came a troubled look—the look of one who is endeavouring to grasp an elusive recollection.

"Ma foi," he muttered. "It seems to come to me as if I had heard something of the sort in a dream. It was—" He paused, and his brows were knit a moment. Then he looked up suddenly, and gradually his face cleared. "Why, yes—I have it!" he exclaimed. "It was in Duhamel's house. While I was lying half unconscious on the couch I heard one of the men telling Duhamel that you had paid them to carry me there and to keep a secret."

"And you had forgotten that?" she asked, with the faintest note of contempt.

"Not forgotten," he answered, "for it was never really there to be remembered. That I had heard such words had more than once occurred to me, but I have always looked upon it as the recollection of something that I had dreamt. I had never looked upon it as a thing that had had a real happening."

"How, then, did you explain your escape?"

"I always imagined that I had been assumed dead."

There was a brief spell of silence. Then—

"And now that you know, Monsieur—?"

She left the question unfinished, and held out her hands to him in a gesture of supplication. His face paled slightly and overclouded. Her influence, against which so long he had steeled himself, reinforced by the debt in which she had shown him that he stood towards her, was prevailing with him despite himself. Stirred suddenly out of the coldness that he had hitherto assumed, he caught the outstretched hands and drew her a step nearer. That was his undoing. Strong man though he unquestionably was, like many another strong man his strength seemed to fall from him at a woman's touch. He had led so austere and stern a life during the past four years; of women he had but had the most passing of glances, and intercourse with none save an old female who acted as

52

his housekeeper in Paris. And here was a woman who was not only beautiful, but the woman who years ago had embodied all his notions of what was most perfect in womanhood; the woman who ever since, and despite all that was past, had reigned in his heart and mind almost in spite of himself, almost unknown to him.

The touch of her hand now, the closeness of her presence, the faint perfume that reached him from her, and that was to him as a symbol of her inherent sweetness, the large blue eyes meeting his in expectation, and the imploring half-pout of her lips, were all seductions against which he had not been human had he prevailed.

Very white in the intensity of the long-quiescent passion she had resuscitated, he cried:

"Mademoiselle, what shall I say to you?"

The four years that were gone seemed suddenly to have slipped away. It was as if they stood again by the brook in the park on that April morn when first he had dared to word his presumptuous love. Even the vocabulary of the Republic was forgotten, and the interdicted title of "Mademoiselle" fell naturally from his lips.

"Say that you can be generous," she implored him softly. "Say that you prefer the debt you owe to the injury you received."

"You do not know the sacrifice you ask," he exclaimed still fighting with himself. "I have waited four years for this, and now—"

"He is my brother," she whispered, in so wonderful a tone that words which of themselves may have seemed no argument at all became the crowning argument of her intercession.

"Soit!" he consented. "For your sake, Mademoiselle, and in payment of the debt I owe you, I will go as I came. I shall not see the Citizen-marquis again. But do you tell him from me that if he sets any value on his life, he had best shake the dust of France from his feet. Too long already has he tarried, and at any moment those may arrive who will make him emigrate not only out of France but out of the world altogether. Besides, the peasantry that has risen once may rise again, and I shall not be here to protect him from its violence. Tell him he had best depart at once."

"Monsieur, I am grateful—very, very deeply grateful. I can say no more. May Heaven reward you. I shall pray the good God to watch over you always. Adieu, Monsieur!"

He stood looking at her a moment still retaining his hold of her hands.

"Adieu, Mademoiselle," he said at last. Then, very slowly—as if so that realising his intent she might frustrate it were she so minded—he raised her right hand. It was not withdrawn, and so he bent low, and pressed his lips upon it.

"God guard you, Mademoiselle," he said at last, and if they were strange words for a Republican and a Deputy, it must be remembered that his bearing during the past few moments had been singularly unlike a Republican's.

He released her hand, and stepping back, doffed his hat. With a final inclination of the head, she turned and walked away in the direction of the terrace.

At a distance La Boulaye followed, so lost in thought that he did not observe Captain Juste until the fellow's voice broke upon his ear.

"You have been long enough, Citizen-deputy," was the soldier's greeting. "I take it there is to be no duel."

"I make you my compliments upon the acuteness of your perception," answered La Boulaye tartly. "You are right. There is to be no encounter."

Juste's air was slightly mocking, and words of not overdelicate banter rose to his lips, to be instantly quelled by La Boulaye.

"Let your drums beat a rally, Citizen-captain," he commanded briskly. "We leave Bellecour in ten minutes.".

And indeed, in less than that time the blue-coats were swinging briskly down the avenue. In the rear rode La Boulaye, his cloak wrapped about him, his square chin buried in his neck-cloth, and his mind deep in meditation.

From a window of the Chateau the lady who was the cause of the young Revolutionist's mental absorption watched the departing soldiers. On either side of her stood Ombreval and her father.

"My faith, little one," said Bellecour good-humouredly. "I wonder what magic you have exercised to rid us of that infernal company."

"Women have sometimes a power of which men know nothing," was her cryptic answer.

Ombreval turned to her with a scowl of sudden suspicion.

"I trust, Mademoiselle, that you did not—" he stopped short. His thoughts were of a quality that defied polite utterance.

"That I did not what, Monsieur?" she asked.

"I trust you remembered that you are to become the Vicomtesse d'Ombreval" he answered, constructing his sentence differently.

"Monsieur!" exclaimed Bellecour angrily.

"I was chiefly mindful of the fact that I had my brother's life to save," said the girl, very coldly, her eye resting upon her betrothed in a glance of so much contempt that it forced him into an abashed silence.

In her mind she was contrasting this supercilious, vacillating weakling with the stern, strong man who lode yonder. A sigh fluttered across her lips. Had things but been different. Had Ombreval been the Revolutionist and La Boulaye the Vicomte, how much better pleased might she not have been. But since it was not so, why sigh? It was not as if she had loved this La Boulaye. How was that possible? Was he not of the canaille, basely born, and a Revolutionist—the enemy of her order—in addition? It were a madness to even dream of the possibility of such a thing, for Suzanne de Bellecour came of too proud a stock, and knew too well the respect that was due to it.

CHAPTER VIII

THE INVALIDS AT BOISVERT

There had been friction between the National Convention and General Dumouriez, who, though a fine soldier, was a remarkably indifferent Republican. The Convention had unjustly ordered the arrest of his commissariat officers, Petit-Jean and Malus, and in other ways irritated a man whose patience was never of the longest.

On the eve, however, of war with Holland, the great ones in Paris had suddenly perceived their error, and had sought—despite the many enemies, from Marat downwards, that Dumouriez counted among their numbers—to conciliate a general whose services they found that they could not dispense with. This conciliation was the business upon which the Deputy La Boulaye had been despatched to Antwerp, and as an ambassador he proved signally successful, as much by virtue of the excellent terms he was empowered to offer as in consequence of the sympathy and diplomacy he displayed in offering them.

The great Republican General started upon his campaign in the Low Countries as fully satisfied as under the circumstances he could hope to be. Malus and Petit-Jean were not only enlarged but reinstated, he was promised abundant supplies of all descriptions, and he was assured that the Republic approved and endorsed his plan of campaign.

La Boulaye, his mission satisfactorily discharged, turned homewards once more, and with an escort of six men and a corporal he swiftly retraced his steps through that blackened, war-ravaged country. They had slept a night at Mons, and they were within a short three leagues of French soil when they chanced to ride towards noon into the little hamlet of Boisvert. Probably they would have gone straight through without drawing rein, but that, as they passed the Auberge de l'Aigle, La Boulaye espied upon the green fronting the wayside hostelry a company of a half-dozen soldiers playing at bowls with cannon-balls.

The sight brought Caron to a sudden halt, and he sat his horse observing them and wondering how it chanced that these men should find themselves so far from the army. Three of them showed signs of having been recently wounded. One carried his arm in a sling, another limped painfully and by the aid of a stick, whilst the head of the third was swathed in bandages. But most remarkable were they by virtue of their clothes. One fellow—he of the bandaged head—wore a coat of yellow brocaded silk, which, in spite of a rent in the shoulder, and sundry stains of wine and oil, was unmistakably of a comparative newness. Beneath this appeared the nankeens and black leggings of a soldier. Another covered his greasy locks with a three-cornered hat, richly laced in gold. A third flaunted under his ragged blue coat a gold-broidered waistcoat and a Brussels cravat. A valuable ring flashed from the grimy finger of a fourth, who, instead of the military white nankeens, wore a pair of black silk breeches. There was one—he of the injured arm— resplendent in a redingote of crimson velvet, whilst he of the limp supported himself upon a gold-headed cane of ebony, which was in ludicrous discord with the tattered blue coat, the phrygian cap, and the toes that peeped through his broken boots.

They paused in their game to inspect, in their turn, the newcomers, and to La Boulaye it seemed that their glances were not free from uneasiness.

"A picturesque company on my life," he mused aloud. Then beckoned the one in the crimson coat.

"Hola, Citizen," he called to him.

The fellow hesitated a moment, then shuffled forward with a sullen air, and stood by Caron's stirrup.

"In God's name, what are you and who are you?" the Deputy demanded.

"We are invalided soldiers from the army of Dumouriez," the man answered him.

"But what are you doing here, at Boisvert?"

"We are in hospital, Citizen."

"Yonder?" asked La Boulaye derisively, pointing with his whip to the "Eagle Inn."

The fellow nodded.

"Yes, Citizen, yonder," he answered curtly.

La Boulaye looked surprised. Then his eyes strayed to the others on the green.

"But you are not all invalids?" he questioned.

"Many of us are convalescent."

"Convalescent? But those three braves yonder are something more than convalescent. They are as well as I am. Why do they not rejoin the troops?"

The fellow looked up with a scowl.

"We take our orders from our officer," he answered sourly.

"Ah!" quoth the Deputy. "There is someone in charge here, then? Who may it be?"

"Captain Charlot," the fellow answered, with an impudent air, which clearly seemed to ask: "What have you to say to that?"

"Captain Charlot?" echoed La Boulaye, in astonishment, for the name was that of the sometime peasant of Bellecour, who had since risen in life, and who, as an officer, had in a few months acquired a brilliant fame for deeds of daring. "Charlot Tardivet?" he inquired.

"Is there any other Captain Charlot in the army of the Republic?" the fellow asked insolently.

"Is he invalided too?" inquired Caron, without heeding the soldier's offensiveness of manner.

"He was severely wounded at Jemappes," was the answer.

"At Jemappes? But, voyons my friend, Jemappes was fought three months ago."

"Why, so all the world knows. What then? The General sent Captain Charlot here to rest and be cured, giving him charge of the invalided soldiers who came with him and of others who were already here."

"And of these," cried La Boulaye, his amazement growing, "have none returned to Dumouriez?"

"Have I not said that we are invalids?"

Caron eyed him with cold contempt.

"How many of you are there?" he asked. And for all that the man began to mislike this questioning, he had not the hardihood to refuse an answer to the stern tones of that stern man on horseback.

"Some fifty, or thereabouts."

La Boulaye said nothing for a moment, then touching the fellow's sleeve with his whip.

"How came you into this masquerade?" he inquired.

"Ma foi," answered the man, shrugging his shoulders, "we were in rags. The commissariat was demoralised, and supplies were not forthcoming. We had to take what we could find, or else go naked."

"And where did you find these things?"

"Diable! Will your questions never come to an end, Citizen? Would you not be better advised in putting them to the Captain himself?"

"Why, so I will. Where is he?"

In the distance a cloud of dust might be perceived above the long, white road. The soldier espied it as La Boulaye put his question.

"I am much at fault if he does not come yonder." And he pointed to the dust-cloud.

"I think," said La Boulaye, turning to his men, "that we will drink a cup of wine at the 'Eagle Inn.'"

Mean though the place was, it was equipped with a stable-

58

yard, to which admittance was gained by a porte-cochere on the right. Wheeling his horse, La Boulaye, without another word to the soldier he had been questioning, rode through it, followed by his escort.

The hostess, who came forward to receive them, was a tall, bony woman of very swarthy complexion, with beady eyes and teeth prominent as a rat's. But if ill-favoured, she seemed, at least, well-intentioned, in addition to which the tricolour scarf of office round La Boulaye's waist was a thing that commanded respect and servility, however much it might be the insignia of a Government of liberty, equality, and fraternity.

She bade the ostler care for their horses, and she brought them her best wine, seeking under an assumed geniality to conceal the unrest born of her speculations as to what might happen did Captain Charlot return ere the Deputy departed.

Charlot did return. Scarce were they seated at their wine when the confused sounds that from the distance had been swelling took more definite shape. The hostess looked uneasy as La Boulaye rose and went to the door of the inn. Down the road marched now a numerous company from which—to judge by their odd appearance—the players at bowls had been drawn. They numbered close upon threescore, and in the centre of them came a great lumbering vehicle, which puzzled La Boulaye. He drew away from the door and posted himself at the window, so that unobserved he might ascertain what was toward. Into the courtyard came that company, pêle-mêle, an odd mixture of rags and gauds, yet a very lusty party, vigorous of limb and loud of voice. With them came the coach, and there was such a press about the gates that La Boulaye looked to see some of them crushed to death. But with a few shouts and oaths and threats at one another they got through in safety, and the unwieldy carriage was brought to a standstill.

They were clamouring about its doors, and to La Boulaye it seemed that they were on the point of quarrelling among themselves, some wanting to enter the coach and others seeking to restrain them, when through the porte-cochere rode Charlot Tardivet himself.

He barked out a sharp word of command, and they grew silent and still, testifying to a discipline which said much for the strength of character of their captain. He was strangely altered, was this Tardivet, and his appearance now was worthy of his followers. Under a gaudily-laced, three-cornered hat his hair hung dishevelled and unkempt, like wisps of straw. He wore a coat of flowered black silk, with a heavy gold edging, and a very bright plum-coloured waistcoat showed above the broad tricolour scarf that sashed his middle. His breeches were white (or had been white in origin), and disappeared into a pair of very lustrous lacquered boots that rose high above his knees. A cavalry sabre of ordinary dimensions hung from a military belt, and a pistol-butt, peeping from his sash, completed the astonishing motley of his appearance. For the rest, he was the same tall and well-knit fellow; but there was more strength in his square chin, more intelligence in the keen blue eyes, and, alas! more coarseness in the mouth, which bristled with a reddish beard of some days' growth.

La Boulaye watched him with interest. He had become intimate with him in the old days in Paris, whither Tardivet had gone, and where, fired by the wrongs he had suffered, he had been one of the apostles of the Revolution. When the frontiers of France had been in danger Tardivet had taken up arms, and by the lustre which he had shed upon the name of Captain Charlotas he was come to be called throughout the army—he had eclipsed the fame of Citizen Tardivet, the erstwhile prophet of liberty. Great changes these in the estate of one who had been a simple peasant; but then the times were times of great changes. Was not Santerre, the brewer, become a great general, and was not Robespierre, the obscure lawyer of Arras, by way of becoming a dictator? Was it, therefore, wonderful that Charlot should have passed from peasant to preacher, from preacher to soldier, and from soldier to—what?

A shrewd suspicion was being borne in upon La Boulaye's mind as he stood by that window, his men behind him watching also, with no less intentness and some uneasiness for themselves— for they misliked the look of the company.

In five seconds Charlot had restored order in the human chaos without. In five minutes there were but ten men left in the yard. The others were gone at Charlot's bidding—a bidding, couched in words that went to confirm La Boulaye's suspicions.

"You will get back to your posts at once," he had said. "Because we have made one rich capture is no reason why you should neglect the opportunities of making others no less rich. You, Moulinet, with twenty men, shall patrol the road to Charleroi, and get as near France as possible. You Boligny, station yourself in the neighbourhood of Conde, with ten men, and guard the road from Valenciennes. You, Aigreville, spread your twenty men from Conde to Tournay, and watch the frontiers closely. Make an inspection of any captures you may take, and waste no time in bringing hither worthless ones. Now go. I will see that each man's share of this is assured him. March!"

There were some shouts of "Vive la Republique!" some of "Vive le Captaine Charlot!" and so they poured out of the yard, and left him to give a few hurried directions to the ten men that remained.

"Sad invalids these, as I live!" exclaimed La Boulaye over his shoulder to his followers. "Ha! There is my friend of the red redingote!"

The fellow with the bandaged head had approached Charlot and was tugging at his sleeve.

"Let be, you greasy rascal," the Captain snapped at him, to add: "What do you say? A Deputy? Where?" The fellow pointed with his thumb in the direction of the hostelry.

"Sacred name of a name!" growled Charlot, and, turning suddenly from the men to whom he had been issuing directions, he sprang up the steps and entered the inn. As he crossed the threshold of the common room he was confronted by the tall figure of La Boulaye.

"I make you my compliments, Charlot," was Caron's greeting, "upon the vigorous health that appears to prevail in your hospital."

Tardivet stood a moment within the doorway, staring at the Deputy. Then his brow cleared, and with a laugh, at once of welcome and amusement, he strode forward and put out his hand.

"My good Caron!" he cried. "To meet you at Boisvert is a pleasure I had not looked for."

"Are you so very sure," asked La Boulaye sardonically, as he took the outstretched hand, "that it is a pleasure?"

"How could it be else, old friend? By St. Guillotine!" he added, clapping the Deputy on the back, "you shall come to my room, and we will broach a bottle of green seal."

In some measure of wonder, La Boulaye permitted himself to be led up the crazy stairs to a most untidy room above, which evidently did duty as the Captain's parlour. A heavy brass lamp, hanging from the ceiling, a few untrustworthy chairs and a deal table, stained and unclean, were the only articles of furniture. But in almost every corner there were untidy heaps of garments Of all sorts and conditions; strewn about the floor were other articles of apparel, a few weapons, a saddle, and three or four boots; here an empty bottle, lying on its side, yonder a couple of full ones by the hearth; an odd book or two and an infinity of playing cards, cast there much as a sower scatters his seeds upon the ground.

There may be a hundred ways of apprehending the character of a man, but none perhaps is more reliable than the appearance of his dwelling, and no discerning person that stepped into Captain Tardivet's parlour could long remain in doubt of its inhabitant's pursuits and habits.

When Dame Capoulade had withdrawn, after bringing them

their wine and casting a few logs upon the fire, La Boulaye turned his back to the hearth and confronted his host.

"Why are you not with the army, Charlot?" he asked in a tone which made the question sound like a demand.

"Have they not told you," rejoined the other airily, engrossed in filling the glasses.

"I understand you were sent here to recover from a wound you received three months ago at Jemappes, and to take charge of other invalided soldiers. But seemingly, your invalids do not number more than a half-dozen out of the fifty or sixty men that are with you. How is it then, that you do not return with these to Dumouriez?"

"Because I can serve France better here," answered Charlot, "and at the same time enrich myself and my followers."

"In short," returned La Boulaye coldly, "because you have degenerated from a soldier into a brigand."

Charlot looked up, and for just a second his glance was not without uneasiness. Then he laughed. He unbuckled his sword and tossed it into a corner, throwing his hat after it.

"It was ever your way to take extreme views, Caron," he observed, with a certain whimsical regret of tone. "That, no doubt, is what has made a statesman of you. You had chosen more wisely had you elected to serve the Republic with your sword instead. Come, my friend," and he pointed to the wine, "let us pledge the Nation."

La Boulaye shrugged his shoulders slightly, and sighed. In the end he came forward and took the wine.

"Long live the Republic!" was Charlot's toast, and with a slight inclination of the head La Boulaye drained his glass.

"It is likely to live without you, Charlot, unless you mend your conduct."

"Diable!" snapped the Captain, a trifle peevishly. "Can you not understand that in my own way I am serving my country. You have called me a brigand. But you might say the same of General Dumouriez himself. How many cities has he not sacked?"

"That is the way of war."

"And so is this. He makes war upon the enemies of France that dwell in cities, whilst I, in a smaller way, make war upon those that travel in coaches. I confine myself to emigres—these damned aristocrats whom it is every good Frenchman's duty to aid in stamping out. Over the frontiers they come with their jewels, their plate, and their money-chests. To whom belongs this wealth? To France. Too long already have they withheld from the sons of the soil that which belongs equally to them, and now they have the effrontery to attempt to carry these riches out of the country. Would any true Republican dare to reproach me for what I do? I am but seizing that which belongs to France, and here dividing it among the good patriots that are with me, the soldiers that have bled for France."

"A specious argument," sneered La Boulaye.

"Specious enough to satisfy the Convention itself if ever I should be called to task," answered Charlot, with heat. "Do you propose to draw the attention of the Executive to my doings?"

La Boulaye's grey eyes regarded him steadily for a moment.

"Know you of any reason why I should not?" he asked.

"Yes, Caron, I do," was the ready answer. "I am well aware of the extent of your power with the Mountain. In Paris I can see that it might go hard with me if you were minded that it should, and you were able to seize me. On the other hand, that such arguments that I have advanced to you would be acceptable to the Government I do not doubt. But whilst they would approve of this that you call brigandage, I also do not doubt that they would claim that the prizes I have seized are by right the property of the Convention, and they might compel me to surrender them. Thus they would pass from my hands into those of some statesman-brigand, who, under the plea of seizing these treasures for the coffers of the nation, would transfer them to his own. Would you rather help such an one to profit than me, Caron? Have you so far forgotten how we suffered together— almost in the self-same cause—at Bellecour, in the old days? Have you forgotten the friendship that linked us later, in Paris, when the Revolution was in its dawn? Have you forgotten what I have endured at the hands of this infernal class that you can feel no sympathy for me? Caron, it is a measure of revenge, and as there is a Heaven, a very mild one. Me they robbed of more than life; them I deprive but of their jewels and their plate, turning them destitute upon the world. Bethink you of my girl-wife, Caron," he added, furiously, "and of how she died of grief and shame a short three months after our hideous nuptials. God in Heaven! When the memory of it returns to me I marvel at my own forbearance. I marvel that I do not take every man and woman of them that fall into my hands and flog them to death as they would have flogged you when you sought—alas to so little purpose—to intervene on my behalf."

He grew silent and thoughtful, and the expression of his face was not nice. At last: "Have I given you reason enough," he asked, "why you should not seek to thwart me?"

"Why, yes," answered La Boulaye, "more than was necessary. I am desolated that I should have brought you to re-open a sorrow that I thought was healed."

"So it is, Caron. How it is I do not know. Perhaps it is my nature; perhaps it is that in youth sorrow is seldom long-enduring; perhaps it is the strenuous life I have lived and the changes that have been wrought in me—for, after all, there is a little in this Captain Tardivet that is like the peasant poor Marie took to husband, four years ago. I am no longer the same man, and among the other things that I have put from me are the sorrows that were of the old Charlot. But some memories cannot altogether die, and if to-day I no longer mourn that poor child, yet the knowledge of the debt that lies 'twixt the noblesse of France and me is ever present, and I neglect no opportunity of discharging a part of it. But enough of that, Caron. Tell me of yourself. It is a full twelvemonth since last we met, and in that time, from what I have heard, you have done much and gone far. Tell me of it, Caron."

They drew their chairs to the hearth, and they sat talking so long that the early February twilight came down upon them while they were still at their reminiscences. La Boulaye had intended reaching Valenciennes that night; but rather than journey forward in the dark he now proposed to lie at Boisvert, a resolution in which he did not lack for encouragement from Charlot.

CHAPTER IX

THE CAPTIVES

Amid the sordid surroundings of Charlot's private quarters the Captain and the Deputy supped that evening. The supper sorted well with the house—a greasy, ill-cooked meal that proved little inviting to the somewhat fastidious La Boulaye. But the wine, plundered, no doubt, in common with the goblets out of which they drank it—was more than good, and whilst La Boulaye showed his appreciation of it, Charlot abused it like a soldier. They sat facing each other across the little deal table, whose stains were now hidden by a cloth, and to light them they had four tapers set in silver candlesticks of magnificent workmanship, and most wondrous weight, which Tardivet informed his guest had been the property of a ci-devant prince of the blood.

As the night wore on Captain Charlot grew boisterous and more confidential. He came at length to speak of the last capture they had made.

"I have taken prizes, Caron," said he, "which a king might not despise. But to-day—" He raised his eyes to the ceiling and wagged his head.

"Well?" quoth La Boulaye. "What about to-day?"

"I have made a capture worth more than all the others put together. It was an indifferent-looking berline, and my men were within an ace of allowing it to pass. But I have a nose, mon cher"—and he tapped the organ with ludicrous significance—"and, bon Dieu, what affair! I can smell an aristocrat a league off. Down upon that coach I swooped like a hawk upon a sparrow. Within it sat two women, thickly veiled, and I give you my word that in a sense I pitied them, for not a doubt of it, but they were in the act of congratulating themselves upon their escape from France. But sentiment may become fatal if permitted to interfere with enterprise. Stifling my regrets I desired them to alight, and they being wise obeyed me without demur. I allowed them to retain their veils. I sought the sight of things other than women's faces, and a brief survey of the coach showed me where to bestow my attention. I lifted the back seat. It came up like the lid of the chest it was, and beneath it I discovered enough gold and silver plate to outweigh in value almost everything that I had ever taken. But that was by no means all. Under the front seat there was a chest of gold—louis d'ors they were, some two or three thousand at least—and, besides that, a little iron-bound box of gems which in itself was worth more than all the rest of the contents of that treasure-casket of a coach. I tell you, Caron, I dropped the lid of that seat in some haste, for I was not minded that my men should become as wise as I. I stepped down and bade, the women re-enter, and hither under strong escort I have brought them."

"And these treasures?" asked La Boulaye.

"They are still in the coach below, with the women. I have told these that they shall spend the night there. To-morrow I shall see to them and give them their liberty—which is a more generous proceeding than might befall them at the hands of another. When they are gone comes the division of the spoil." He closed one eye slowly, in a very ponderous wink. "To my men I shall relegate the gold and silver plate as well as the money. For myself I shall only retain the little iron-bound box. My followers will account me more than generous and themselves more than satisfied. As for me, La Boulaye—by St. Guillotine, I am tempted to emigrate also and set up as an aristocrat myself in Prussia or England, for in that little box there is something more than a fortune. I asked you to-day whether you were minded to lay information against me in Paris. My faith, I am little concerned whether you do or not, for I think that before you can reach Paris, Captain Charlot Tardivet will be no more than a name in the Republican army. Abroad I shall call myself Charlot du Tardivet, and I shall sleep in fine linen and live on truffles and champagne. Caron, your health!"

He drained his glass, and laughed softly to himself as he set it down.

"Do you trust your men?" asked La Boulaye.

"Eh? Trust them? Name of a name! They know me. I have placed the ten most faithful ones on guard. They answer to the rest of us with their necks for the safety of their charge. Come hither, Caron."

He rose somewhat unsteadily, and lurched across to the window. La Boulaye followed him, and gazing out under his indication, he beheld the coach by the blaze of a fire which the men had lighted to keep them from freezing at their post.

"Does that look secure?"

"Why, yes—secure enough. But if those fellows were to take it into their heads that it would be more profitable to share the prize among ten than among sixty?"

"Secreanom!!" swore Charlot impatiently. "You do my wits poor credit. For what do you take me? Have I gone through so much, think you, without learning how little men are to be trusted? Faugh! Look at the porte-cochere. The gates are closed—aye, and

66

locked, mon cher, and the keys are here, in my pocket. Do you imagine they are to be broken through without arousing anyone? And then, the horses. They are in the stables over there, and again, the keys are in my pocket. So that, you see, I do not leave everything to the honesty of my ten most faithful ones."

"You have learned wisdom, not a doubt of it," laughed the Deputy.

"In a hard school, Caron," answered the Captain soberly. "Aye, name of a name, in a monstrous hard school."

He turned from the window, and the light of the tapers falling on his face, showed it heavily scored with lines of pain, testifying to the ugly memories which the Deputy's light words had evoked. Then suddenly he laughed, half-bitterly, half humourously.

"La, la!" said he. "The thing's past. Charlot Tardivet the bridegroom of Bellecour and Captain Charlot of Dumouriez' army are different men-very different."

He strode back to the table, filled his goblet, and gulped down the wine. Then he crossed to the fire and stood with his back to La Boulaye for a spell. When next he faced his companion all signs of emotion had cleared from his countenance. It was again the callous, reckless face of Captain Charlot, rendered a trifle more reckless and a trifle more callous by the wine-flush on his cheeks and the wine-glitter in his eye.

"Caron" said he, with a half-smile, "shall we have these ladies in to supper?"

"God forbid!" ejaculated La Boulaye.

"Nay, but I will," the other insisted, and he moved across to the window.

As he passed him, La Boulaye laid a detaining hand upon his arm.

"Not that, Charlot," he begged impressively, his dark face very set. "Plunder them, turn them destitute upon the world, if you will, but remember, at least, that they are women."

Charlot laughed in his face.

"It is something to remember, is it not? They remembered it of our women, these aristocrats!"

There was so much ugly truth in the Captain's words, and such a suggestion of just, if bitter, retribution in his mental attitude, that La Boulaye released his arm, at a loss for further arguments wherewith to curb him.

"Paydi!" Charlot continued, "I have a mind for a frolic. Does not justice give me the right to claim that these aristocrats shall amuse me?"

With an oath he turned abruptly, and pulled the casement open.

"Guyot!" he called, and a voice from below made answer to him.

"You will make my compliments to the citoyennes in the coach, Guyot, and tell them that the Citizen-captain Tardivet requests the honour of their company to supper."

Then he went to the door, and calling Dame Capoulade, he bade her set two fresh covers; in which he was expeditiously obeyed. La Boulaye stood by the fire, his pale face impassive now and almost indifferent. Charlot returned to the window to learn from Guyot that the citoyennes thanked the Citizen-captain, but that they were tired and sought to be excused, asking nothing better than to be allowed to remain at peace in their carriage.

"Sacred name of a name!" he croaked, a trifle thickly, for the wine he had taken was mastering him more and more. "Are they defying us? Since they will not accept an invitation, compel them to obey a command. Bring them up at once, Guyot."

"At once, Captain," was the answer, and Guyot went about the business.

Charlot closed the window and approached the table.

"They are coquettish these scented dames," he mocked, as he poured himself out some wine. "You are not drinking Caron."

"It is perhaps wise that one of us should remain sober," answered the Deputy quietly, for in spite of a certain sympathy with the feelings by which Charlot was actuated, he was in dead antipathy to this baiting of women that seemed toward.

Charlot made no answer. He drained his goblet and set it down with a bang. Then he flung himself into a chair, and stretching out his long, booted legs he began to hum the refrain of the "Marseillaise." Thus a few moments went by. Then there came a sound of steps upon the creaking stairs, and the gruff voice of the soldier urging the ladies to ascend more speedily.

At last the door opened and two women entered, followed by Guyot. Charlot lurched to his feet.

"You have come, Mesdames," said he, forgetting the mode of address prescribed by the Convention, and clumsily essaying to make a leg. "Be welcome! Guyot, go to the devil."

For a moment or two after the soldier's departure the women remained in the shadow, then, at the Captain's invitation, which they dared not disobey, they came forward into the halo of candle-light. Simultaneously La Boulaye caught his breath, and took a step forward. Then he drew back again until his shoulders touched the

68

overmantel and there he remained, staring at the newcomers, who as yet, did not appear to have observed him.

They wore no headgear, and their scarfs were thrown back upon their shoulders, revealing to the stricken gaze of La Boulaye the countenances of the Marquise de Bellecour and her daughter.

And now, as they advanced into the light, Charlot recognised them too. In the act of offering a chair he stood, arrested, his eyes devouring first one, then the other of then, with a glance that seemed to have grown oddly sobered. The flush died from his face, and his lips twitched like those of a man who seeks to control his emotions. Then slowly the colour crept back into his cheeks, a curl of mockery appeared on the coarse mouth, and the eyes beamed evilly.

They tense silence was broken by the bang with which he dropped the chair he had half raised. As he leaned forward now, La Boulaye read in his face the thought that had leapt into the Captain's mind, and had it been a question of any woman other than Zuzanne de Bellecour, the Deputy might have indulged in the consideration of what a wonderful retribution was there here. Into the hands of the man whose bride the Marquis de Bellecour had torn from him were now delivered by a wonderful chance the wife and daughter of that same Bellecour. And at Boisvert this briganding Captain was as much to-night the lord of life and death, and all besides, as had been the Marquis of Bellecour of old. But he pondered not these things, for all that the stern irony of the coincidence did not escape him. That evil look in Charlot's eyes, that sinister smile on Charlot's lips, more than suggested what manner of vengeance the Captain would exact—and that, for the time, was matter enough to absorb the Deputy's whole attention.

And the women did not see him. They were too much engrossed in the figure fronting them, and agonisedly, with cheeks white and bosoms heaving, they waited, in their dread suspense. At last, drawing himself to the full of his stalwart height, the Captain laughed grimly and spoke.

"Mesdames," said he, his very tone an insult in its brutal derision, "we Republicans have abolished God, and until tonight I have held the Republic right, arguing that if a God there was, His leanings must be aristocratic, since He never seemed to concern Himself with the misfortunes of the lowly-born. But tonight, mesdames, I know that the Republic is at fault. There is a God—a God of justice and retribution, who has delivered you, of all people in the world, into my hands. Look on me well, Ci-devant Marquise de Bellecour, and you, Mademoiselle de Bellecour. Look in my face and see if you know me again. Not you. You never heeded me as you rode by in those proud days. But heard you ever tell of one Charlot Tardivet, a base vassal whose wife your husband, Madame, and your father, Mademoiselle, took from him on his bridal morn? Heard you ever tell of that poor girl—one Marie Tardivet—who died of grief as a consequence of that brutality? But no; such matters were too trivial for your notice if you saw them, or for your memory if you ever heard tell of them. What was the life of a peasant more than that of any other animal of the land, that the concern of it should perturb the sereneness of your aristocratic being? Mesdames, that Charlot Tardivet am I; that Marie Tardivet was my wife. I knew not whom you were when I bade you sup at my table but now that I know it—what do you look for at my hands?"

It was the Marquise who answered him. She was deathly pale, and her words came breathlessly: for all that their import was very bold.

"We look for the recollection that we are women and unless you are as cowardly as—"

"Citoyenne," he broke in harshly, answering her as he had answered La Boulaye, "was my wife less a woman think you? Pah! There is yet another here who was wronged," he announced, and he waved his hand in the direction of La Boulaye, who stood, stiff and pale, by the hearth.

The women turned, and at sight of the Deputy a cry escaped Suzanne. It was a cry of hope, for here was one who would surely lend them aid. It was a fact, she thought, upon which the Captain had not counted. But La Boulaye stood straight and cold, and not by so much as an inclination of the head did he acknowledge that grim introduction. Charlot, mistaking Mademoiselle's exclamation, laughed softly.

"Well may you cry out, Citoyenne," said he, "for him I see you recognise. He is the man who sought to rescue my wife from the clutches of your lordly and most noble father. For his pains he was flogged until they believed him dead. Is it not very fitting that he should be with me now to receive you?"

"But he, at least, is in my debt," cried Mademoiselle, now making a step forward, and sustained by an excitement born of hope. "Whatever may be my father's sins, M. la Boulaye, at least, will not seek to visit them upon the daughter, for he owes his life to me, and he will not forget the debt."

Charlot's brows were suddenly knit with vexation. He half-turned to La Boulaye, as if to speak; but ere he could utter a word—

"The debt has been paid, Citoyenne," said Caron impassively.

Before that cold answer, so coldly delivered, Mademoiselle recoiled.

70

"Paid!" she echoed mechanically.

"Aye, paid," he rejoined. "You claimed your brother's life in payment, and I gave it to you. Do you not think that we are quits? Besides," he ended suddenly, "Captain Tardivet is the master here. Address your appeals to him, Citoyenne."

With terror written on her face, she turned from him to meet the flushed countenance of Charlot, who, with arms akimbo and his head on one side, was regarding her at once with mockery and satisfaction.

"What do you intend by us, Monsieur?" she questioned in a choking voice.

He smiled inscrutably.

"Allay your fears, Citoyenne; you will find me very gentle."

"I knew you would prove generous," she cried.

"But, yes, Citoyenne," he rejoined, in the tones we employ to those who fear unreasonably. "I shall prove generous; as generous as—as was my lord your father."

La Boulaye trembled, but his face remained calmly expressionless as he watched that grim scene.

"Monsieur!" Suzanne cried out in horror.

"You will not dare, you scum!" blazed the Marchioness.

Charlot shrugged his shoulders and laughed, whereupon Madame de Bellecour seemed to become a being transformed. Her ample flesh, which but a moment back had quivered in fear, quivered now more violently still in anger. The colour flowed back into her cheeks until they flamed an angry crimson, and her vituperations rang in so loud and fierce a voice that at last, putting his hands to his ears, Charlot crossed to the door.

"Silence!" he roared at her, so savagely that her spirit forsook her on the instant. "I will put an end to this," he swore, as he opened the door. "Hold there! Is Guyot below?"

"Here, Captain," came a voice.

Charlot retraced his steps, leaving the door wide, his eyes dwelling upon Suzanne until she shrank under its gaze, as she might have done from the touch of some unclean thing. She drew near to her mother, in whom the brief paroxysm of rage was now succeeded by a no less violent paroxysm of weeping. On the stairs sounded Guyot's ascending steps.

"Mother," whispered Suzanne, setting her arms about her in a vain attempt to comfort. Then she heard Charlot's voice curtly bidding Guyot to reconduct the Marquise to her carriage.

Madame de Bellecour heard it also, and roused herself once more.

71

"I will not go," she stormed, anger flashing again from the tear-laden eyes. "I will not leave my daughter."

Charlot shrugged his shoulders callously.

"Take her away, Guyot," he said, shortly, and the sturdy soldier obeyed him with a roughness that took no account of either birth or sex.

When the Marquise's last scream had died away in the distance, Charlot turned once more to Suzanne, and it seemed that he sought to compose his features into an expression of gentleness beyond their rugged limitations. But the glance of his blue eyes was kind, and mistaking the purport of that kindness, Mademoiselle began an appeal to his better feelings.

Straight and tall, pale and delicate she stood, her beauty rendered, perhaps, the more appealing by virtue of the fear reflected on her countenance. Her blue eyes were veiled behind their long black lashes, her lips were tremulous, and her hands clasped and unclasped as she now made her prayer to the Republican. But in the hardened heart of Charlot no breath of pity stirred. He beheld her beauty and he bethought him of his wrongs. For the rest, perhaps, had she been less comely he had been less vengeful.

And yonder by the hearth stood La Boulaye like a statue, unmoved and immovable. The Captain was speaking to her, gently and soothingly, but her thoughts became more taken with the silence of La Boulaye than with the speech of Charlot. Even in that parlous moment she had leisure to despise herself for having once— on the day on which, in answer to her intercessions, he had spared her brother's life—entertained a kindly, almost wistful, thought concerning this man whom she now deemed a dastard.

CHAPTER X

THE BAISER LAMOURETTE

Presently Charlot turned to La Boulaye, and for all that he uttered no word, his glance left nothing to be said. In response to it Caron stirred at last, and came leisurely over to the table.

"A mouthful of wine, and I'm gone, Charlot," said he in level, colourless tones, as taking up a flagon he filled himself a goblet.

"Fill for me, too," cried the Captain; "aye, and for the Citoyenne here. Come, my girl, a cup of wine will refresh you."

But Suzanne shrank from the invitation as much as from the tenor of it and the epithet he had applied to her. Observing this, he laughed softly.

"Oh! As you will. But the wine is good-from cellar of a ci-devant Duke. My service to you, Citoyenne," he pledged her, and raising his cup, he poured the wine down a throat that was parched by the much that he had drunk already, But ere the goblet was half-empty, a sharp, sudden cry from La Boulaye came to interrupt his quaffing. He glanced round, and at what he saw he spilled the wine down his waistcoat, then let the cup fall to the ground, as with an oath he flung himself upon the girl.

She had approached the table whilst both men were drinking, and quietly possessed herself of a knife; and, but that it was too blunt to do the service to which she put it, Charlot's intervention would have come too late. As it was he caught her wrist in time, and in a rage he tore the weapon from her fingers, and flung it far across the room.

"So, pretty lady!" he gasped, now gripping both her wrists. "So! we are suicidally inclined, are we! We would cheat Captain Charlot, would we? Fi donc!" he continued with horrid playfulness. "To shed a blood so blue upon a floor so unclean! Name of a name of a name!"

Accounting herself baffled at every point, this girl, who had hitherto borne herself so stoutly as to have stoically sought death as a last means of escape, began to weep softly. Whereupon:

"Nay, nay, little-woman," murmured the Captain, in such accents as are employed to a petted child, and instinctively, in his intent to soothe he drew her nearer. And now the close contact thrilled him; her beauty, and some subtle perfume that reached him from her, played havoc with his senses. Nearer he drew her in silence, his face white and clammy, and his hot, wine laden breath coming quicker every second. And unresisting she submitted, for she was beyond resistance now, beyond tears even. From between wet lashes her great eyes gazed into his with a look of deadly, piteous affright; her lips were parted, her cheeks ashen, and her mind was dimly striving to formulate a prayer to the Holy Mother, the natural protectress of all imperilled virgins.

Nearer she felt herself drawn to her tormentor, in whose thoughts there dwelt now little recollection of the vengeful character of his purpose. For a second her wrists were released; then she felt his arms going round her as the coils of a snake go round its prey. With a sudden reassertion of self, with a panting gasp of horror, she tore herself free. An oath broke from him as he sprang after her. Then the unexpected happened. Above his head something bright flashed up, then down. There was a dull crack, and the Captain stopped short in his rush; his hands were jerked to the height of his breast, and like a pole-axed beast he dropped and lay prone at her feet.

Across his fallen body she beheld La Boulaye standing impassively, the ghost of a smile on his thin lips, and in his hand one of the heavy silver candlesticks from the table.

Whilst a man might count a dozen they stood so with no word spoken. Then:

"It was a cowardly blow, Citoyenne," said the Deputy in accents of regret; "but what choice had I?" He set down the candlestick, and kneeling beside Charlot, he felt for the Captain's heart. "The door, Citoyenne," he muttered. "Lock it."

Mechanically, and without uttering a word, she hastened to do his bidding. As the key grated in the lock he rose.

"It has only stunned him," he announced. "Now to prepare an explanation for it."

He drew a chair under the old brass lamp, that hung from the ceiling. He mounted the chair, and with both hands he seized the chain immediately above the lamp. Drawing himself up, he swung there for just a second; then the hook gave way, and amid a shower of plaster La Boulaye half-tumbled to the ground.

"There," said he, as he dropped the lamp with its chain and hook upon the floor by Charlot. "It may not be as convincing as we might wish, but I think that it will prove convincing enough to the dull wits of the landlady, and of such of Charlot's followers as may enter here. I am afraid," he deplored, "that it will be some time before he recovers. He was so far gone in wine that it needed little weight to fell him."

Her glance met his once more, and she took a step towards him with hands outstretched.

74

"Monsieur, Monsieur!" she cried. "If you but knew how in my thoughts I wronged you a little while ago."

"You had all reason to," he answered, taking her hands, and there came the least softening of his stern countenance. "It grieved me to add to your affliction. But had I permitted him to do so much as suspect that I was anything but your implacable enemy, I had no chance of saving you. He would have dismissed me, and I must have obeyed or been compelled, for he is master here, and has men enough to enforce what he desires."

And now she would have thanked him for having saved her, but he cut her short almost roughly.

"You owe me no thanks," he said. "I have but done for you what my manhood must have bidden me do for any woman similarly situated. For to-night I have saved you, Citoyenne. I shall make an effort to smuggle you and your mother out of Boisvert before morning, but after that you must help yourselves."

"You will do this?" she cried, her eyes glistening.

"I will attempt it."

"By what means, Monsieur Caron?"

"I do not yet know. I must consider. In the meantime you had best return to your coach. Later to-night I shall have you and your mother brought to me, and I will endeavour to so arrange matters that you shall not again return to your carriage."

"Not return to it?" she exclaimed. "But are we then to leave it here?"

"I am afraid there is no help for that."

"But, Monsieur, you do not know; there is a treasure in that carriage. All that we have is packed in it, and if we go without it we go destitute."

"Better, perhaps, to go destitute than not to go at all, Mademoiselle. I am afraid there is no choice for you."

His manner was a trifle impatient. It irritated him that in such a moment she should give so much thought to her valuables. But in reality she was thinking of them inasmuch as they concerned her mother, who was below, and her father and brother who awaited them in Prussia, whither they had separately emigrated. The impatience in his tone stung her into a feeling of resentment, that for the moment seemed to blot out the much that she owed him. A reproachful word was trembling on her lips, when suddenly he put out his hand.

"Hist!" he whispered, the concentrated look of one who listens stamped upon his face. His sharp ears had detected some sound which—perhaps through her preoccupation—she had not noticed. He stepped quickly to the Captain's side, and taking up the lamp by its chain, he leapt into the air like a clown, and came down on his heels with a thud that shook the chamber. Simultaneously he dropped the lamp with a clatter, and sent a shout re-echoing through the house.

The girl stared at him with parted lips and the least look of fear in her eyes. Was he gone clean mad of a sudden?

But now the sound which had warned him of someone's approach reached her ears as well. There were steps on the stairs, which at that alarming noise were instantly quickened. Yet ere they had reached the top La Boulaye was at the door vociferating wildly.

Into the room came the hostess, breathless and grinning with anxiety, and behind her came Guyot, who, startled by the din, had hastened up to inquire into its cause.

At sight of the Captain stretched upon the floor there was a scream from Mother Capoulade and an oath from the soldier.

"Mon Dieu! what has happened?" she cried, hurrying forward.

"Miserable!" exclaimed La Boulaye, with well-feigned anger. "It seems that your wretched hovel is tumbling to pieces, and that men are not safe beneath its roof." And he indicated the broken plaster and the fallen lamp.

"How did it happen, Citoyenne-deputy?" asked Guyot; for all that he drew the only possible inference from what he saw.

"Can you not see how it happened?" returned La Boulaye, impatiently. "As for you, wretched woman, you will suffer for it, I promise you. The nation is likely to demand a high price for Captain Charlot's injuries."

"But, bon Dieu, how am I to blame?" wailed the frightened woman.

"To blame," echoed La Boulaye, in a furious voice. "Are you not to blame that you let rooms in a crazy hovel? Let them to emigres as much as you will, but if you let them to good patriots and thereby endanger their lives you must take the consequences. And the consequences in this case are likely to be severe, malheureuse."

He turned now to Guyot, who was kneeling by the Captain, and looking to his hurt.

"Here, Guyot," he commanded sharply, "reconduct the Citoyenne to her coach. I will perhaps see her again later, when the Captain shall have recovered consciousness. You, Citoyenne Capoulade, assist me to carry him to bed."

Each obeyed him, Guyot readily, as became a soldier, and the hostess trembling with the dread which La Boulaye's words had instilled into her. They got Charlot to bed, and when a half-hour or so later he recovered consciousness, it was to find Guyot watching at his bed-side. Bewildered, he demanded an explanation of his

76

present position and of the pain in his head, which brought him the memory of a sudden and unaccountable blow he had received, which was the last thing that he remembered. Guyot, who had never for a moment entertained a doubt of the genuineness of the mise-en-scene La Boulaye had prepared, answered him with the explanation of how he had been struck by the falling lamp, whereupon Charlot fell to cursing lamps and crumblings with horrid volubility. That done he would have risen, but that La Boulaye, entering at that moment, insisted that he should remain abed.

"Are you mad?" the Deputy expostulated, "or is it that you do not appreciate the nature of your hurt? Diable! I have known a man die through insisting to be about with a cracked skull that was as nothing to yours."

"Name of a name!" gasped Charlot, who in such matters was profoundly ignorant and correspondingly credulous. "Is it so serious?"

"Not serious if you lie still and sleep. You will probably be quite well by to-morrow. But if you move to-night the consequences may well be fatal."

"But I cannot sleep at this hour," the Captain complained. "I am very wakeful."

"We will try to find you a sleeping potion, then," said La Boulaye. "I hope the hosteen may have something that will answer the purpose. Meanwhile, Guyot, do not allow the Captain to talk. If you would have him well to-morrow, remember that it is of the first importance that he should have utter rest tonight."

With that he went in quest of Dame Capoulade to ascertain whether she possessed any potion that would induce sleep. He told her that the Captain was seriously injured, and that unless he slept he might die, and, quickened by the terror of what might befall her in such a case, the woman presently produced a small phial full of a brown, viscous fluid. What it might be he had no notion, being all unversed in the mysteries of the pharmacopoeia; but she told him that it had belonged to her now defunct husband, who had always said that ten drops of it would make a man sleep the clock round.

He experimented on the Captain with ten drops, and within a quarter of an hour of taking the draught of red wine in which it was administered, Charlot's deep breathing proclaimed him fast asleep.

That done, La Boulaye sent Guyot below to his post once more, and returning to the room in which they had supped, he paced up and down for a full hour, revolving in his mind the matter of saving Mademoiselle and her mother. At last, towards ten o'clock, he opened the casement, and calling down to Guyot, as Charlot had done, he bade him bring the women up again. Now Guyot knew of

77

the high position which Caron occupied in the Convention, and he had seen the intimate relations in which he stood to Tardivet, so that unhesitatingly he now obeyed him.

La Boulaye closed the window, and crossed slowly to the fire. He stirred the burning logs with his boot, then stood there waiting. Presently the stairs creaked, next the door opened, and Guyot ushered in Mademoiselle.

"The elder citoyenne refuses to come, Citizen-deputy," said the soldier. "They both insisted that it was not necessary, and that the Citoyenne here would answer your questions."

Almost on the point of commanding the soldier to return for the Marquise, Caron caught the girl's eye, and her glance was so significant that he thought it best to hear first what motives she had for thus disobeying him.

"Very well," he said shortly. "You may go below, Guyot. But hold yourself in readiness lest I should have need of you."

The soldier saluted and disappeared. Scarce was he gone when Mademoiselle came hurrying forward.

"Monsieur Caron," she cried "Heaven is surely befriending us. The soldiers are drinking themselves out of their wits. They will be keeping a slack watch presently."

He looked at her for a moment, fathoming the purport of what she said.

"But," he demanded at last, "why did not the Marquise obey my summons, and accompany you?"

"She was afraid to leave the coach, Monsieur. Moreover, she agreed with me that it would not be necessary."

"Not necessary?" he echoed. "But it is necessary. When last you were here I told you I did not intend you should return to the coach. This is my plan, Citoyenne. I shall keep Guyot waiting below while you and your mother are fortifying yourselves by supper here. Then I shall dismiss him with a recommendation that he keep a close watch upon the carriage, and the information that you will not be returning to it to-night. A half-hour later or so, when things are quiet, I shall find a way out for you by the back, after which the rest must remain in your hands. More I cannot do."

"You can," she cried; "you can."

"If you will enlighten me," said he, with the faintest touch of irony.

She looked at his stern, sardonic face and solemn grey eyes, and for a moment it almost seemed to her that she hated him more than anybody in the world. He was so passionless, so master of himself, and he addressed her in a tone which, whilst it suggested that he accounted himself most fully her equal, made her feel that he was really her better by much. If one of these two was an aristocrat, surely that one was the Citizen-deputy La Boulaye.

"If you had but the will you would do it, Monsieur," she answered him. "It is not mine to enlighten you; I know not how."

"I have the very best will in the world, Citoyenne," said he. "Of that I think that I am giving proof."

"Aye, the will to do nothing that will shame your manhood," she rejoined. "That is all you think of. It was because your manhood bade you that you came to my rescue—so you said when you declined my thanks. It is this manhood of yours, I make no doubt, that is now prevailing upon you to deliver two unprotected women out of the hands of these brigands."

"In Heaven's name, Citoyenne," quoth the astonished Deputy, "out of what sentiment would you have me act, and, indeed, so that I save you, how can it concern you by what sentiment I am prompted?"

She paused a moment before replying. Her eyes were downcast, and some of the colour faded from her cheeks. She came a step nearer, which brought her very close to him.

"Monsieur," she faltered very shyly, "in the old days at Bellecour you would have served me out of other sentiments."

He started now in spite of himself, and eyed her with a sudden gleam of hope, or triumph, or mistrust, or perhaps of all three. Then his glance fell, and his voice was wistful.

"But the old days are dead, Mademoiselle."

"The days, yes," she answered, taking courage from his tone. "But love Monsieur, is everlasting—it never dies, they say."

And now it was La Boulaye who drew closer, and this man who had so rigidly schooled himself out of all emotions, felt his breath quickening, and his pulses throbbing faster and faster. To him it seemed that she was right, and that love never died—for the love for her, which he believed he had throttled out of existence long ago, seemed of a sudden to take life as vigorously as ever. And then it was as if some breeze out of the past bore to his nostrils the smell of the violets and of the moist earth of that April morning when she had repulsed him in the woods of Bellecour. His emotion died down. He drew back, and stood rigid before her.

"And if it were to live, Citoyenne," he said—the resumption of the Republican form of address showed that he had stepped back into the spirit as well as in the flesh "what manner of fool were I to again submit it to the lash of scorn it earned when first it was discovered?"

"But that belonged to the old days," she cried, "and it is dead with the old days.'

"It is vain to go back, Citoyenne," he cut in, and his voice rang harsh with determination.

She bit her lip under cover of her bent head. If she had hated him before how much more did she not hate him now? And but a moment back it had seemed to her that she had loved him. She had held out her hands to him and he had scorned them; in her eagerness she had been unmaidenly, and all that she had earned had been humiliation. She quivered with shame and anger, and sinking into the nearest chair she burst into a passion of tears.

Thus by accident did she stumble upon the very weapon wherewith to make an utter rout of all Caron's resolutions. For knowing nothing of the fountain from which those tears were springing, and deeming them the expression of a grief pure and unalloyed—saving, perhaps, by a worthy penitence—he stepped swiftly to her side.

"Mademoiselle," he murmured, and his tone was as gentle and beseeching as it had lately been imperious. "Nay, Mademoiselle, I implore you!"

But her tears continued, and her sobs shook the slender frame as if to shatter it. He dropped upon his knees. Scarcely knowing what he did, he set his arm about her waist in a caress of protection.

A long curl of her black, unpowdered hair lay against his cheek.

"Mademoiselle," he murmured, and she took comfort at the soothing tone.

From it she judged him malleable now, that had been so stern and unyielding before. She raised her eyes, and through her tears she turned their heavenly blue full upon the grey depths of his.

"You will not believe me, Monsieur," she complained softly. "You will not believe that I can have changed with the times; that I see things differently now. If you were to come to me again as in the woods at Bellecour—" She paused abruptly, her cheeks flamed scarlet, and she covered them with her hands.

"Suzanne!" he cried, seeking to draw those hands away. "Is it true, this? You care, beloved!"

She uncovered her face at last. Again their eyes met.

"I was right," she whispered. "Love never dies, you see."

"And you will marry me, Suzanne?" he asked incredulously.

She inclined her head, smiling through her tears, and he would have caught her to him but that she rose of a sudden.

"Hist!" she cried, raising her finger: "someone is coming."

He listened, holding his breath, but no sound stirred. He went to the door and peered out. All was still. But the interruption served to impress him with the fact that time was speeding, and that all unsuspicious though Guyot might be as yet, it was more than possible that his suspicions would be aroused if she remained there much longer.

He mentioned this, and he was beginning to refer to his plan for their escape when she thrust it aside, insisting that they must depart in their coach, so that their treasure might also be saved.

"Be reasonable, Suzanne," he cried. "It is impossible."

A cloud of vexation swept across her averted face.

"Nay, surely not impossible," she answered. "Listen, Caron, there are two treasures in that coach. One is in money and in gold and silver plate; the other is in gems, and amounts to thrice the value of the rest. This latter is my dowry. It is a fortune with which we can quit France and betake ourselves wherever our fancy leads us. Would you ask me to abandon that and come to you penniless, compelled thereby to live in perpetual terror in a country where at any moment an enemy might cast at me the word aristocrate, and thereby ruin me?"

There was no cupidity in La Boulaye's nature, and even the prospect of an independent fortune would have weighed little with him had it not been backed by the other argument she employed touching the terror that would be ever with her did they dwell in France.

He stood deep in thought, his hand to his brow, thrusting back the long black hair from his white forehead, what time she recapitulated her argument.

"But how?" he exclaimed, in exasperation "Tell me how?"

"That is for you to discover, Caron."

He thrust his hands deep into his pockets, and set himself to pace the chamber. And now his fingers came in contact with something foreign. Idly he drew it forth, and it proved to be the phial Mother Capoulade had given him, and from which he had poured the ten drops for the Captain's sleeping potion. His eyes brightened with inspiration. Here was a tool whose possibilities were vast. Then his brows were knit again.

"Wait," he said slowly. "Let me think."

CHAPTER XI

THE ESCAPE

Resting his elbow on the table, and with his hand to his brow, Caron sat deep in thought, his forefinger and thumb pressed against his closed eyelids. From beyond the board Mademoiselle watched him anxiously and waited. At last he looked up.

"I think I have it," he announced, rising. "You say that the men are drinking heavily. That should materially assist us."

She asked him what plan he had conceived, but he urged that time pressed; she should know presently; meanwhile, she had best return immediately to her carriage. He went to the door to call Guyot, but she stayed him.

"No, no, Monsieur," she exclaimed. "I will not pass through the common-room again in that fellow's company. They are all in there, carousing, and—and I dare not."

As if to confirm her words, now that he held the door open, he caught some sounds of mirth and the drone of voices from below.

"Come with me, then," said he, taking up one of the candles. "I will escort you."

Together they descended the narrow staircase, La Boulaye going first, to guide her, since two might not go abreast. At the foot there was a door, which he opened, and then, at the end of a short passage—in which the drone of voices sounded very loud and in particular one, cracked voice that was raised in song—they gained the door of the common-room. As La Boulaye pushed it open they came upon a scene of Bacchanalian revelry. On a chair that had been set upon the table they beheld Mother Capoulade enthroned like a Goddess of Liberty, and wearing a Phrygian cap on her dishevelled locks. Her yellow cheeks were flushed and her eyes watery, whilst hers was the crazy voice that sang.

Around the table, in every conceivable attitude of abandonment, sat Captain Charlot's guard—every man of the ten—and with them the six men and the corporal of La Boulaye's escort, all more or less in a condition of drunkenness.

"Le jour de gloire est arrive?" sang the croaking voice of Dame Capoulade, and there it stopped abruptly upon catching sight of La Boulaye and his companion in the doorway. Mademoiselle shivered out of loathing; but La Boulaye felt his pulses quickened with hope, for surely all this was calculated to assist him in his purpose.

At the abrupt interruption of the landlady's version of the

"Marseillaise" the men swung round, and upon seeing the Deputy they sought in ludicrous haste to repair the disorder of their appearance.

"So!" thundered Caron. "This is the watch you keep? This is how you are to be trusted? And you, Guyot," he continued, pointing his finger at the man. "Did I not bid you await my orders? Is this how you wait? You see that I am compelled to reconduct the Citoyenne myself, for I might have called you in vain all night."

Guyot came forward sheepishly, and a trifle unsteady in his gait.

"I did not hear you call, Citizen," he muttered.

"It had been a miracle if you had with this din," answered La Boulaye. "Here, take the Citoyenne back to her carriage."

Obediently Guyot led the Citoyenne across the room and out into the courtyard, and the men, restrained by La Boulaye's severe presence, dared scarcely so much as raise their eyes to her as she passed out.

"And now to your posts," was Caron's stern command. "By my soul, if you were men of mine I would have you flogged for this. Out with you!" And he pointed imperiously to the door.

"It is a bitter night, Citizen," grumbled one of them.

"Do you call yourselves soldiers, and does a touch of frost make cowards of you? Outside, you old wives, at once! I'll see you at your post before I go to bed."

And with that he set himself to drive them out, and they went, until none but his own half-dozen remained. These he bade dispose themselves about the hearth, in which they very readily obeyed him.

On a side-table stood a huge steaming can which had attracted La Boulaye's attention from the moment that he had entered the room. He went to peer into this, and found it full almost to the brim of mulled red wine.

With his back to those in the room, so as to screen his actions, he had uncorked the phial as he was approaching the can. Now, as he made pretence first to peer into it and then to smell its contents, he surreptitiously emptied the potion into it, wondering vaguely to himself whether the men would ever wake again if they had drunk it. Slipping the phial into his sash he turned to Mother Capoulade, who had descended from the table and stood looking very foolish.

"What is this?" he demanded angrily.

"It was a last cup of wine for the men," she faltered. "The night is bitterly cold, Citizen," she added, by way of excusing herself.

"Bah!" snarled Caron, and for a moment he stood there as if deliberating. "I am minded to empty it into the kennel," he announced.

"Citizen!" cried the woman, in alarm. "It is good wine, and I have spiced it."

"Well," he relented, "they may have it. But see that it is the last to-night."

And with that he strode across the room, and with a surly "Good-night" to his men, he mounted the stairs once more.

He waited perhaps ten minutes in the chamber above, then he went to the casement, and softly opened the window. It was as he expected. With the exception of the coach standing in the middle of the yard, and just discernible by the glow of the smouldering fire they had built there but allowed to burn low, the place was untenanted. Believing him to have retired for the night, the men were back again in the more congenial atmosphere of the hostelry, drinking themselves no doubt into a stupor with that last can of drugged wine. He sat down to quietly mature his plans, and to think out every detail of what he was about to do. At the end of a half-hour, silence reigning throughout the house, he rose. He crept softly into Charlot's chamber and possessed himself of the Captain's outer garments. These he carried back to the sitting-room, and extracted from the coat pocket two huge keys tied together with a piece of string. He never doubted that they were the keys he sought, one opening the stable door and the other the gates of the porte-cochere.

He replaced the garments, and then to make doubly sure, he waited yet—in a fever of impatience—another half-hour by his watch.

It wanted a few minutes to midnight when, taking up his cloak and a lantern he had lighted, he went below once more. In the common-room he found precisely the scene he had expected. Both Charlot's men and his own followers lay about the floor in all conceivable manner of attitudes, their senses locked deep in the drunken stupor that possessed them. Two or three had remained seated, and had fallen across the table, when overcome. Of these was Mother Capoulade, whose head lay sideways on her curled arms, and from whose throat there issued a resonant and melodious snore. Most of the faces that La Boulaye could see were horribly livid and bedewed with sweat, and again it came into his mind to wonder whether he had overdone things, and they would wake no more. On the other hand, an even greater fear beset him, that the drug might have been insufficient. By way of testing it, he caught one fellow who lay across his path a violent kick in the side. The man grunted in his sleep, and stirred slightly, to relapse almost at once into his helpless attitude, and to resume his regular breathing, which the blow had interrupted.

La Boulaye smiled his satisfaction, and without further hesitancy passed out into the yard. He had yet a good deal to say to Mademoiselle, but he could not bring himself to speak to her before her mother, particularly as he realised how much the Marquise might be opposed to him. He opened the carriage door.

"Mademoiselle," he called softly, "will you do me the favour to alight for an instant? I must speak to you."

"Can you not say what you have to say where you are?" came the Marquise's voice.

"No, Madame," answered La Boulaye coldly, "I cannot."

"Oh, it is 'Madame' and 'Mademoiselle' now, eh? What have you done to the man, child, to have earned us so much deference."

"May I remind Mademoiselle," put in La Boulaye firmly, "that time presses, and that there is much to be done?"

"I am here, Monsieur" she answered, as without more ado, and heedless of her mother's fresh remarks, she stepped from the carriage.

La Boulaye proffered his wrist to assist her to alight, then reclosed the door, and led her slowly towards the stable.

"Where are the soldiers?" she whispered.

"Every soul in the inn is asleep," he answered. "I have drugged them all, from the Captain down to the hostess. The only one left is the ostler, who is sleeping in one of the outhouses here. Him you must take with you, not only because it is not possible to drug him as well, but also because the blame of your escape must rest on someone, and it may as well rest on him as another."

"But why not on you?" she asked.

"Because I must remain."

"Ah!" It was no more than a breath of interrogation, and her face was turned towards him as she awaited an explanation.

"I have given it much thought, Suzanne, and unless someone remains to cover, as it were, your retreat, I am afraid that your flight might be vain, and that you would run an overwhelming risk of recapture. You must remember the resourcefulness of this fellow, Tardivet, and his power in the country here. If he were to awake to the discovery that I had duped him, he would be up and after us, and I make little doubt that it would not be long ere he found the scent and ran us to earth. Tomorrow I shall discover your flight and the villainy of the ostler, and I shall so organise the pursuit that you shall not be overtaken."

There was a moment's pause, during which La Boulaye seemed to expect some question. But none came, so he proceeded:

"Your original intention was to make for Prussia, where you say that your father and your brother are awaiting you."

85

"Yes, Monsieur. Beyond the Moselle—at Treves."

"You must alter your plans," said he shortly. "Your mother, no doubt, will insist upon repairing thither, and I will see that the road is left open for her escape. At Soignies you, Suzanne, can hire yourself a berline, that will take you back to France."

"Back to France?" she echoed.

"Yes, back to France. That is the unlikeliest road on which to think of pursuing you, and thus you will baffle Charlot. Let your mother proceed on her journey to Prussia, but tell her to avoid Charleroi, and to go round by Liege. Thus only can she hope to escape Tardivet's men that are patrolling the road from France. As for you, Suzanne, you had best go North as far as Oudenarde, so as to circumvent the Captain's brigands on that side. Then make straight for Roubaix, and await me at the 'Hotel des Cloches.'"

"But, Monsieur, I shudder at the very thought of re-entering France."

"As Mademoiselle de Bellecour, a proscribed aristocrat, that is every reason for your fears. But I have given the matter thought and I can promise you that as the Citoyenne La Boulaye, wife of the Citizen-deputy Caron La Boulaye, you will be as safe as I should be myself, if you are questioned, and, in response, you will find nothing but eagerness to serve you on every hand."

She spoke now of the difficulties her mother would make, but he dismissed the matter by reminding her that her mother could not detain her by force. Again she alluded to her dowry, but that also he dismissed, bidding her leave it behind. Her family would need the money, to be realised by the jewels. As for herself, he assured her that as his wife she would not want, and showed her how idle was her dread of living in France.

"And now, Mademoiselle," he said, more briskly, "let us see to this ostler."

He opened the door of the outhouse, and uncovering his lantern he raised it above his head. Its yellow light revealed to them a sleeper on the straw in a corner. La Boulaye entered and stirred the man with his foot.

The fellow sat up blinking stupidly and dragging odd wisps of straw from his grey hair.

"What's amiss?" he grunted.

As briefly as might be La Boulaye informed him that he was to receive a matter of five hundred francs if he would journey into Prussia with the ci-devant Marquise de Bellecour.

Five hundred francs? It was a vast sum, the tenth of which had never been his at any one time of his wretched life. For five hundred francs he would have journeyed into Hades, and La

Boulaye found him willing enough to go to Prussia, and had no need to resort to the more forcible measures he had come prepared to employ.

Accompanied by the ostler, they now passed to the stables, and when La Boulaye had unlocked the door and cut the bonds that pinioned the Marquis's coachman, they got the horses, and together they harnessed them as quietly as might be.

Then working with infinite precaution, and as little sound as possible, they brought them out into the yard and set them in the shafts of the carriage. The rest was easy work, and a quarter of an hour later the heavy vehicle rumbled through the porte-cochere and started on its way to Soignies.

La Boulaye dropped the keys into a bucket and went within. In the common-room nothing had changed, and the men lay about precisely as he had left them. Reassured, he went above and took a peep at the Captain, whom he found snoring lustily.

Satisfied that all was well, Caron passed quietly to his own chamber, and with an elation of soul such as had never been his since boyhood, he fell asleep amid visions of Suzanne and the new life he was to enter upon in her sweet company.

CHAPTER XII

THE AWAKENING

La Boulaye awakened betimes next morning. It may be that the matter on his mind and the business that was toward aroused him; certainly it was none of the sounds that are common to an inn at early morn, for the place was as silent as a tomb.

Some seconds he remained on his back, staring at the whitewashed ceiling and listening to the patter of the rain against his window. Then, as his mind gathered up the threads of recollection, he leapt from his bed and made haste to assume a garment or two.

He stood a moment at his casement, looking out into the empty courtyard. From a leaden sky the rain was descending in sheets, and the gargoyle at the end of the eaves overhead was discharging a steady column of water into the yard. Caron shivered with the cold of that gloomy February morning, and turned away from the window. A few moments later he was in Tardivet's bedchamber, vigorously shaking the sleeping Captain.

"Up, Charlot! Awake!" he roared in the man's ear.

"What o'clock?" he asked with a yawn. Then a sudden groan escaped him, and he put his hand to his head. "Thousand devils!" he swore, "what a headache!"

But La Boulaye was not there on any mission of sympathy, nor did he waste words in conveying his news.

"The coach is gone," he announced emphatically.

"Coach? What coach?" asked the Captain, knitting his brows.

"What coach?" echoed La Boulaye testily. "How many coaches were there? Why, the Bellecour coach; the coach with the treasure."

At that Charlot grew very wide-awake. He forgot his headache and his interest in the time of day.

"Gone?" he bellowed. "How gone? Pardieu, it is not possible!"

"Look for yourself," was La Boulaye's answer as he waved his hand in the direction of the window. "I don't know what manner of watch your men can have kept that such a thing should have come about. Probably, knowing you ill a-bed, they abused the occasion by getting drunk, and probably they are still sleeping it off. The place is silent enough."

But Tardivet scarcely heard him. From his window he was staring into the yard below, too thunderstruck by its emptiness to even have recourse to profanity. Stable door and porte-cochere alike stood open. He turned suddenly and made for his coat. Seizing it, he thrust his hand in one pocket after another. At last:

"Treachery!" he cried, and letting the garment fall to the ground, he turned upon La Boulaye a face so transfigured by anger that it looked little like the usually good-humoured countenance of Captain Tardivet "My keys have been stolen. By St. Guillotine, I'll have the thief hanged."

"Did anybody know that the keys were in your pocket?" asked the ingenuous Caron.

"I told you last night."

"Yes, yes; I remember that. But did anybody else know?"

"The ostler knew. He saw me lock the doors."

"Why, then, let us find the ostler," urged Caron. "Put on some clothes and we will go below."

Mechanically Charlot obeyed him, and as he did so he gave his feelings vent at last. From between set teeth came now a flow of oaths and imprecations as steady as the flow of water from the gargoyle overhead.

At last they hastened down the stairs together, and in the common-room they found the sleeping company much as La Boulaye had left it the night before. In an access of rage at what he saw, and at the ample evidences of the debauch that had reduced them to this condition, Charlot began by kicking the chair from under Mother Capoulade. The noise of her fall and the scream with which she awoke served to arouse one or two others, who lifted their heads to gaze stupidly about them.

But Charlot was busy stirring the other slumberers. He had found a whip, and with this he was now laying vigorously about him.

"Up, you swine!" he blazed at them. "Afoot, you drunken scum!"

His whip cracked, and his imprecations rang high and lurid. And La Boulaye assisted him in his labours with kicks and cuffs and a tongue no less vituperative.

At last they were on their feet—a pale, bewildered, shamefaced company—receiving from the infuriated Charlot the news that whilst they had indulged themselves in their drunken slumbers their prisoners had escaped and carried off the treasure with them. The news was received with a groan of dismay, and several turned to the door to ascertain for themselves whether it was indeed exact. The dreary emptiness of the rain-washed yard afforded them more than ample confirmation.

"Where is your pig of an ostler, Mother Capoulade?" demanded the angry Captain.

Quivering with terror, she answered him that the rascal should be in the shed by the stables, where it was his wont to sleep. Out into the rain, despite the scantiness of his attire, went Charlot, followed closely by La Boulaye and one or two stragglers. The shed proved empty, as Caron could have told him—and so, too, did the stables. Here, at the spot where Madame de Bellecour's coachman had been left bound, the Captain turned to La Boulaye and those others that had followed him.

"It is the ostler's work," he announced. "There was knavery and treachery writ large upon his ugly face. I always felt it, and this business proves how correct were my instincts. The rogue was bribed when he discovered how things were with you, you greasy sots. But you, La Boulaye," he cried suddenly, "were you drunk, too?"

"Not I," answered the Deputy.

"Then, name of a name, how came that lumbering coach to leave the yard without awakening you?"

"You ask me to explain too much," was La Boulaye's cool evasion. "I have always accounted myself a light sleeper, and I could not have believed that such a thing could really have taken place without disturbing me. But the fact remains that the coach has gone, and I think that instead of standing here in idle speculation as to how it went, you might find more profitable employment in considering how it is to brought back again. It cannot have gone very far."

If any ray of suspicion had begun to glimmer in Charlot's brain, that suggestion of La Boulaye's was enough to utterly extinguish it.

They returned indoors, and without more ado Tardivet set himself to plan the pursuit. He knew, he announced, that Prussia was their destination. He had discovered it at the time of their capture from certain papers that he had found in a portmanteau of the Marquise's. He discussed the matter with La Boulaye, and it was now that Caron had occasion to congratulate himself upon his wisdom in having elected to remain behind.

The Captain proposed to recall the fifty men that were watching the roads from France, and to spread them along the River Sambre, as far as Liege, to seek information of the way taken by the fugitives. As soon as any one of the parties struck the trail it was to send word to the others, and start immediately in pursuit.

Now, had Charlot been permitted to spread such a net as this, the Marquise must inevitably fall into it, and Caron had pledged his word that she should have an open road to Prussia. With a map spread upon the table he now expounded to the Captain how little necessity there was for so elaborate a scheme. The nearest way to Prussia was by Charleroi, Dinant, and Rochefort, into Luxembourg, and—he contended—it was not only unlikely, but incredible, that the Marquise should choose any but the shortest road to carry her out of Belgium, seeing the dangers that must beset her until the frontiers of Luxembourg were passed.

"And so," argued La Boulaye, "why waste time in recalling your men? Think of the captives you might miss by such an act! It were infinitely better advised to assume that the fugitives have taken the Charleroi-Dinant road, and to despatch, at once, say, half-a-dozen men in pursuit."

Tardivet pondered the matter for some moments.

"Yom are right," he agreed at last. "If they have resolved to continue their journey, a half-dozen men should suffice to recapture them. I will despatch these at once..."

La Boulaye looked up at that.

"If they have resolved to continue their journey?" he echoed. "What else should they have resolved?"

Tardivet stroked his reddish hair and smiled astutely.

"In organising a pursuit," said he, "the wise pursuer will always put himself in the place of the fugitives, and seek to reason as they would probably reason. Now, what more likely than that these ladies, or their coachman, or that rascally ostler, should have thought of doubling back into France? They might naturally argue that we; should never think of pursuing them in that direction. Similarly placed, that is how I should reason, and that is the course I should adopt, making for Prussia through Lorraine. Perhaps I do their intelligences too much honour—yet, to me, it seems such an obvious course."'

La Boulaye grew cold with apprehension. Yet impassively he asked:

"But what of your men who are guarding the frontiers?"

"Pooh! A detour might circumvent them. The Marquise might go as far north as Roubaix or Comines, or as fair south as Rocroy, or even Charlemont. Name of a name, but it is more than likely!" he exclaimed, with sudden conviction. "What do you say, Caron?"

"That you rave," answered La Boulaye coldly.

"Well, we shall see. I will despatch a message to my men, bidding them spread themselves as far north as Comiines and as far south as Charlemont. Should the fugitives have made such a detour as I suggested there will be ample time to take them."

La Boulaye still contemned the notion with a fine show of indifference, but Tardivet held to his purpose, and presently despatched the messengers as he had proposed. At that Caron felt his pulses quickening with anxiety for Mademoiselle. These astute measures must inevitably result im her capture—for was it not at Roubaix that he had bidden her await him? There was but one thing to be done, to ride out himself to meet her along the road from Soignies to Oudenarde, and to escort her into France. She should go ostensibly as his prisoner, and he was confident that not all the brigands of Captain Tardivet would suffice to take her from him.

Accordingly, he announced his intention of resuming his interrupted journey, and ordered his men to saddle and make ready. Meanwhile, having taken measures to recapture the Marquise should she have doubled back into France, Charlot was now organising an expedition to scour the road to Prussia, against the possibility of her having adhered to her original intention of journeying that way. Thus he was determined to take no risks, and leave her no loophole of escape.

Tardivet would have set himself at the head of the six horsemen of this expedition, but that La Boulaye interfered, and this time to some purpose. He assured the Captain that he was still far from recovered, and that to spend a day in the saddle might have the gravest of consequences for him.

"If the occasion demanded it," he concluded, "I should myself urge you to chance the matter of your health. But the occasion does not. The business is of the simplest, and your men can do as much without you as they could with you."

Tardivet permitted himself to be persuaded, and Caron had again good cause to congratulate himself that he had remained behind to influence him. He opined that the men, failing to pick up the trail at Charleroi, would probably go on as far as Dinant before abandoning the chase; then they would return to Boisvert to announce their failure, and by that time it would be too late to reorganise the pursuit. On the other hand, had Tardivet accompanied them, upon failing to find any trace of the Marquise at Charleroi, La Boulaye could imagine him pushing north along the Sambre, and pressing the peasantry into his service to form an impassable cordon.

And so, having won his way in this at least, and seen the six men set out under the command of Tardivet's trusted Guyot, Caron took his leave of the Captain. He was on the very point of setting out when a courier dashed up to the door of the "Eagle," and called for a cup of wine. As it was brought him he asked the hostess whether the Citizen-deputy La Boulaye, Commissioner to the army of Dumouriez, had passed that way. Upon being informed that the Deputy was even then within the inn, the courier got down from his horse and demanded to be taken to him.

The hostess led him into the common-room, and pointed out the Deputy. The courier heaved a sigh of relief, and removing his sodden cloak he bade the landlady get it dried and prepare him as stout a meal as her hostelry afforded.

"Name of a name!" he swore, as he pitched his dripping hat into a corner. "But it is good to find you at last, Citizen-deputy? I had expected to meet you at Valenciennes. But as you were not there, and as my letters were urgent, I have been compelled to ride for the past six hours through that infernal deluge. Enfin, here you are, and here is my letter—from the Citizen-deputy Maximilien Robespierre—and here I'll rest me for the next six hours."

Bidding the fellow by all means rest and refresh himself, La Boulaye broke the seal, and read the following:

Dear Caron,

My courier should deliver you this letter as you are on the Point of reentering France, on your return from the mission which you have discharged with so much glory to yourself and credit to me who recommended you for the task. I make you my compliments on the tact and adroitness you have employed to bring this stubborn Dumouriez into some semblance of sympathy with the Convention.

And now, my friend, I have another task for you, which you can discharge on your homeward journey. You will make a slight detour, passing into Artois and riding to the Chateau d'Ombreval, which is situated some four miles south of Arras. Here I wish you not only to Possess yourself of the person of the ci-devant Vicomte d'Ombreval, bringing him to Paris as your Prisoner, but further, to make a very searching investigation of that aristocrat's papers, securing any documents that you may consider of a nature treasonable to the French Republic, One and Indivisible.

The letter ended with the usual greetings and Robespierre's signature.

La Boulaye swore softly to himself as he folded the epistle.

"It seems," he muttered to Charlot, "that I am to turn catch-poll in the service of the Republic."

"To a true servant of the Nation," put in the courier, who had overheard him, "all tasks that may tend to the advancement of the

93

Republic should be eagerly undertaken. Diable! Have not I ridden in the rain these six hours past?"

La Boulaye paid no heed to him; he was too inured to this sort of insolence since the new rule had levelled all men. But Charlot turned slowly to regard the fellow.

He was a tall man of rather slender stature, but indifferently dressed in garments that were splashed from head to foot with mud, and from which a steam was beginning to rise as he stood now with his back to the fire. Charlot eyed him so narrowly that the fellow shifted his position and dropped his glance in some discomfort. His speech, though rough of purport, had not been ungentle of delivery. But his face was dirty—the sure sign of an ardent patriot—his hair hung untidy about his face, and he wore that latest abomination of the ultra-revolutionist, a dense black beard and moustache.

"My friend," said Charlot, "although we are ready to acknowledge you our equal, we should like you to understand that we do not take lessons in duty even from our equals. Bear you that in mind if you seek to have a peaceful time while you are here, for it so happens that I am quartered at this inn, and have a more important way with me than this good-natured Deputy here."

The fellow darted Charlot a malevolent glance.

"You talk of equality and you outrage equality in a breath," he growled. "I half suspect you of being a turncoat aristocrat." And he spat ostentatiously on the ground.

"Suspect what you will, but voice no suspicions here, else you'll become acquainted with the mighty short methods of Charlot Tardivet. And as for aristocrats, my friend, there are none so rabid as the newly-converted. I wonder how long it is since you became a patriot?"

Before the fellow could make any answer the corporal in command of La Boulaye's escort entered to inform Caron that the men were in the saddle.

At that the Deputy hurriedly took his leave of Tardivet, and wrapping his heavy cloak tightly about him he marched out into the rain, and mounted.

A few moments later they clattered briskly out of Boisvert, the thick grey mud flying from their horses' hoofs as they went, and took the road to France. For a couple of miles they rode steadily along under the unceasing rain and in the teeth of that bleak February wind. Then at a cross-road La Boulaye unexpectedly called a halt.

"My friends," he said to his escort, "we have yet a little business to discharge in Belgium before we cross the frontier."

With that he announced his intention of going North, and so

94

briskly did he cause them to ride, that by noon—a short three hours after quitting Boisvert—they had covered a distance of twenty-five miles, and brought up their steaming horses before the Hotel de Flandres at Leuze.

At this, the only post-house in the place, La Boulaye made inquiries as to whether any carriage had arrived from Soignies that morning, to receive a negative answer. This nowise surprised him, for he hardly thought that Mademoiselle could have had time to come so far. She must, however, be drawing nearer, and he determined to ride on to meet her. From Leuze to Soignies is a distance of some eight or nine leagues by a road which may roughly be said to be the basis of a triangle having its apex at Boisvert.

After his men had hurriedly refreshed themselves, La Boulaye ordered them to horse again, and they now cantered out, along this road, to Soignes. But as mile after mile was covered without their coming upon any sign of such a carriage as Mademoiselle should be travelling in, La Boulaye almost unconsciously quickened the pace until in the end they found themselves careering along as fast as their jaded horses would bear them, and speculating mightily upon the Deputy's odd behaviour.

Soignies itself was reached towards four o'clock, and still they had not met her whom La Boulaye expected. Here, in a state of some wonder and even of some anxiety, Caron made straight for the Auberge des Postes. Bidding his men dismount and see to themselves and their beasts, he went in quest of the host, and having found him, bombarded him with questions.

In reply he elicited the information that at noon that day a carriage such as he described had reached Soignies in a very sorry condition. One of the wheels had come off on the road, and although the Marquise's men had contrived to replace it and to rudely secure it by an improvised pin, they had been compelled to proceed at a walk for some fifteen miles of the journey, which accounted for the lateness of their arrival at Soignies. They had remained at the Auberge des Postes until the wheel had been properly mended, and it was not more than an hour since they had resumed their journey along the road to Liege.

"But did both the citoyennes depart?" cried La Boulaye, in amazement, and upon receiving an affirmative reply it at once entered his mind that the Marquise must have influenced her daughter to that end—perhaps even employed force.

"Did there appear to be any signs of disagreement between them?" was his next question.

"No, Citizen, I observed nothing. They seemed in perfect accord."

"The younger one did not by any chance inquire of you whether it would be possible to hire a berline?" asked Caron desperately.

"No," the landlord answered him, with wondering eyes. "She appeared as anxious as her mother for the repairing of the coach in which they came, that they might again depart in it."

La Boulaye stood a moment in thought, his brows drawn together, his breathing seeming suspended, for into his soul a suspicion had of a sudden been thrust—a hideous suspicion. Abruptly he drew himself up to the full of his active figure, and threw back his head, his resolve taken.

"Can I have fresh horses at once?" he inquired. "I need eight."

The landlord thoughtfully scratched his head.

"You can have two at once, and the other six in a half-hour."

"Very well," he answered. "Saddle me one at once, and have the other seven ready for my men as soon as possible."

And whilst the host sent the ostler to execute the order, Caron called for a cup of wine and a crust of bread. Munching his crust he entered the common-room where his men were at table with a steaming ragout before them.

"Garin," he said to the corporal, "in a half-hour the landlord will be able to provide you with fresh horses. You will set out at once to follow me along the road to Liege. I am starting immediately."

Garin, with the easy familiarity of the Republican soldier, bade him take some thought of his exhausted condition, and snatch at least the half-hour's rest that was to be theirs. But La Boulaye was out of the room before he had finished. A couple of minutes later they heard a clatter of departing hoofs, and La Boulaye was gone along the road too Liege in pursuit of the ladies of Bellecour.

CHAPTER XIII

THE ROAD TO LIEGE

"Of what are you thinking, little fool?" asked the Marquise peevishly, her fat face puckered into a hundred wrinkles of ill-humour.

"Of nothing in particular, Madame," the girl answered patiently.

The Marquise sniffed contemptuously, and glanced through the window of the coach upon the dreary, rain sodden landscape.

"Do you call the sometime secretary Citizen-cutthroat La Boulaye, nothing in particular?" she asked. "Ma foi! I wonder that you do not die of self-contempt after what passed between you at Boisvert."

"Madame, I was not thinking of him," said Suzanne.

"More shame to you, then," was the sour retort, for the Marquise was bent upon disagreeing with her. "Have you a conscience, Suzanne, that you could have played such a Delilah part and never give a thought to the man you have tricked?"

"You will make me regret that I told you of it," said the girl quietly.

"You are ready enough to regret anything but the act itself. Perhaps you'll be regretting that you did not take a berline at Soignies, as you promised the citizen-scoundrel that you would, and set out to join him?"

"It is hardly generous to taunt me so, Madame, I do very bitterly regret what has taken place. But you might do me the justice to remember that what I did I did as much for others as for myself. As much, indeed, for you as for myself."

"For me?" echoed the Marquise shrilly. "Tiens, that is droll now! For me? Was it for me that you made love to the citizen-blackguard? Are you so dead to shame that you dare remind me of it?"

Mademoiselle sighed, and seemed to shrink back into the shadows of the carriage. Her face was very pale, and her eyes looked sorely troubled.

"It is something that to my dying day I shall regret," she murmured. "It was vile, it was unworthy! Yet if I had not used the only weapon to my hand—" She ceased, the Marquise caught the sound of a sob.

"What are you weeping for, little fool?" she cried.

"As much as anything for what he must think of me when he realises how shamefully I have used him."

"And does it matter what the canaille thinks? Shall it matter what the citizen-assassin thinks?"

"A little, Madame," she sighed. "He will despise me as I deserve. I almost wish that I could undo it, and go back to that little room at Boisvert the prisoner of that fearful man, Tardivet, or else that—" Again she paused, and the Marquise turned towards her with a gasp.

"Or else that what?" she demanded. "Ma foi, it only remains that you should wish you had kept your promise to this scum."

"I almost wish it, Madame. I pledged my word to him."

"You talk as if you were a man," said her mother; "as if your word was a thing that bound you. It is a woman's prerogative to change her mind. As for this Republican scum—"

"You shall not call him that," was the rejoinder, sharply delivered; for Suzanne was roused at last. "He is twenty times more noble and brave than any gentleman, that I have ever met. We owe our liberty to him at this moment, and sufficiently have I wronged him by my actions—"

"Fool, what are you saying?" cried the enraged Marquise. "He, more noble and brave than any gentleman that you ever met? He— this kennel-bred citizen-ruffian of a revolutionist? Are you mad, girl, or—" The Marquise paused a moment and took a deep breath that was as a gasp of sudden understanding. "Is it that you are in love with this wretch!"

"Madame!" The exclamation was laden with blended wonder, dignity, and horror.

"Well?" demanded Madame de Bellecour severely. "Answer me, Suzanne. Are you in love with this La Boulaye?"

"Is there the need to answer?" quoth the girl scornfully. "Surely you forget that I am Mademoiselle de Bellecour, daughter of the Marquise de Bellecour, and that this man is of the canaille, else you had never asked the question."

With an expression of satisfaction the Marquise was sinking back in the carriage, when of a sudden she sat bolt upright.

"Someone is riding very desperately," she cried, a note of alarm ringing in her voice.

Above the thud of the coach-horses' hoofs and the rumble of their vehicle sounded now the clatter of someone galloping madly in their wake. Mademoiselle looked from the window into the gathering dusk.

"It will be some courier, Madame," she answered calmly. "None other would ride at such a pace."

"I shall know no rest until we are safely in a Christian country again," the Marquise complained.

The hoof-beats grew nearer, and the dark figure of a horseman dashed suddenly past the window. Simultaneously, a loud, harsh command to halt rang out upon the evening air.

The Marquise clutched at her daughter's arm with one hand, whilst with the other she crossed herself, as though their assailant were some emissary of the powers of evil.

"Mother in Heaven, deliver us!" she gasped, turning suddenly devout.

"Mon Dieu!" cried Mademoiselle, who had recognised the voice that was now haranguing the men on the box—their driver and the ostler of the 'Eagle Inn.' "It is La Boulaye himself."

"La Boulaye?" echoed the Marquise. Then, in a frenzy of terror: "There are the pistols there, Suzanne," she cried. "You can shoot. Kill him! Kill him!"

The girl's lips came tightly together until her mouth seemed no more than a straight line. Her cheeks grew white as death, but her eyes were brave and resolute. She put forth her hand and seized one of the pistols as the carriage with a final jolt came to a standstill.

An instant later the door was dragged open, and La Boulaye stood bowing in the rain with mock ceremoniousness and a very contemptuous smile on his stern mouth. He had dismounted, and flung the reins of his horse over the bough of a tree by the roadside. The Marquise shuddered at sight of him, and sought to shrink farther back into the cushions of the carriage.

"Citoyenne," he was saying, very bitterly, "when I made my compact with you yesternight, I did not reckon upon being compelled to ride after you in this fashion. I have some knowledge of the ways of your people, of their full words and empty deeds; but you I was fool enough to trust. By experience we learn. I must ask you to alight, Citoyenne."

"To what purpose, Monsieur?" she asked, in a voice which she strove to render cold and steady.

"To the purpose that your part of the bargain be carried out. Your mother and your treasure were to find their way into Prussia upon condition that you return with me to France."

"It was a bargain of coercion, Monsieur," she answered attempting to brazen it out. "I was a woman in a desperate situation."

"Surely your memory is at fault, Citoyenne," he answered, with a politeness that was in itself a mockery.

"Your situation was so little desperate that I had offered to effect the rescue both of your mother and yourself without asking

99

any guerdon. Your miserable treasure alone it was that had to be sacrificed. You will recall that the bargain was of your own proposing."

There was a pause, during which he stood waiting for her reply. Her blue eyes made an attempt to meet his steady gaze, but failed. Her bosom rose and fell in the intensity of her agitation.

"I was a woman distraught, Monsieur. Surely you will not hold me to words uttered in an hour of madness. It was a bargain I had no right to make, for I am no longer free to dispose of myself. I am betrothed to the Vicomte Anatole d'Ombreval. The contract has already been signed, and the Vicomte will be meeting us at Treves."

It was as if she had struck him, and amazement left him silent a moment. In a dim, subconscious way he seemed to notice that the name she mentioned was that of the man he was bidden to arrest. Then, with an oath:

"I care naught for that," he cried. "As God lives, you shall fulfil your word to me."

"Monsieur, I refuse," she answered, with finality. "Let me request you to close the door and suffer us to proceed."

"Your mother and your treasure may proceed—it was thus we bargained. But you shall come with me. I will be no girl's dupe, no woman's fool, Citoyenne."

When he said that he uttered the full truth. There was no love in his voice or in his heart at that moment. Than desire of her nothing was further from his mind. It was his pride that was up in arms, his wounded dignity that cried out to him to avenge himself upon her, and to punish her for having no miserably duped him. That she was unwilling to go with him only served to increase his purpose of taking her, since the more unwilling she was the more would she be punished.

"Citoyenne, I am waiting for you to alight," he said peremptorily.

"Monsieur, I am very well as I am," she answered him, and leaning slightly from the coach—"Drive on, Blaise," she commanded.

But La Boulaye cocked a pistol.

"Drive so much as a yard," he threatened "and I'll drive you to the devil." Then, turning once more to Suzanne: "Never in my life, Citoyenne have I employed force to a woman," he said. "I trust that you will not put me to the pain of commencing now."

"Stand back, Monsieur," was her imperious answer. But heedless he advanced, and thrusting his head under the lintel of the carriage door he leaned forward, to seize her. Then, before he could so much as conjecture what she was about, her hand went up grasping a heavy horse-pistol by the barrel, and she brought the butt of it down with a deadly precision between his brows.

He reeled backwards, threw up his arms, and measured his length in the thick grey mud of the road.

Her eyes had followed him with a look of horror, and until she saw him lying still on his back did she seem to realise what she had done.

"My dear, brave girl," murmured her mother's voice but she never heard it. With a sob she relaxed her grasp of the pistol and let it fall from the carriage.

"Shall I drive on, Mademoiselle?" inquired Blaise from the box.

But without answering him she had stepped down into the mud, and was standing bare-headed in the rain beside the body of Caron.

Silently, she stooped and groped for his heart. It was beating vigorously enough, she thought. She stooped lower and taking him under the arms, she half bore, half dragged him to the side of the road, as if the thin, bare hedge were capable of affording him shelter. There she stood a moment looking down at him. Then with a sob she suddenly stooped, and careless of the eyes observing her, she kissed him full upon the mouth.

A second later she fled like a frightened thing back to the carriage, and, closing the door, she called in a strangled voice too drive on.

She paid little heed to the praise that was being bestowed upon her by her mother—who had seen nothing of the kiss. But she lay back in her corner of the coach, and now her lashes were wet at the thought of Caron lying out there in the road. Now her cheeks grew red with shame at the thought that she, the nobly-born Mademoiselle de Bellecour, should have allowed even pity to have so far overcome her as to have caused her to touch with her lips the lips of a low-bred revolutionist.

CHAPTER XIV

THE COURIER

It was well for La Boulaye that he had tethered his horse to a tree before approaching the coach. That solitary beast standing by the roadside in the deepening gloom attracted the attention of his followers, when—a half-hour or so later—they rode that way, making for Liege, as La Boulaye had bidden them.

At their approach the animal neighed, and Garin, hearing the sound, reined in and peered forward into the gloom, to descry the horse's head and back outlined above the blur of the hedge. His men halted behind him whilst he approached the riderless beast and made—as well as he could in the darkness—an examination of the saddle. One holster he found empty, at which he concluded that the rider, whoever he had been, had met with trouble; from the other he drew a heavy pistol, which, however, gave him no clue.

"Get down," he ordered his men, "and search the roads hereabouts. I'll wager a horse to a horseshoe that you will find a body somewhere."

He was obeyed, and presently a cry from one of the searchers announced a discovery. It was succeeded by another exclamation.

"Sacre nom!" swore the trooper. "It is the Citizen-deputy!"

In an instant Garin had leapt to the ground and with the others crowding about him, their bridles over their arms and their horses in a bunch behind them, he was bending under the dripping hedge to examine the body that lay supine in the sodden road. A vigorous oath escaped him when he assured himself that it was indeed La Boulaye.

"Is he dead?" cried the men in chorus.

"No—not dead" grumbled the corporal. "But there is a lump on his brow the size of an egg, and God knows how long he has been lying here in this bed of mud."

They had no restoratives, and the only thing was to convey him to the nearest habitation and demand shelter. They held a short council on the matter, and in the end Garin bade four of them take him up and carry him in a cloak. Some two miles back they had passed a house, and thither the corporal now bade them retrace their steps. They made an odd procession; first went two mounted troopers leading the horses of the others, then the four on foot, carrying the Deputy in a cloak, and lastly, Garin riding in the rear.

In this manner they went back along the dark road, and for

close upon a half-hour—for their progress was slow—they trudged along in silence. At last there was a short exclamation from one of the riders, as half a mile away an illuminated window beamed invitingly. Encouraged by it, they quickened their steps a little. But almost at the same time La Boulaye stirred on the cloak, and the men who carried him heard him speak. At first it was an incoherent mutter, then his words came more distinctly.

"Hold! Where are you carrying me? Who the devil are you?"

It was Garin's voice that came instantly to reassure him. Caron essayed to sit up, but finding it impracticable, he shortly bade his men set him down. They halted. Garin dismounted and came to the Deputy's side, and it was found that his condition was none so grave after all, for he was able to stand unaided. When, however, he attempted to walk, he reeled, and would of a certainty have fallen, but that Garin put out his arm to support him.

"Steady there, Citizen," the corporal admonished him.

"Get my horse!" he commanded briefly.

"But, name of a name! you are not fit to ride," Garin protested.

La Boulaye, however, would listen to no reason. With the recovery of his faculties came the consideration of how miserably Suzanne had duped him, and of how she had dealt with him when he had overtaken her. He burned now to be avenged, and at all costs he would ride after and recapture her. He announced, therefore, to the corporal that they must push on to Liege. Garin gasped at his obstinacy, and would have sought to have dissuaded him, but that La Boulaye turned on him with a fierceness that silenced his expostulations.

It was left to Nature to enforce what Garin could not achieve. When La Boulaye came to attempt to mount he found it impossible. He was stiff and numb from his long exposure in the rain, and when he moved with any vigour his head swam dizzily and throbbed with pain.

At last he was forced to realise—with inward girding—that he must relinquish his determination, and he acknowledged himself ready to take the corporal's advice and make for the house whose lighted window shone like a beacon in the darkness that had descended. He even allowed them to prevail upon him to lie down in the cloak again, and thus they carried him the remainder of the way. In his heart he still bore the hope that short rest, restoratives, and fresh clothes would fit him for the pursuit once more, and that if he set out within the next few hours he might yet come up with Mademoiselle before she had passed beyond his reach. Should the

103

morning still find him unequal to the task of going after her, he would despatch Garin and his men.

At last they reached the cottage—it was little more—and Garin rapped on the door with his whip. It was opened by a woman, who told them, in answer to the corporal's request for shelter, that her husband was from home, and that she had no accommodation for them. It would seem that the woman had housed soldiers of the Republic before, and that her experiences had not been of a nature calculated to encourage her in the practice. But La Boulaye now staggered forward and promised her generous payment if she would receive them.

"Payment?" she cried. "In worthless assignats that nobody will take from me. I know the ways of you."

"Not in assignats," La Boulaye promised her, "but in coin."

And having mollified her somewhat with that assurance, he proceeded to urge her to admit them. Yonder was a shed where the horses could be stabled for the night. But still the woman demurred.

"I lack the room," she said, with some firmness.

"But at least," put in Garin, "you could house the Citizen here. He has been hurt, and he is scarcely able to stand. Come, woman, if you will consent to that, we others can lie with the horses in the shed."

This in the end they gained by renewed promises of good payment. She brewed a broth for them, and for La Boulaye she found a suit of her absent husband's clothes, whilst his own wet garments were spread to dry before the fire. Some brandy, too, she found and brought him, and the draught did much to restore him.

When they had supped, Garin and the troopers withdrew to the outhouse, leaving La Boulaye in sole possession of the cottage hearth. And there, in a suit of the absent farmer's grey homespun, his legs encased in coarse woollen stockings and sabots upon his feet, sat the young Deputy alone with his unpleasant thoughts. The woman had brought him a pipe, and, although the habit was foreign to him as a rule, he had lighted it and found the smoking somewhat soothing. Ruefully he passed his hand across his bandaged brow, and in pondering over all that had taken place since yesternight at Boisvert, his cheeks grew flushed at once with anger and with shame.

"To have been so duped!"

And now—his mind growing clearer as he recovered in vigour—it occurred to him that by to-morrow it would be too late to give pursuit. Once she crossed the Sambre at Liege, or elsewhere, who could tell him by what road she would elect to continue her journey? He had not sufficient men at his disposal to send out parties along each of the possible roads. That her ultimate destination was Treves he knew. But once there she was beyond his reach, at safety from the talons of the French Republic.

He sat on and thought, what time his brows came closer together and his teeth fastened viciously upon the stem of the pipe. By the table sat the woman, knitting industriously, and ever and anon glancing inquiry at her stern, thoughtful guest, and the click of her needles was the only sound that disturbed the stillness of the room. Outside the wind was wailing like the damned, and the rain which had recommenced with new vigour, rattled noisily upon the panes.

Suddenly above the din of the elements a shout sounded in the night. The Deputy raised his head, and glanced towards the woman. A moment later they heard the gate creak, and steps upon the path that led to the cottage door.

"Your husband?" inquired La Boulaye.

"No, monsieur. He has gone to Liege, and will not return until to-morrow. I do not know who it can be."

There was alarm on her face, which La Boulaye now set himself to allay.

"At least you are well protected, Citoyenne. My men are close at hand, and we can summon them if there be the need."

Reassured she rose, and at the same moment a knock sounded on the door. She went to open it, and from his seat by the hearth La Boulaye heard a gentle, mincing voice that was oddly familiar to him.

"Madame," it said, "we are two poor, lost wayfarers, and we crave shelter for the night. We will pay you handsomely."

"I am desolated that I have no room, Messieur," she answered, with courteous firmness.

"Pardi!" interpolated another voice. "We need no room. A bundle of straw and a corner is all we seek. Of your charity, Madame, is this a night on which to leave a dog out of doors?"

A light of recollection leaped suddenly to La Boulaye's eyes, and with a sudden gasp he stooped to the hearth.

"But I cannot, Messieurs," the woman was saying, when the second voice interrupted her.

"I see your husband by the fire, Madame. Let us hear what he has to say."

The woman coloured to the roots of her hair. She stepped back a pace, and was about to answer them when, chancing to glance in La Boulaye's direction, she paused. He had risen, and was standing with his back to the fire. There was a black smudge across his face, which seemed to act as a mask, and his dark eyes glowed with an intensity of meaning which arrested her attention, and silenced the answer which was rising to her lips.

In the brief pause the new-comers had crossed the threshold, and stood within the rustic chamber. The first of these was he whose gentle voice La Boulaye had recognised—old M. des Cadoux, the friend of the Marquis de Bellecour. His companion, to the Deputy's vast surprise, was none other than the bearded courier who had that morning delivered him at Boisvert the letter from Robespierre. What did these two together, and upon such manifest terms of equality? That, it should be his business to discover.

"Come in, Messieurs," he bade them, assuming the role of host. "We are unused to strangers, and Mathilde there is timid of robbers. Draw near the fire and dry yourselves. We will do the best we can for you. We are poor people, Messieurs; very poor."

"I have already said that we will pay you handsomely my friend," quoth Des Cadoux, coming forward with his companion. "Do your best for us and you shall not regret it. Have you aught to eat in the house?"

The woman was standing by the wall, her face expressing bewilderment and suspicion. Suspicious she was, yet that glance of La Boulaye's had ruled her strangely, and she was content to now await developments.

"We will see what we can do," answered La Boulaye, as he made room for them by the hearth. "Come, Mathilde, let us try what the larder will yield."

"I am afraid that Madame still mistrusts us," deplored Des Cadoux.

La Boulaye laughed for answer as he gently but firmly drew her towards the door leading to the interior of the house. He held it for her to pass, what time his eyes were set in an intent but puzzled glance upon the courier. There was something about the man that was not wholly strange to La Boulaye. That morning, when he had spoken in the gruff accents of one of the rabble, no suspicion had entered the Deputy's mind that he was other than he seemed, for all that he now recalled how Tardivet had found the fellow's patriotism a little too patriotic. Now that he spoke in the voice that was naturally usual to him, it seemed to La Boulaye that it contained a note that he had heard before.

Still puzzled, he passed out of the room to be questioned sharply by the woman of the house touching his motives for passing himself off as her husband and inviting the new-comers to enter.

"I promise you their stay will be a very brief one," he answered. "I have suspicions to verify the ends to serve, as you shall see. Will you do me the favour to go out by the back and call my men? Tell the corporal to make his way to the front of the house, and to hold himself in readiness to enter the moment I call him."

"What are you about to do?" she asked and the face, as he saw it by the light of the candle she held, wore an expression of sullen disapproval.

He reassured her that there would be no bloodshed, and suggested that the men were dangerous characters whom it might be ill for her to entertain. And so at last he won his way, and she went to do his errand, whilst he reentered the kitchen.

He found Des Cadoux by the fire, intent upon drying as much of himself as possible. The younger man had seized upon the bottle of brandy that had been left on the table, and was in the act of filling himself a second glass. Nothing could be further from the mind of either than a suspicion of the identity of this rustically-clad and grimy-faced fellow.

"Mathilde will be here in a moment," said Caron deferentially. "She is seeking something for you."

Had he told them precisely what she was seeking they had been, possibly, less at ease.

"Let her hasten," cried the courier, "for I am famished."

"Have patience, Anatole," murmured the ever-gentle Cadoux. "The good woman did not expect us."

Anatole! The name buzzed through Caron's brain. To whom did it belong? He knew of someone who bore it. Yet question himself though he might, he could at the moment find no answer. And then the courier created a diversion by addressing him.

"Fill yourself a glass, mon bonhomme," said he. "I have a toast for you."

"For me, Monsieur," cried La Boulaye, with surprised humility. "It were too great an honour."

"Do as you are bidden, man," returned this very peremptory courier. "There; now let us see how your favour runs. Cry 'Long Live the King!'"

Holding the brandy-glass, which the man had forced upon him, La Boulaye eyed him whimsically for a second.

"There is no toast I would more gladly drink," said he at last, "if I considered it availing. But—alas—you propose it over-late."

"Diable! What may you mean?"

"Why, that since the King is dead, it shall profit us little to cry, 'Long Live the King!'"

"The King, Monsieur, never dies," said Cadoux sententiously.

"Since you put it so, Monsieur," answered La Boulaye, as if convinced, "I'll honour the toast." And with the cry they asked of him he drained his glass.

107

"And so, my honest fellow," said Des Cadoux, producing his eternal snuff-box, "it seems that you are a Royalist. We did but test you with that toast, my friend."

"What should a poor fellow know of politics, Messieurs?" he deprecated. "These are odd times. I doubt me the world has never seen their like. No man may safely know his neighbour. Now you, sir," he pursued, turning to the younger man, "you have the air of a sans-culotte, yet from your speech you seem an honest enough gentleman."

The fellow laughed with unction.

"The air of a sans-culotte?" he cried. "My faith, yes. So much so, that this morning I imposed myself as a courier from Paris upon no less an astute sleuth-hound of the Convention than the Citizen-deputy La Boulaye."

"Is it possible?" cried Caron, his eyes opening wide in wonder. "But how, Monsieurs? For surely a courier must bear letters, and—"

"So did I, so did I, my friend," the other interrupted, with vain glory. "I knocked a patriotic courier over the head to obtain them. He was genuine, that other courier, and I passed myself out of France with his papers."

"Monsieur is amusing himself at the expense of my credulity," La Boulaye complained.

"My good man, I am telling you facts," the other insisted.

"But how could such a thing be accomplished?" asked Caron, seating himself at the table, and resting his chin upon his hand, his gaze so full of admiration as to seem awestruck.

"How? I will tell you. I am from Artois."

"You'll be repeating that charming story once too often," Des Cadoux cautioned him.

"Pish, you timorous one!" he laughed, and resumed his tale. "I am from Artois, then. I have some property there, and it lately came to my ears that this assembly of curs they call the Convention had determined to make an end of me. But before they could carry out their design, those sons of dogs, my tenants, incited by the choice examples set them by other tenantry, made a descent on my Chateau one night, and did themselves the pleasure of burning it to the ground. By a miracle I escaped with my life and lay hidden for three weeks in the house of an old peasant who had remained faithful. In that time I let my beard grow, and trained my hair into a patriotic unkemptness. Then, in filthy garments, like any true Republican, I set out to cross the frontier. As I approached it, I was filled with fears that I might not win across, and then, in the moment of my doubtings, I came upon that most opportune of couriers. I had the notion to change places with him, and I did. He

108

was the bearer of a letter to the Deputy La Boulaye, of whom you may have heard, and this letter I opened to discover that it charged him to effect my arrest."

If La Boulaye was startled, his face never betrayed it, not by so much as the quiver of an eyelid. He sat on, his jaw in his palm, his eyes admiringly bent upon the speaker.

"You may judge of my honesty, and of how fully sensible I was of the trust I had undertaken, when I tell you that with my own hand I delivered the letter this morning to that animal La Boulaye at Boisvert." He seemed to swell with pride in his achievement. "Diable!" he continued. "Mine was a fine piece of acting. I would you could have seen me play the part of the patriot. Think of the irony of it! I won out of France with the very papers ordering my arrest. Ma foi! You should have seen me befool that dirt of a deputy! It was a performance worthy of Talma himself." And he looked from Cadoux to La Boulaye for applause.

"I doubt not," said the Deputy coldly. "It must have been worth witnessing. But does it not seem a pity to spoil everything and to neutralise so wonderful an achievement for the mere sake of boasting of it to a poor, ignorant peasant, Monsieur le Vicomte Anatole d'Ombreval?"

With a sudden cry, the pseudo courier leapt to his feet, whilst Des Cadoux turned on the stool he occupied to stare alarmedly at the speaker.

"Name of God! Who are you?" demanded Ombreval advancing a step.

With his sleeve La Boulaye rubbed part of the disfiguring smear from his face as he stood up and made answer coolly:

"I am that dirt of a Deputy whom you befooled at Boisvert." Then, raising his voice, "Garin!" he shouted, and immediately the door opened and the soldiers filed in.

Ombreval stood like a statue, thunderstruck with amazement at this most unlooked-for turning of the tables, his face ashen, his weak mouth fallen open and his eyes fearful.

Des Cadoux, who had also risen, seemed to take in the situation at a glance. Like a well-bred gamester who knows how to lose with a good grace the old gentleman laughed drily to himself as he tapped his snuff-box.

"We are delightfully taken, cher Vicomte," he murmured, applying the tobacco to his nostril as he spoke. "It's odds you won't be able to repeat that pretty story to any more of your friends. I warned you that you inclined to relate it too often."

With a sudden oath, Ombreval—moved to valour by the blind

rage that possessed him—sprang at La Boulaye. But, as suddenly, Garin caught his arms from behind and held him fast.

"Remove them both," La Boulaye commanded. "Place them in safety for the night, and see that they do not escape you, Garin, as you value your neck."

Des Coudax shut his snuff-box with a snap.

"For my part, I am ready, Monsieur—your pardon—Citizen," he said, "and I shall give you no trouble. But since I am not, I take it, included in the orders you have received, I have a proposal to make which may prove mutually convenient."

"Pray make it, Citizen," said La Boulaye.

"It occurs to me that it may occasion you some measure of annoyance to carry me all the way to Paris—and certainly, for my part, I should much prefer not to undertake the journey. For one thing, it will be fatiguing, for another, I have no desire to look upon the next world through the little window of the guillotine. I wish, then, to propose, Citizen," pursued the old nobleman, nonchalantly dusting some fragments of tobacco from his cravat, "that you deal with me out of hand."

"How, Citizen?" inquired La Boulaye.

"Why, your men, I take it are tolerable marksmen. I think that it might prove more convenient to both of us if you were to have me shot as soon as there is light enough."

La Boulaye's eyes rested in almost imperceptible kindness upon Des Cadoux. Here, at least, was an aristocrat with a spirit to be admired and emulated.

"You are choosing the lesser of two evils, Citizen," said the Deputy.

"Precisely," answered Des Cadoux.

"But possibly, Citizen, it may be yours to avoid both. You shall hear from me in the morning. I beg that you will sleep tranquilly in the meantime. Garin, remove the prisoners."

CHAPTER XV

LA BOULAYE BAITS HIS HOOK

For fully an hour after their prisoners had been removed La Boulaye paced the narrow limits of the kitchen with face inscrutable and busy mind. He recalled what Suzanne had said touching her betrothal to Ombreval, whom she looked to meet at Treves. This miserable individual, then, was the man for whose sake she had duped him. But Ombreval at least was in Caron's power, and it came to him now that by virtue of that circumstance he might devise a way to bring her back without the need to go after her. He would send her word—aye, and proof—that he had taken him captive, and it should be hers to choose whether she would come to his rescue and humble herself to save him or leave him to his fate. In that hour it seemed all one to La Boulaye which course she followed, since by either, he reasoned, she must be brought to suffer. That he loved her was with him now a matter that had sunk into comparative insignificance. The sentiment that ruled his mind was anger, with its natural concomitant—the desire to punish.

And when morning came the Deputy's view of the situation was still unchanged. He was astir at an early hour, and without so much as waiting to break his fast, he bade Garin bring in the prisoners. Their appearance was in each case typical. Ombreval was sullen and his dress untidy, even when allowance had been made for the inherent untidiness of the Republican disguise which he had adopted to so little purpose. Des Cadoux looked well and fresh after his rest, and gave the Deputy an airy "Good morning" as he entered. He had been at some pains, too, with his toilet, and although his hair was slightly disarranged and most of the powder was gone from the right side, suggesting that he had lain on it, his appearance in the main was creditably elegant.

"Citizen Ombreval," said La Boulaye, in that stern, emotionless voice that was becoming characteristic of him, "since you have acquainted yourself with the contents of the letter you stole from the man you murdered, you cannot be in doubt as to my intentions concerning you."

The Vicomte reddened with anger.

"For your intentions I care nothing," he answered hotly—rendered very brave by passion—"but I will have you consider your words. Do you say that I stole and murdered? You forget, M. le Republican, that I am a gentlemen."

111

"Meaning, of course, that the class that so described itself could do these things with impunity without having them called by their proper names, is it not so? But you also forget that the Republic has abolished gentlemen, and with them, their disgraceful privileges."

"Canaille!" growled the Vicomte, his eyes ablaze with wrath.

"Citizen-aristocrat, consider your words!" La Boulaye had stepped close up to him, and his voice throbbed with a sudden anger no whit less compelling than Ombreval's. "Fool! let me hear that word again, applied either to me or to any of my followers, and I'll have you beaten like a dog."

And as the lesser ever does give way before the greater, so now did the anger that had sustained Ombreval go down and vanish before the overwhelming passion of La Boulaye. He grew pale to the lips at the Deputy's threat, and his eyes cravenly avoided the steady gaze of his captor.

"You deserve little consideration at my hands, Citizen," said La Boulaye, more quietly, "and yet I have a mind to give you a lesson in generosity. We start for Paris in half-an-hour. If anywhere you should have friends expecting you, whom you might wish to apprise of your position, you may spend the half-hour that is left in writing to them. I will see that your letter reaches its destination."

Ombreval's pallor seemed to intensify. His eyes looked troubled as they were raised to La Boulaye's. Then they fell again, and there was a pause. At last—.

"I shall be glad to avail myself of your offer," he said, in a voice that for meekness was ludicrously at variance with his late utterances.

"Then pray do so at once." And La Boulaye took down an inkhorn a quill, and a sheaf of paper from the mantel-shelf behind him. These he placed on the table, and setting a chair, he signed to the aristocrat to be seated.

"And now, Citizen Cadoux," said La Boulaye, turning to the old nobleman, "I shall be glad if you will honour me by sharing my breakfast while Citizen Ombreval is at his writing."

Des Cadoux looked up in some surprise.

"You are too good, Monsieur," said he, inclining his head. "But afterwards?"

"I have decided," said La Boulaye, with the ghost of a smile, "to deal with your case myself, Citizen."

The old dandy took a deep breath, but the glance of his blue eyes was steadfast, and his lips smiled as he made answer:

"Again you are too good. I feared that you would carry me to Paris, and at my age the journey is a tiresome one. I am grateful, and meanwhile,—why, since you are so good as to invite me, let us breakfast, by all means."

They sat down at a small table in the embrasure of the window, and their hostess placed before them a boiled fowl, a dish of eggs, a stew of herbs, and a flask of red wine, all of which La Boulaye had bidden her prepare.

"Why, it is a feast," declared Des Cadoux, in excellent humour, and for all that he was under the impression that he was to die in half-an-hour he ate with the heartiest good-will, chatting pleasantly the while with the Republican—the first Republican with whom it had ever been his aristocratic lot to sit at table. And what time the meal proceeded Ombreval—with two soldiers standing behind his chair-penned his letter to Mademoiselle de Bellecour.

Had La Boulaye—inspired by the desire to avenge himself for the treachery of which he had been the victim—dictated that epistle, t could not have been indicted in a manner better suited to his ends. It was a maudlin, piteous letter, in which, rather than making his farewells, the Vicomte besought the aid of Suzanne. He was, he wrote, in the hands of men who might be bribed, and since she was rich—for he knew of the treasure with which she had escaped—he based his hopes upon her employing a portion of her riches to obtaining his enlargement. She, he continued, was his only hope, and for the sake of their love, for the sake of their common nobility, he besought her not to fail him now. Carried away by the piteousness of his entreaties the tears welled up to his eyes and trickled down his cheeks, one or two of them finding their way to the paper thus smearing it with an appeal more piteous still if possible than that of his maudlin words.

At last the letter was ended. He sealed it with a wafer and wrote the superscription:

"To Mademoiselle de Bellecour. At the 'Hotel des Trois Rois,' Treves."

He announced the completion of his task, and La Boulaye bade him go join Des Cadoux at the next table and take some food before setting out, whilst the Deputy himself now sat down to write.

"Citoyenne," he wrote, "the man to whom you are betrothed, for whose sake you stooped to treachery and attempted murder, is in my hands. Thus has Heaven set it in my power to punish you, if the knowledge that he travels to the guillotine is likely to prove a punishment. If you would rescue him, come to me in Paris, and, conditionally, I may give you his life."

That, he thought should humble her. He folded his letter round Ombreval's and having sealed the package, he addressed it as Ombreval had addressed his own missive.

"Garin," he commanded briefly, "remove the Citizen Ombreval."

When he had been obeyed, and Garin had conducted the Vicomte from the room, La Boulaye turned again to Des Cadoux. They were alone, saving the two soldiers guarding the door.

The old man rose, and making the sign of the cross, he stepped forward, calm and intrepid of bearing.

"Monsieur," he announced to La Boulaye, who was eyeing him with the faintest tinge of surprise, "I am quite ready."

"Have you always been so devout, Citizen?" inquired the Deputy.

"Alas! no Monsieur. But there comes a time in the life of every man when, for a few moments at least, he is prone to grow mindful of the lessons learnt in childhood."

The surprise increased in La Boulaye's countenance. At last he shrugged his shoulders, after the manner of one who abandons a problem that has grown too knotty.

"Citizen des Cadoux," said he, "I have deliberated that since I have received no orders from Paris concerning you, and also since I am not by profession a catch-poll there is no reason whatever why I should carry you to Paris. In fact, Citizen, I know of no reason why I should interfere with your freedom at all. On the contrary when I recall the kindness you sought to do me that day, years ago, at Bellecour, I find every reason why I should further your escape from the Revolutionary tribunal. A horse, Citizen, stands ready saddled for you, and you are free to depart, with the one condition, however, that you will consent to become my courier for once, and carry a letter for me—a matter which should occasion you, I think, no deviation from your journey."

The old dandy, in whose intrepid spirit the death which he had believed imminent had occasioned no trembling, turned pale as La Boulaye ceased. His blue eyes were lifted almost timidly to the Deputy's face, and his lip quivered.

"You are not going to have me shot, then?" he faltered.

"Shot?" echoed La Boulaye, and then he remembered the precise words of the request which Des Cadoux had preferred the night before, but which, at the time, he had treated lightly. "Ma foi, you do not flatter me!" he cried. "Am I a murderer, then? Come, come, Citizen, here is the letter that you are to carry. It is addressed to Mademoiselle de Bellecour, at Treves, and encloses Ombreval's farewell epistle to that lady."

"But, gladly, Monsieur," exclaimed Des Cadoux.

And then, as if to cover his sudden access of emotion, of which he was most heartily ashamed, he fumbled for his snuff-box, and, having found it, he took an enormous pinch.

They parted on the very best of terms did these two—the aristocrat and the Revolutionary—actuated by a mutual esteem tempered in each case with gratitude.

When at last Des Cadoux had taken a sympathetic leave of Ombreval and departed, Caron ordered the Vicomte to be brought before him again, and at the same time bade his men make ready for the road.

"Citizen," said La Boulaye, "we start for Paris at once. If you will pass me your word of honour to attempt no escape you shall travel with us in complete freedom and with all dignity."

Ombreval looked at him with insolent surprise, his weak supercilious mouth growing more supercilious even than its wont. He had recovered a good deal of his spirit by now.

"Pass you my word of honour?" he echoed. "Mon Dieu! my good fellow a word of honour is a bond between gentlemen. I think too well of mine to pass it to the first greasy rascal of the Republic that asks it of me."

La Boulaye eyed him a second with a glance before which the aristocrat grew pale, and already regretted him of his words. The veins in the Deputy's temples were swollen.

"I warned you," said he, in a dull voice. Then to the soldiers standing on either side of Ombreval—"Take him out," he said, "mount him on horseback. Let him ride with his hands pinioned behind his back, and his feet lashed together under the horse's belly. Attend to it!"

"Monsieur," cried the young man, in an appealing voice, "I will give you my word of honour not to escape. I will—"

"Take him out," La Boulaye repeated, with a dull bark of contempt. "You had your chance, Citizen-aristocrat."

Ombreval set his teeth and clenched his hands.

"Canaille!" he snarled, in his fury.

"Hold!" Caron called after the departing men.

They obeyed, and now this wretched Vicomte, of such unstable spirit dropped all his anger again, as suddenly as he had caught it up. Fear paled his cheek and palsied his limbs once more, for La Boulaye's expression was very terrible.

"You know what I said that I would have done to you if you used that word again?" La Boulaye questioned him coldly.

"I—I was beside myself, Monsieur," the other gasped, in the intensity of his fear. And at the sight of his pitiable condition the anger fell away from La Boulaye, and he smiled scornfully.

"My faith," he sneered. "You are hot one moment and cold the next. Citizen, I am afraid that you are no better than a vulgar coward. Take him away," he ended, waving his hand towards the door, and as he watched them leading him out he reflected bitterly that this was the man to whom Suzanne was betrothed—the man whom, not a doubt of it, she loved, since for him she had stooped so low. This miserable craven she preferred to him, because the man, so ignoble of nature, was noble by the accident of birth.

PART III

THE EVERLASTING RULE

Love rules the court, the camp, the grove,
And men below and saints above,
For love is Heaven and Heaven is love.

—*The Lay of the Last Minstrel.*

CHAPTER XVI

CECILE DESHAIX

In his lodgings at the corner of the Rue-St. Honore and the Rue de la Republique—lately changed, in the all-encompassing metamorphosis, from "Rue Royale" sat the Deputy Caron La Boulaye at his writing-table.

There was a flush on his face and a sparkle in the eyes that looked pensively before him what time he gnawed the feathered end of his quill. In his ears still rang the acclamations that had greeted his brilliant speech in the Assembly that day. He was of the party of the Mountain—as was but natural in a protege of the Seagreen Robespierre—a party more famed for its directness of purpose than elegance of expression, and in its ranks there was room and to spare for such orators as he. The season was March of '93—a season marked by the deadly feud raging 'twixt the Girondins and the Mountain, and in that battle of tongues La Boulaye was covering himself with glory and doing credit to his patron, the Incorruptible. He was of a rhetoric not inferior to Vergniaud's—that most eloquent Girondon—and of a quickness of wit and honesty of aim unrivalled in the whole body of the Convention, and with these gifts he harassed to no little purpose those smooth-tongued legislators of the Gironde, whom Dumouriez called the Jesuits of the Revolution. His popularity with the men of the Mountain and with the masses of Paris was growing daily, and the crushing reply he had that day delivered to the charges preferred by Vergniaud was likely to increase his fame.

Well, therefore, might he sit with flushed cheeks and sparkling eyes chewing the butt of his pen and smiling to himself at the memory of the enthusiasm of which he had been the centre a half-hour ago. Here, indeed, was something that a man might live for, something that a man might take pride in, and something that might console a man for a woman's treachery. What, indeed, could woman's love give him that might compare with this? Was it not more glorious far to make himself the admired, the revered, the very idol of those stern men, than the beloved of a simpering girl? The latter any coxcomb with a well-cut coat might encompass, but the former achievement was a man's work.

And yet, for all that he reasoned thus speciously and philosophically, there was a moment when his brow grew clouded and his eyes lost their sparkle. He was thinking of that night in the inn at Boisvert, when he had knelt beside her and she had lied to him. He was thinking of the happiness, that for a few brief hours had been his, until he discovered how basely she had deceived him, and for all the full-flavour of his present elation it seemed to him that in that other happiness which he now affected to despise by contrast, there had dwelt a greater, a more contenting sweetness.

Would she come to Paris? He had asked himself that question every day of the twenty that were spent since his return. And in the meantime the Vicomte d'Ombreval lay in the prison of the Luxembourg awaiting trial. That he had not yet been arraigned he had to thank the efforts of La Boulaye. The young Deputy had informed Robespierre that for reasons of his own he wished the ci-devant Vicomte, to be kept in prison some little time, and the Incorruptible, peering at him over his horn-rimmed spectacles, had shrugged his shoulders and answered:

"But certainly, cher Caron, since it is your wish. He will be safe in the Luxembourg."

He had pressed his protege for a reason, but La Boulaye had evaded the question, promising to enlighten him later.

Since then Caron had waited, and now it was more than time that Mademoiselle made some sign. Or was it that neither Ombreval's craven entreaties nor his own short message had affected her? Was she wholly heartless and likely to prove as faithless to the Vicomte in his hour of need as she had proved to him?

With a toss of the head he dismissed her from his thoughts, and dipping his quill, he began to write.

From the street came the dull roll of beaten drums and the rhythmical fall of marching feet. But the sound was too common in revolutionary Paris to arrest attention, and he wrote on, heeding it as little as he did the gruff voice of a pastry-cook crying his wares, the shriller call of a milkman, or the occasional rumblings of passing vehicles. But of a sudden one of those rumblings ceased abruptly at his door. He heard the rattle of hoofs and the grind of the wheel against the pavement, and looking up, he glanced across at the ormolu timepiece on his overmantel. It was not yet four o'clock.

Wondering whether the visitor might be for him or for the tenant of the floor above, he sat listening until his door opened and his official—the euphemism of "servant" in the revolutionary lexicon—came to announce that a woman was below, asking to see him.

Now for all that he believed himself to have become above emotions where Mademoiselle de Bellecour was concerned, he felt his pulses quicken at the very thought that this might be she at last.

"What manner of woman, Brutus?" he asked.

"A pretty woman, Citizen," answered Brutus, with a grin. "It is the Citoyenne Deshaix."

La Boulaye made an impatient gesture.

"Fool, why did you not say so," he cried sharply.

"Fool, you did not ask me," answered the servant, with that touching, fraternal frankness adopted by all true patriots. He was a thin, under-sized man of perhaps thirty years of age, and dressed in black, with a decency—under La Boulaye's suasion—that was rather at variance with his extreme democracy. His real name was Ferdinand, but, following a fashion prevailing among the ultra-republicans, he had renamed himself after the famous Roman patriot.

La Boulaye toyed a moment with his pen, a frown darkening his brow. Then:

"Admit her," he sighed wearily.

And presently she came, a pretty woman, as Brutus had declared, very fair, and with the innocent eyes of a baby. She was small of stature, and by the egregious height of her plume-crowned head-dress it would seem as if she sought by art to add to the inches she had received from Nature. For the rest she wore a pink petticoat, very extravagantly beflounced, and a pink corsage cut extravagantly low. In one hand she carried a fan—hardly as a weapon against heat, seeing that the winter was not yet out—in the other a huge bunch of early roses.

"Te voile!" was her greeting, merrily—roguishly—delivered, and if the Revolution had done nothing else for her, it had, at least, enabled her to address La Boulaye by the "Thou" of intimacy which the new vocabulary prescribed.

La Boulaye rose, laid aside his pen, and politely, if coolly, returned her greeting and set a chair for her.

"You are," said he, "a very harbinger of Spring, Citoyenne, with your flowers and your ravishing toilette."

"Ah! I please you, then, for once," said she without the least embarrassment. "Tell me—how do you find me?" And, laughing, she turned about that he might admire her from all points of view.

He looked at her gravely for a moment, so gravely that the laughter began to fade from her eyes.

"I find you charming, Citoyenne," he answered at last. "You remind me of Diana."

"Compliments?" quoth she, her eyebrows going up and her eyes beaming with surprise and delight. "Compliments from La Boulaye! But surely it is the end of the world. Tell me, mon ami,"

120

she begged, greedily angling for more, "in what do I remind you of the sylvan goddess?"

"In the scantiness of your raiment, Citoyenne," he answered acidly. "It sorts better with Arcadia than with Paris."

Her eyebrows came down, her cheeks flushed with resentment and discomfiture. To cover this she flung her roses among the papers of his writing-table, and dropping into a chair she fanned herself vigorously.

"Citoyenne, you relieve my anxieties," said he. "I feared that you stood in danger of freezing."

"To freeze is no more than one might expect in your company," she answered, stifling her anger.

He made no reply. He moved to the window, and stood drumming absently on the panes. He was inured to these invasions on the part of Cecile Deshaix and to the bold, unwomanly advances that repelled him. To-day his patience with her was even shorter than its wont, haply because when his official had announced a woman he had for a moment permitted himself to think that it might be Suzanne. The silence grew awkward, and at last he broke it.

"The Citizen Robespierre is well?" he asked, without turning.

"Yes," said she, and for all that there was chagrin to spare in the glance with which she admired the back of his straight and shapely figure, she contrived to render her voice airily indifferent. "We were at the play last night."

"Ah!" he murmured politely. "And was Talma in veine?"

"More brilliant than ever," answered she.

"He is a great actor, Citoyenne."

A shade of annoyance crossed her face.

"Why do you always address me as Citoyenne?" she asked, with some testiness.

He turned at last and looked at her a moment.

"We live in a censorious world, Citoyenne," he answered gravely.

She tossed her head with an exclamation of impatience.

"We live in a free world, Citizen. Freedom is our motto. Is it for nothing that we are Republicans?"

"Freedom of action begets freedom of words," said he, "and freedom of words leads to freedom of criticism—and that is a thing to which no wise woman will expose herself, no matter under what regime we live. You would be well-advised, Citoyenne, in thinking of that when you come here."

"But you never come to us, Caron," she returned, in a voice of mild complaint. "You have not been once to Duplay's since your return from Belgium. And you seem different, too, since your journey to the army." She rose now and approached him. "What is it, cher Caron?" she asked, her voice a very caress of seductiveness, her eyes looking up into his. "Is something troubling you?"

"Troubling me?" he echoed, musingly. "No. But then I am a busy man, Citoyenne."

A wave of red seemed to sweep across her face, and her heel beat the parquet floor.

"If you call me Citoyenne again I shall strike you," she threatened him.

He looked down at her, and she had the feeling that behind the inscrutable mask of his countenance he was laughing at her.

"It would sort well with your audacity," he made answer coolly.

She felt in that moment that she hated him, and it was a miracle that she did not do as she had threatened, for with all her meek looks she owned a very fiercest of tempers. She drew back a pace or two, and her glance fell.

"I shall not trouble you in future," she vowed. "I shall not come here again."

He bowed slightly.

"I applaud the wisdom of your resolve—Cit—Cecile. The world, as I have said, is censorious."

She looked at him a second, then she laughed, but it was laughter of the lips only; the eyes looked steely as daggers and as capable of mischief.

"Adieu, Citizen La Boulaye," she murmured mockingly.

"Au revoir, Citoyenne Deshaix," he replied urbanely.

"Ough!" she gasped, and with that sudden exclamation of pent-up wrath, she whisked about and went rustling to the door.

"Citoyenne," he called after her, "you are forgetting your flowers."

She halted, and seemed for a second to hesitate, looking at him oddly. Then she came back to the table and took up her roses. Again she looked at him, and let the bouquet fall back among the papers.

"I brought them for you, Caron," she said, "and I'll leave them with you. We can at least be friends, can we not?"

"Friends? But were we ever aught else?" he asked.

"Alas! no," she said to herself, whilst aloud she murmured: "I thought that you would like them. Your room has such a gloomy, sombre air, and a few roses seem to diffuse some of the sunshine on which they have been nurtured."

"You are too good, Cecile" he answered, and, for all his coldness, he was touched a little by this thoughtfulness.

She looked up at the altered tone, and the expression of her face seemed to soften. But before she could make answer there was a rap at the door. It opened, and Brutus stood in the doorway.

"Citizen," he announced, in his sour tones, "there is another woman below asking to see you."

La Boulaye started, as again his thoughts flew to Suzanne, and a dull flush crept into his pale cheeks and mounted to his brow. Cecile's eyes were upon him, her glance hardening as she observed these signs. Bitter enough had it been to endure his coldness whilst she had imagined that it sprang from the austerity of his nature and the absorption of his soul in matters political. But now that it seemed she might have cause to temper her bitterness with jealousy her soul was turned to gall.

"What manner of woman, Brutus?" he asked after a second's pause.

"Tall, pale, straight, black hair, black eyes, silk gown—and savours the aristocrat a league off," answered Brutus.

"Your official seems gifted with a very comprehensive eye," said Cecile tartly.

But La Boulaye paid no heed to her. The flush deepened on his face, then faded again, and he grew oddly pale. His official's inventory of her characteristics fitted Mademoiselle de Bellecour in every detail.

"Admit her, Brutus," he commanded, and his voice had a husky sound. Then, turning to Cecile, "You will give me leave?" he said, cloaking rude dismissal in its politest form.

"Assuredly," she answered bitterly, making shift to go. "Your visitor is no doubt political?" she half-asked half-asserted.

But he made no answer as he held the door for her, and bowed low as she passed out. With a white face and lips tightly compressed she went, and half-way on the stairs she met a handsome woman, tall and of queenly bearing, who ascended. Her toilette lacked the elaborateness of Cecile's, but she carried it with an air which not all the modistes of France could have succeeded in imparting to the Citoyenne Deshaix.

So dead was Robespierre's niece to every sense of fitness that, having drawn aside to let the woman pass, she stood gazing after her until she disappeared round the angle of the landing. Then, in a fury, she swept from the house and into her waiting coach, and as she drove back to Duplay's in the Rue St. Honore she was weeping bitterly in her jealous rage.

CHAPTER XVII

LA BOULAYE'S PROMISE

La Boulaye remained a moment by the door after Cecile's departure; then he moved away towards his desk, striving to master the tumultuous throbbing of his pulses. His eye alighted on Cecile's roses, and, scarce knowing why he did it, he picked them up and flung them behind a bookcase. It was but done when again the door opened, and his official ushered in Mademoiselle de Bellecour.

Oddly enough, at sight of her, La Boulaye grew master of himself. He received her with a polite and very formal bow—a trifle over-graceful for a patriot.

"So, Citoyenne," said he, and so cold was his voice that it seemed even tinged with mockery, "you are come at last."

"I could not come before, Monsieur," she answered, trembling. "They would not let me." Then, after a second's pause: "Am I too late, Monsieur?" she asked.

"No," he answered her. "The ci-devant Vicomte d'Ombreval still lies awaiting trial. Will you not be seated?"

"I do not look to remain long."

"As you please, Citoyenne. I have delayed Ombreval's trial thinking that if not my letter why then his might bring you, sooner or later, to his rescue. It may interest you to hear," he continued with an unmistakable note of irony, "that that brave but hapless gentleman is much fretted at his incarceration."

A shadow crossed her face, which remained otherwise calm and composed —the beautiful, intrepid face that had more than once been La Boulaye's undoing.

"I am glad that you have waited, Monsieur. In so doing you need have no doubts concerning me. M. d'Ombreval is my betrothed, and the troth I plighted him binds me in honour to succour him now."

La Boulaye looked steadily at her for a moment.

"Upon my soul," he said at last, a note of ineffable sarcasm vibrating in his voice, "I shall never cease to admire the effrontery of your class, and the coolness with which, in despite of dishonourable action, you make high-sounding talk of honour and the things to which it binds you. I have a dim recollection, Citoyenne, of something uncommonly like your troth which you plighted me one night at Boisvert. But so little did that promise bind you that when I

124

sought to enforce your fulfilment of it you broke my head and left me to die in the road."

His words shook her out of her calm. Her bosom rose and fell, her eyes seemed to grow haggard and her hands were clasped convulsively.

"Monsieur," she answered, "when I gave you my promise that night I had every intention of keeping it. I swear it, as Heaven is my witness."

"Your actions more than proved it," he said dryly.

"Be generous, Monsieur," she begged. "It was my mother prevailed upon me to alter my determination. She urged that I should be dishonoured if I did not."

"That word again!" he cried. "What part it plays in the life of the noblesse. All that it suits you to do, you do because honour bids you, all to which you have bound yourselves, but which is distasteful, you discover that honour forbids, and that you would be dishonoured did you persist. But I am interrupting you, Citoyenne. Did your mother advance any arguments?"

"The strongest argument of all lay here, in my heart, Monsieur," she answered him, roused and hardened by his scorn. "You must see that it had become with me a matter of choosing the lesser of two evils. Upon reflection I discovered that I was bound to two men, and it behoved me to keep the more binding of my pledges."

"Which you discovered to be your word to Ombreval," he said, and his voice grew unconsciously softer, for he began to realise the quandary in which she had found herself.

She inclined her head assentingly.

"To him I had given the earlier promise, and then, again, he was of my own class whilst you—"

"Spare me, Citoyenne," he cried. "I know what you would say. I am of the rabble, and of little more account in a matter of honour than a beast of the field. It is thus that you reason, and yet, mon Dieu! I had thought that ere now such notions had died out with you, and that, stupid enough though your class has proved itself, it would at least have displayed the intelligence to perceive that its day is ended, its sun set." He turned and paced the apartment as he spoke. "The Lilies of France have been shorn from their stems, they have withered by the roadside, and they have been trampled into the dust by the men of the new regime, and yet it seems that you others of the noblesse have not learnt your lesson. You have not yet discovered that here in France the man who was born a tiller of the soil is still a man, and, by his manhood, the equal of a king, who, after all, can be no more than a man, and is sometimes less. Enfin!"

125

he ended brusquely. "This is not the National Assembly, and I talk to ears untutored in such things. Let us deal rather with the business upon which you are come."

She eyed him out of a pale face, with eyes that seemed fascinated. That short burst of the fiery eloquence that had made him famous revealed him to her in a new light: the light of a strength and capacity above and beyond that which, already, she had perceived was his.

"Will you believe, Monsieur, that it cost me many tears to use you as I did? If you but knew—" And there she paused abruptly. She had all but told him of the kiss that she had left upon his unconscious lips that evening on the road to Liege. "Mon Dieu how I hated myself!" And she shuddered as she spoke.

He observed all this, and with a brusqueness that was partly assumed he hastened to her rescue.

"What is done is done, Citoyenne. Come, let us leave reminiscences. You are here to atone, I take it."

At that she started. His words reminded her of those of his letter.

"Monsieur La Boulaye—"

"If it is all one to you, Citoyenne, I should prefer that you call me citizen."

"Citizen, then," she amended. "I have brought with me the gems which I told you would constitute my dowry. In his letter to me the Vicomte suggested that—" She paused.

"That some Republican blackguard might be bribed," he concluded, very gently.

His gentleness deceived her. She imagined that it meant that he might not be unwilling to accept such a bribe, and thereupon she set herself to plead with him. He listened dispassionately, his hands behind his back, his eyes bent upon her, yet betraying nothing of his thoughts. At last she brought her prayer for Ombreval's life to an end, and produced a small leather bag which she set upon the table, beseeching him to satisfy himself as to the value of the contents.

Now at last he stirred. His face grew crimson to the roots of his hair, and his eyes seemed of a sudden to take fire. He seized that little bag and held it in his hand.

"And so, Mademoiselle de Bellecour," said he, in a concentrated voice, "you have learnt so little of me that you bring me a bribe of gems. Am I a helot, that you should offer to buy my very soul? Do you think my honour is so cheap a thing that you can have it for the matter of some bits of glass? Or do you imagine that we of the new regime, because we do not mouth the word at every turn, have no such thing as honour? For shame!" He paused, his wrath boiling over as he sought words in which to give it utterance. And then, words failing him to express the half of what was in him, he lifted the bag high above his head, and hurled it at her feet with a force that sent half the glittering contents rolling about the parquet floor. "Citoyenne, your journey has been in vain. I will not treat with you another instant."

She recoiled before his wrath, a white and frightened thing that but an instant back had been so calm and self-possessed. She gave no thought to the flashing jewels scattered about the floor. Through all the fear that now possessed her rose the consideration of this man—this man whom she had almost confessed half-shamedly to herself that she loved, that night on the Liege road; this man who at every turn amazed her and filled her with a new sense of his strength and dignity.

Then, bethinking her of Ombreval and of her mission, she took her courage in both hands, and, advancing a step, she cast herself upon her knees before Caron.

"Monsieur, forgive me," she besought him. "I meant you no insult. How could I, when my every wish is to propitiate you? Bethink you, Monsieur, I have journeyed all the way from Prussia to save that man, because my hon—because he is my betrothed. Remember, Monsieur, you held out to me the promise in your letter that if I came you would treat with me, and that I might buy his life from you."

"Why, so I did," he answered, touched by her humiliation and her tears. "But you went too fast in your conclusions."

"Forgive me that. See! I am on my knees to you. Am I not humbled enough? Have I not suffered enough for the wrong I may have done you?"

"It would take the sufferings of a generation to atone for the wrongs I have endured at the hands of your family, Citoyenne."

"I will do what you will, Monsieur. Bethink you that I am pleading for the life of the man I am to marry."

He looked down upon her now in an emotion that in its way was as powerful as her own. Yet his voice was hard and sternly governed as he now asked her,

"Is that an argument, Mademoiselle? Is it an argument likely to prevail with the man who, for his twice-confessed love of you, has suffered sore trials?"

He felt that in a way she had conquered him; his career, which but that day had seemed all-sufficing to him, was now fallen into the limbo of disregard. The one thing whose possession would render his life a happy one, whose absence would leave him now a lasting unhappiness, knelt here at his feet. Forgotten were the wrongs he had suffered, forgotten the purpose to humble and to punish. Everything was forgotten and silenced by the compelling voice of his blood, which cried out that he loved her. He stooped to her and caught her wrists in a grip that made her wince. His voice grew tense.

"If you would bribe me to save his life, Suzanne, there is but one price that you can pay."

"And that?" she gasped her eyes looking up with a scared expression into his masterful face.

"Yourself," he whispered, with an ardour that almost amounted to fierceness.

She gazed a second at him in growing alarm, then she dragged her hands from his grasp, and covering her face she fell a-sobbing.

"Do not misunderstand me," he cried, as he stood erect over her. "If you would have Ombreval saved and sent out of France you must become my wife."

"Your wife?" she echoed, pausing in her weeping, and for a moment an odd happiness seemed to fill her. But as suddenly as it had arisen did she stifle it. Was she not the noble daughter of the noble Marquis de Bellecour and was not this a lowly born member of a rabble government? There could be no such mating. A shudder ran through her. "I cannot, Monsieur, I cannot!" she sobbed.

He looked at her a moment with a glance that was almost of surprise, then, with a slight compression of the lips and the faintest raising of the shoulders, he turned from her and strode over to the window. There was a considerable concourse of people on their way to the Place de la Republique, for the hour of the tumbrils was at hand.

A half-dozen of those unsexed viragos produced by the Revolution, in filthy garments, red bonnets and streaming hair, were marching by to the raucous chorus of the "Ca ira!"

He turned from the sight in disgust, and again faced his visitor.

"Citoyenne," he said, in a composed voice, "I am afraid that your journey has been in vain."

She rose now from her knees, and advanced towards him.

"Monsieur, you will not be so cruel as to send me away empty-handed?" she cried, scarce knowing what she was saying.

But he looked at her gravely, and without any sign of melting.

"On what," he asked, "do you base any claim upon me?"

"On what?" she echoed, and her glance was troubled with perplexity. Then of a sudden it cleared. "On the love that you have confessed for me," she cried.

He laughed a short laugh-half amazement, half scorn.

128

"Mon Dieu!" he exclaimed, tossing his arms to Heaven, "a fine claim that, as I live; a fine argument by which to induce me to place another man in your arms. I am to do it because I love you!"

They gazed at each other now, she with a glance of strained anxiety, he with the same look of half-contemptuous wonder. And then a creaking rumble from below attracted his attention, and he looked round. He moved forward and threw the window wide, letting in with the March air an odd medley of sounds to which the rolling of drums afforded a most congruous accompaniment.

"Look, Citoyenne," he said, and he pointed out the first tumbril, which was coming round the corner of the Rue St. Honore.

She approached with some shrinking begotten by a suspicion of what she was desired to see.

In the street below, among a vociferating crowd of all sorts and conditions, the black death-cart moved on its way to the guillotine. It was preceded by a company of National Guards, and followed by the drummers and another company on foot. Within the fatal vehicle travelled three men and two women, accompanied by a constitutional priest—one of those renegades who had taken the oath imposed by the Convention. The two women sat motionless, more like statues than living beings, their faces livid and horribly expressionless, so numbed were their intelligences by fear. Of the men, one stood calm and dignified, another knelt at his prayers, and was subject, therefore, to the greater portion of the gibes the mob was offering these poor victims; the third, a very elegant gentleman in a green coat and buckskin breeches, leant nonchalantly upon the rail of the tumbril and exchanged gibes with the people. All five of them were in the prime of life, and, by their toilettes and the air that clung to them, belonged unmistakably to the noblesse.

One glance did Mademoiselle bestow upon that tragic spectacle, then with a shudder she drew back, her face going deathly white.

"Why did you bid me look?" she moaned.

"That for yourself you might see," he answered pitilessly, "the road by which your lover is to journey."

"Mon Dieu!" she cried, wringing her hands, "it is horrible. Oh! You are not men, you Revolutionists. You are beasts of prey, tigers in human semblance."

He shrugged his shoulders.

"Great injustices beget great reactions. Great wrongs can only be balanced by great wrongs. For centuries the power has lain with the aristocrats, and they have most foully abused it. For centuries the people of France have writhed beneath the armed heel of the nobility, and their blood, unjustly and wantonly shed, has saturated

129

the soil until from that seed has sprung this overwhelming retribution. Now—now, when it is too late—you are repenting; now, when at last some twenty-five million Frenchmen have risen with weapons in their hands to purge the nation of you. We are no worse than were you; indeed, not so bad. It is only that we do in a little while—and, therefore, while it lasts in greater quantity—what you have been doing through countless generations."

"Spare me these arguments, Monsieur," she cried, recovering her spirit. "The 'whys' and 'wherefores' of it are nothing to me. I see what you are doing, and that is enough. But," and her voice grew gentle and pleading, her hands were held out to him, "you are good at heart, Monsieur; you are generous and you can be noble. You will give me the life that I have come to beg of you; the life you promised me."

"Yes, but upon terms, Mademoiselle, and those terms you have heard."

She looked a moment into that calm, set face, into the dark grey eyes that looked so solemn and betrayed so little of what was passing within.

"And you say that you love me?" she cried.

"Helas!" he sighed. "It is a weakness I cannot conquer.

"Look well down into your heart, M. La Boulaye," she answered him, "and you will find how egregious is your error. You do not love me; you love yourself, and only yourself. If you loved me you would not seek to have me when I am unwilling. Above all things, you would desire my happiness—it is ever so when we truly love—and you would seek to promote it. If, indeed, you loved me you would grant my prayer, and not torture me as you are doing. But since you only love yourself, you minister only to yourself, and seek to win me by force since you desire me."

She ceased, and her eyes fell before his glance, which remained riveted upon her face. Immovable he stood a moment or two, then he turned from her with a little sigh, and leaning his elbow upon the window-sill, he gazed down into the crowds surging about the second tumbril. But although he saw much there that was calculated to compel attention, he heeded nothing. His thoughts were very busy, and he was doing what Mademoiselle had bidden him. He was looking into himself. And from that questioning he gathered not only that he loved her, but that he loved her so well and so truly that—in spite even of all that was passed—he must do her will, and deliver up to her the man she loved.

His resolve was but half taken when he heard her stirring in the room behind him. He turned sharply to find that she had gained the door.

"Mademoiselle!" he called after her. She stopped, and as she turned, he observed that her lashes were wet. But in her heart there arose now a fresh hope, awakened by the name by which he had recalled her. "Whither are you going?" he asked.

"Away, Monsieur," she answered. "I was realising that my journey had indeed been in vain."

He looked at her a second in silence. Then stepping forward:

"Mademoiselle," he said, very quietly, "your arguments have prevailed, and it shall be as you desire. The ci-devant Vicomte d'Ombreval shall go free."

Her face seemed to grow of a sudden paler, and for an instant she stood still as if robbed of understanding. Then she came forward with hands outheld.

"Said I not that you were good and generous? Said I not that you could be noble, Monsieur?" she cried, as she caught his resisting hand and sought to carry it to her lips. "God will bless you, Monsieur—"

He drew his hand away, but without roughness. "Let us say no more, Mademoiselle," he begged.

"But I will," she answered him. "I am not without heart, Monsieur, and now that you have given me this proof of the deep quality of your love, I—" She paused, as if at a loss for words.

"Well, Mademoiselle?" he urged her.

"I have it in my heart to wish that—that it were otherwise," she said, her cheeks reddening under his gaze. "If it were not that I account myself in honour bound to wed M. le Vicomte—"

"Stop!" he interrupted her. He had caught at last the drift of what she was saying. "There is no need for any comedy, Suzanne. Enough of that had we at Boisvert."

"It is not comedy," she cried with heat. "It was not altogether comedy at Boisvert."

"True," he said, wilfully misunderstanding her that he might the more easily dismiss the subject, "it went nearer to being tragedy." Then abruptly he asked her:

"Where are you residing?"

She paused before replying. She still wanted to protest that some affection for him dwelt in her heart, although curbed (to a greater extent even than she was aware) by the difference in their stations, and checked by her plighted word to Ombreval. At last, abandoning a purpose which his countenance told her would be futile:

"I am staying with my old nurse at Choisy," she answered him. "Henriette Godelliere is her name. She is well known in the village, and seems in good favour with the patriots, so that I account myself safe. I am believed to be her niece from the country."

"Hum!" he snorted. "The Citoyenne Godelliere's niece from the country in silks?"

"That is what someone questioned, and she answered that it was a gown plundered from the wardrobe of some emigrated aristocrats."

"Have a care, Suzanne," said he. "The times are dangerous, and it is a matter of a week ago since a man was lanterne for no other reason than because he was wearing gloves, which was deemed an aristocratic habit. Come, Mademoiselle, let us gather up your gems. You were going without them some moments ago."

And down upon his knees he went, and, taking up the little bag which had been left where he had flung it, he set himself to restore the jewels to it. She came to his assistance, in spite of his protestations, and so, within a moment or two, the task was completed, and the little treasure was packed away in the bosom of her gown.

"To-morrow," he said, as he took his leave of her at the door, "I shall hope to bring the ci-devant Vicomte to Choisy, and I will see that he is equipped with a laissez-passer that will carry both of you safely out of France."

She was beginning to thank him all over again, but he cut her short, and so they parted.

Long after she was gone did he sit at his writing-table, his head in his hands and his eyes staring straight before him. His face looked grey and haggard; the lines that seared it were lines of pain.

"They say," he murmured once, thinking aloud, as men sometimes will in moments of great stress, "that a good action brings its own reward. Perhaps my action is not a good one, after all, and that is why I suffer."

And, burying his head in his arms, he remained thus with his sorrow until his official entered to inquire if he desired lights.

CHAPTER XVIII

THE INCORRUPTIBLE

It was towards noon of the following day when Caron La Boulaye presented himself at the house of Duplay, the cabinet-maker in the Rue St. Honore, and asked of the elderly female who admitted him if he might see the Citizen-deputy Robespierre.

A berline stood at the door, the postillion at the horses' heads, and about it there was some bustle, as if in preparation of a departure. But La Boulaye paid no heed to it as he entered the house.

He was immediately conducted upstairs to the Incorruptible's apartment—for he was too well known to so much as need announcing. In answer to the woman's knock a gentle, almost plaintive voice from within bade them enter, and thus was Caron ushered into the humble dwelling of the humble and ineffective-looking individual whose power already transcended that of any other man in France, and who was destined to become still more before his ephemeral star went out.

Into that unpretentious and rather close-smelling room—for it was bed-chamber as well as dining-room and study—stepped La Boulaye unhesitatingly, with the air of a man who is intimate with his surroundings and assured of his welcome in them. In the right-hand corner stood the bed on which the clothes were still tumbled; in the centre of the chamber was a table all littered with the disorder of a meal partaken; on the left, by the window, sat Robespierre at his writing-table, and from the overmantel at the back of the room a marble counterpart of Robespierre's own head and shoulders looked down upon the newcomer. There were a few pictures on the whitewashed walls, and a few objects of art about the chamber, but in the main it had a comfortless air, which may in part have resulted from the fact that no fire had been lighted.

The great man tossed aside his pen, and rose as the door closed after the entering visitor. Pushing his horn-rimmed spectacles up on to his forehead he stretched out his hand to La Boulaye.

"It is you, Caron," he murmured in that plaintive voice of his. It was a voice that sorted well with the humane man who had resigned a judgeship at Arras sooner than pass a death-sentence, but hardly so well with him who, as Public Prosecutor in Paris, had brought some hundreds of heads to the sawdust. "I have been desiring to congratulate you upon your victory of yesterday," he continued, "even as I have been congratulating myself upon the fact that it was I who found you and gave you to the Nation. I feared that I might not see you ere I left."

"You are leaving Paris?" asked La Boulaye, without heeding the compliments in the earlier part of the other's speech.

"For a few days. Business of the Nation, my friend. But you— let us talk of you. Do you know that I am proud of you, cher Caron? Your eloquence turned Danton green with jealousy, and as for poor Vergniaud, it extinguished him utterly. Ma foi! If you continue as you have begun, the day may not be far distant when you will become the patron and I the Protege." And his weak eyes beamed pleasantly from out of that unhealthy pale face.

Outwardly he had changed little since his first coming to Paris, to represent the Third Estate of Artoise, saving, his cheeks were grown more hollow. Upon his dress he still bestowed the same unpretentious care that had always characterised it, which, in one of the most prominent patriots of the Mountain, amounted almost to foppishness. Blue coat, white waistcoat, silk hose and shoes buckled with silver, gave him an elegant exterior that must have earned him many a covert sneer from his colleagues. His sloping forehead was crowned by a periwig, sedulously curled and powdered—for all that with the noblesse this was already a discarded fashion.

La Boulaye replied to his patron's compliments with the best grace he could command considering how full of another matter was his mind.

"I may congratulate myself, Maximilien," he added, "upon my good fortune in coming before you took your departure. I have a request to prefer, a favour to ask."

"Tut! Who talks of favours? Not you, Caron, I hope. You have but to name what you desire, and so that it lies within my power to accord it, the thing is yours."

"There is a prisoner in the Luxembourg in whom I am interested. I seek his enlargement."

"But is that all?" cried the little man, and, without more ado, he turned to his writing-table and drew a printed form from among the chaos of documents. "His name?" he asked indifferently, as he dipped his quill in the ink-horn and scratched his signature at the foot of it.

"An aristocrat," said Caron, with some slight hesitancy.

"Eh?" And the arched brows drew together for an instant. "But no matter. There are enough and to spare even for Fouquier-Tinvillle's voracious appetite. His name?"

"The ci-devant Vicomte Antole d'Ombreval."

134

"Qui-ca?" The question rang sharp as a pistol-shot, sounding the more fearful by virtue of the contrast with the gentle tones in which Robespierre had spoken hitherto. The little man's face grew evil. "d'Ombreval?" he cried. "But what is this man to you? It is by your favour alone that I have let him live so long, but now—" He stopped short. "What is your interest in this man?" he demanded, and the question was so fiercely put as to suggest that it would be well for La Boulaye that he should prove that interest slight indeed.

But whatever feelings may have been swaying Caron at the moment, fear was not one of them.

"My interest in him is sufficiently great to cause me to seek his freedom at your hands," he answered, with composure.

Robespierre eyed him narrowly for a moment, peering at him over his spectacles which he had drawn down on to his tip-tilted nose. Then the fierceness died out of his mien and manner as suddenly as it had sprung up. He became once more the weak-looking, ineffectual man that had first greeted La Boulaye: urbane and quiet, but cold-cold as ice.

"I am desolated, my dear Caron, but you have asked me for the one man in the prisons of France whose life I cannot yield you. He is from Artois, and there is an old score 'twixt him and me, 'twixt his family and mine. They were the grands seigneurs of the land on which we were born, these Ombrevals, and I could tell you of wrongs committed by them which would make you shudder in horror. This one shall atone in the small measure we can enforce from him. It was to this end that I ordered you to effect his capture. Have patience, dear Caron, and forgive me that I cannot grant your request. As I have said, I am desolated that it should be so. Ask me, if you will, the life of any other—or any dozen others—and they are yours. But Ombreval must die."

Caron stood a moment in silent dismay. Here was an obstacle upon which he had not counted when he had passed his word to Suzanne to effect the release of her betrothed. At all costs he must gain it, he told himself, and to that end he now set himself to plead, advancing, as his only argument—but advancing it with a fervour that added to its weight—that he stood pledged to save the ci-devant Vicomte. Robespierre looked up at him with a shade of polite regret upon his cadaverous face, and with polite regret he deplored that Caron should have so bound himself.

So absorbed were they, the one in pleading, the other in resisting, that neither noticed the opening of the door, nor yet the girl who stood observing them from the threshold.

"If this man dies," cried La Boulaye at last, "I am dishonoured."

"It is regrettable," returned Robespierre, "that you should

have pledged your word in the matter. You will confess, Caron, that it was a little precipitate. Enfin," he ended, crumpling the document he had signed and tossing it under the table, "you must extricate yourself as best you can. I am sorry, but I cannot give him to you."

Caron's face was very white and his hands were clenched convulsively. It is questionable whether in that moment he had not flung himself upon the Incorruptible, and enforced that which hitherto he had only besought, but that in that instant the girl stepped into the room.

"And is it really you, Caron?" came the melodious voice of Cecile.

La Boulaye started round to confront her, and stifled a curse at the untimely interruption which Robespierre was blessing as most timely.

"It is—it is, Citoyenne," he answered shortly, to add more shortly still: "I am here on business with the Citizen, your uncle."

But before the girl could so much as appreciate the rebuke he levelled at her intrusion, her uncle had come to the rescue.

"The business, however, is at an end. Take charge of this good Caron, Cecile, whilst I make ready for my journey."

Thus, sore at heart, and chagrined beyond words, La Boulaye was forced to realise his defeat, and to leave the presence of the Incorruptible. But with Cecile he went no farther than the landing.

"If you will excuse me, Citoyenne," he said abstractedly, "I will take my leave of you."

"But I shall not excuse you, Caron," she said, refusing to see his abstraction. "You will stay to dinner—"

"I am sorry beyond measure, but—"

"You shall stay," she interrupted. "Come, Caron. It is months since you were with us. We will make a little fete in honour of your yesterday's triumph," she promised him, sidling up to him with a bewitching glance of blue eyes, and the most distracting toss of golden curls upon an ivory neck.

But to such seductions Caron proved as impervious as might a man of stone. He excused himself with cold politeness. The Nation's business was awaiting him; he might not stay.

"The Nation's business may await you a little longer," she declared, taking hold of his arm with both hands, and had she left it at that it is possible that she had won her way with him. But most indiscreetly she added:

"Come, Caron, you shall tell me who was your yesterday's visitor. Do you know that the sight of her made me jealous? Was it not foolish in me?"

And now, from cold politeness, La Boulaye passed to hot

impoliteness. Roughly he shook her detaining hands from him, and with hardly so much as a word of farewell, he passed down the stairs, leaving her white with passion at the slight he had thereby put upon her.

The beauty seemed to pass out of her face much as the meekness was wont to pass out of her uncle's when he was roused. Her blue eyes grew steely and cruel as she looked after him.

"Wait, Caron," she muttered to herself, "I will cry quits with you." And then, with a sob of anger, she turned and mounted the stairs to her apartments.

CHAPTER XIX

THE THEFT

La Boulaye sat once more in the Rue Nationale and with his head in his hands, his elbows supported by the writing-table, he stared before him, his face drawn with the pain and anger of the defeat he had sustained where no defeat had been expected.

He had been so assured that he had but to ask for Ombreval's life, and it would be accorded him; he had promised Suzanne with such confidence—boasting almost—that he could do this, and to do it he had pledged his word. And now? For very shame he could not go to her and tell her that despite his fine promises despite his bold bargaining, he was as powerless to liberate Ombreval as was she herself.

And with reflection he came to see that even did he bear her such a tale she would not believe it. The infinite assurance of his power, implicit in everything that he had said to her, must now arise in her memory, and give the lie to his present confession of powerlessness. She would not believe him, and disbelieving him, she would seek a motive for the words that she would deem untrue. And that motive she would not find far to seek. She would account his present attitude the consummation of a miserable subterfuge by which he sought to win her confidence and esteem. She would—she must—believe that he had but made a semblance of befriending her so disinterestedly only that he might enlist her kindness and regard, and turn them presently to his own purposes. She would infer that he had posed as unselfish—as self-sacrificing, almost—only that he might win her esteem, and that by telling her now that Robespierre was inflexible in his resolve to send Ombreval to the guillotine, he sought to retain that esteem whilst doing nothing for it. That he had ever intended to save Ombreval she would not credit. She would think it all a cunning scheme to win his own ends. And now he bethought him of the grief that would beset her upon learning that her journey had indeed been fruitless. He smote the table a blow with his clenched hand, and cursed the whole Republic, from Robespierre down to the meanest sans-culotte that brayed the Ca ira in the streets of Paris.

He had pledged his word, and for all that he belonged to the class whose right to honour was denied by the aristocrats, his word he had never yet broken. That circumstance—as personified by Maximilien Robespierre—should break it for him now was matter enough to enrage him, for than this never had there been an occasion on which such a breach could have been less endurable.

He rose to his feet, and set himself to pace the chamber, driven to action of body by the agonised activity of his mind. From the street rose the cry of the pastry-cook going his daily rounds, as it had risen yesterday, he remembered, when Suzanne had been with him. And now of a sudden he stood still. His lips were compressed, his brows drawn together in a forbidding scowl, and his eyes narrowed until they seemed almost closed. Then with his clenched right hand he smote the open palm of the other. His resolve was taken. By fair means or foul, with Robespierre's sanction or without it, he would keep his word. After not only the hope but the assurance he had given Suzanne that her betrothed should go free, he could do no less than accomplish the Vicomte's enlargement by whatever means should present themselves.

And now to seek a way. He recalled the free pardon to which Robespierre had gone the length of appending his signature. He remembered that it had not been destroyed; Robespierre had crumpled it in his hand and tossed it aside. And by now Robespierre would have departed, and it should not be difficult for him—the protege and intimate of Robespierre—to gain access to the Incorruptible's room.

If only he could find that document and fill in the name of Ombreval the thing would be as good as done. True, he would require the signatures of three other Deputies; but one of these he could supply himself, and another two were easily to be requisitioned, seeing that already it bore Robespierre's.

And then as suddenly as the idea of the means had come to him, came now the spectre of the consequences to affright him. How would it fare with him on Robespierre's return? How angered would not Robespierre be upon discovering that his wishes had been set at naught, his very measures contravened—and this by fraud? And than Robespierre's anger there were few things more terrible in '93. It was an anger that shore away heads as recklessly as wayside flowers are flicked from their stems by the idler's cane.

For a second it daunted him. If he did this thing he must seek refuge in flight; he must leave France, abandon the career which was so full of promise for him, and wander abroad, a penniless fortune-hunter. Well might the prospect give him pause. Well might it cause him to survey that pale, sardonic countenance that eyed him gloomily from the mirror above his mantel shelf, and ask it mockingly if it thought that Suzanne de Bellecour—or indeed, any woman living—were worthy of so great a sacrifice.

What had she done for him that he should cast away everything for her sake? Once she had told him that she loved him, only to betray him. Was that a woman for whom a man should wanton his fortunes? And then he smiled derisively, mocking his reflections in the mirror even as he mocked himself.

"Poor fool," he muttered, "it is not for the sake of what you are to her. Were it for that alone, you would not stir a finger to gratify her wishes. It is for the sake of what she is to you, Caron."

He turned from the mirror, his resolve now firm, and going to the door he called his official. Briefly he instructed Brutus touching the packing of a valise, which he would probably need that night.

"You are going a journey, Citizen?" inquired Brutus, to which La Boulaye returned a short answer in the affirmative. "Do I accompany you?" inquired the official, to which La Boulaye shook his head.

At that Brutus, who, for all his insolence of manner, was very devotedly attached to his employer, broke into remonstrances, impertinent of diction but affectionate of tenor. He protested that La Boulaye had left him behind, and lonely, during his mission to the army in Belgium, and he vowed that he would not be left behind again.

"Well, well; we shall see, Brutus," answered the Deputy, laying his hand upon the fellow's shoulder. "But I am afraid that this time I am going farther than you would care to come."

The man's ferrety eyes were raised of a sudden to La Boulaye's face in a very searching glance. Caron's tone had been laden with insinuation.

"You are running way," cried the official.

"Sh! My good Brutus, what folly! Why should I run away—and from whom, pray?"

"I know not that. But you are. I heard it in your voice. And you do not trust me, Citizen La Boulaye," the fellow added, in a stricken voice. "I have served you faithfully these two years, and yet you have not learnt to trust me."

"I do, I do, my friend. You go too fast with your conclusions. Now see to my valise, and on my return perhaps I'll tell you where I am going, and put your fidelity to the test."

"And you will take me with you?"

"Why, yes," La Boulaye promised him, "unless you should prefer to remain in Paris."

With that he got away and leaving the house, he walked briskly up the street, round the corner, and on until he stood once more before Duplay's.

"Has the Citizen Robespierre departed yet?" he inquired of the woman who answered his peremptory knock.

"He has been gone this hour, Citizen La Boulaye," she answered. "He started almost immediately after you left him."

"Diable!" grumbled Caron, with well-feigned annoyance. "Quel contretemps! I have left a most important document in his room, and, of course, it will be locked."

"But the Citoyenne Cecile has the key," answered the woman, eager to oblige him.

"Why, yes—naturally! Now that is fortunate. Will you do me the favour to procure the key from he Citoyenne for a few moments, telling her, of course, that it is I who need it?"

"But certainly, Montez, Citoyen." And with a wave of the hand towards the stairs she went before him.

He followed leisurely, and by the time he had reached Robespierre's door her voice floated down to him from above, calling the Incorruptible's niece. Next he heard Cecile's voice replying, and then a whispered conference on the landing overhead, to the accompaniment of the occasional tinkle of a bunch of keys.

Presently the domestic returned, and unlocking the door, she held it open for La Boulaye to pass. From her attitude it seemed to Caron as if she were intentioned—probably she had been instructed—to remain there while he obtained what he sought. Now he had no mind that she should see him making his quest among the wasted papers on the floor, and so:

"I shall not be more than a few minutes," he announced quietly. "I will call you when I am ready to depart."

Thus uncompromisingly dismissed, she did not venture to remain, and, passing in, La Boulaye closed the door. As great as had been his deliberation hitherto was now the feverish haste with which he crossed to the spot where he had seen the document flung. He caught up a crumpled sheet and opened it out It was not the thing he sought. He cast it aside and took up another with no better luck. To crumple discarded papers seemed the habit of the Incorruptible, for there was a very litter of them on the ground. One after another did Caron investigate without success. He was on his knees now, and his exploration had carried him as far as the table; another moment and he was grovelling under it, still at his search, which with each fresh disappointment grow more feverish.

Yonder—by the leg of the Incorruptible's chair—he espied the ball of paper, and to reach it he stretched to his full length, lying prone beneath a table in an attitude scarce becoming a Deputy of the French Republic. But it was worth the effort and the disregard of dignity, for when presently on his knees he smoothed out that document, he discovered it to be the one he sought the order upon the gaolers of the Luxembourg to set at liberty a person or persons whose names were to be filled in, signed by Maximilien Robespierre.

He rose, absorbed in his successful find, and he pursued upon the table the process of smoothing the creases as much as possible from that priceless document. That done he took up a pen and attached his own signature alongside of Robespierre's; then into the blank space above he filled the name of Anatole d'Ombreval ci-devant Vicomte d'Ombreval. He dropped the pen and took up the sand-box. He sprinkled the writing, creased the paper, and dusted the sand back into the receptacle. And then of a sudden his blood seemed to freeze, and beads of cold sweat stood out upon his brow. There had been the very slightest stir behind him, and with it had come a warm breath upon his bowed neck. Someone was looking over his shoulder. An instant he remained in that bowed attitude with head half-raised. Then suddenly straightening himself he swung round and came face to face with Cecile Deshaix.

Confronting each other and very close they now stood and each was breathing with more than normal quickness. Her cheeks were white, her nostrils dilated and quivering, her blue eyes baleful and cruel, whilst her lips wore never so faint a smile. For a second La Boulaye looked the very picture of foolishness and alarm. Then it seemed as if he drew a curtain, and his face assumed the expressionless mask that was habitual to it in moments of great tension. Instinctively he put behind him his hands which held the paper. Cecile's lips took on an added curl of scorn as she observed the act.

"You thief!" she said, very low, but very fiercely. "That was the paper that you left behind you, was it?"

"The paper that I have is certainly the paper that I left behind," he answered serenely, for he had himself well in hand by now. "And as for dubbing me a thief so readily"—he paused, and shrugged his shoulders—"you are a woman," he concluded, with an air suggesting that that fact was a conclusion to all things.

"Fool!" she blazed. "Do you think to overcome me by quibbles? Do you think to dupe me with words and shrugs?"

"My dear Cecile" he begged half-whimsically, "may I implore you to use some restraint? Inured as I am to the unbounded licence of your tongue and to the abandon that seems so inherent in you, let me assure you that—"

"Ah! You can say Cecile now?" she cried, leaving the remainder of his speech unheeded. "Now that you need me; now that you want me to be a party to your treacherous designs against my uncle. Oh, you can say 'Cecile' and 'dear Cecile' instead of your everlasting 'Citoyenne'.

"It seems I am doomed to be always misunderstood by you," he laughed, and at the sound she started as if he had struck her.

Had she but looked in his eyes she had seen no laughter there; she might have realised that murder rather than mirth was in his soul—for, at all costs, he was determined to hold the paper he had been at such pains to get.

"I understand you well enough," she cried hotly, her cheeks flaming red of a sudden. "I understand you, you thief, you trickster. Do you think that I heard nothing of what passed this morning between my uncle and you? Do you think I do not know whose name you have written on that paper? Answer me," she commanded him.

"Since you know so much, what need for any questions?" quoth he coolly, transferring the coveted paper to his pocket as he spoke. "And since we are so far agreed that I am not contradicting anything you say—nor, indeed, intend to—perhaps you will see the convenience of ending an interview that promises to be fruitless. My dear Cecile, I am very grateful to you for the key of this room. I beg that you will make my compliments to the Citizen your uncle upon his return, and inform him of how thoroughly you ministered to my wants."

With that and a superb air of insouciance, he made shift to go. But fronting him she barred his way.

"Give me that paper, sclerat," she demanded imperiously. "You shall not go until you surrender it. Give it to me or I will call Duplay."

"You may call the devil for aught I care, you little fool," he answered her, very pleasantly. "Do you think Duplay will be mad enough to lay hands upon a Deputy of the Convention in the discharge of the affairs of the Nation?"

"It is a lie!"

"Why, of course it is," he admitted sweetly. "But Duplay will not be aware of that."

"I shall tell him."

"Tut! He won't believe you. I'll threaten him with the guillotine if he does. And I should think that Duplay has sufficient dread of the national barber not to risk having his toilet performed by him. Now, be reasonable, and let me pass."

Enraged beyond measure by his persiflage and very manifest contempt of her, she sprang suddenly upon him, and caught at the lapels of his redingote.

"Give me that paper!" she screamed, exerting her entire strength in a vain effort to boldly shake him.

Coldly he eyed this golden-haired virago now, and looked in vain for some trace of her wonted beauty in the stormy distortion of her face.

"You grow tiresome with your repetitions," he answered her

impatiently, as, snatching at her wrists, he made her release her hold. "Let me go." And with that he flung her roughly from him.

A second she staggered, then, recovering her balance and without an instant's hesitation, she sped to the door. Imagining her intent to be to lock him in La Boulaye sprang after her. But it seemed that his mind had been more swift to fasten upon the wiser course than had hers. Instead, she snatched the key and closed the door on the inside. She wasted a moment fumbling at the lock, and even as he caught her by the waist the key slipped in, and before he dragged her back she had contrived to turn it, and now held it in her hand. He laughed a trifle angrily as she twisted out of his grasp, and stood panting before him.

"You shall not leave this room with that paper," she gasped, her anger ever swelling, and now rendering her speech almost incoherent.

He set his arms akimbo, and surveyed her whimsically.

"My dear Cecile," quoth he, "if you will take no thought for my convenience, I beg that, at least, you will take some for your good name. Thousand devils woman! Will you have it said in Paris that you were found locked in a room with me? What will your uncle—your virtuous, prudish, incorruptible uncle—say when he learns of it? If he does not demand a heavy price from you for so dishonouring him, he is not the man I deem him. Now be sensible, child, and open that door while there is yet time, and before anybody discovers us in this most compromising situation."

He struck the tone most likely to win him obedience, and that he had judged astutely her face showed him. In the place of the anger that had distorted it there came now into that countenance a look of surprise and fear. She saw herself baffled at every point. She had threatened him with Duplay—the only man available—and he had shown her how futile it must prove to summon him. And now she had locked herself in with him, thinking to sit there until he should do her will, and he showed her the danger to herself therein, which had escaped her notice.

There was a settle close behind her, and on to this she sank, and bending her head she opened the floodgates of her passionate little soul, and let the rage that had so long possessed her dissolve in tears. At sight of that sudden change of front La Boulaye stamped his foot. He appreciated the fact that she was about to fight him with weapons that on a previous occasion—when, however, it is true, they were wielded by another—had accomplished his undoing.

And for all that he steeled his heart, and evoked the memory of Suzanne to strengthen him in his purpose: he approached her with a kindly exterior. He sat him down beside her; he encompassed her waist with his arm, and drawing her to him he set himself to

144

soothe her as one soothes a wilful child. Had he then recalled what her attitude had been towards him in the past he had thought twice before adopting such a course. But in his mind there was no sentiment that was not brotherly, and far from his wishes was it to invest his action with any other than a fraternal kindness.

But she, feeling that caressing arm about her, and fired by it in her hapless passion for this man, was quick to misinterpret him, and to translate his attitude into one of a kindness far beyond his dreams. She nestled closer to him; at his bidding her weeping died down and ceased.

"There, Cecile, you will give me the key now?" he begged.

She glanced up at him shyly through wet lashes—as peeps the sun through April clouds.

"There is nothing I will not do for you, Caron," she murmured. "See, I will even help you to play the traitor on my uncle. For you love me a little, cher Caron, is it not so?"

He felt himself grow cold from head to foot, and he grew sick at the thought that by the indiscretion of his clumsy sympathy he had brought this down upon his luckless head. Mechanically his arm relaxed the hold of her waist and fell away. Instinctively she apprehended that all was not as she had thought. She turned on the seat to face him squarely, and caught something of the dismay in his glance of the loathing almost (for what is more loathsome to a man than to be wooed by a woman he desires not?) Gradually, inch by inch, she drew away from him, ever facing him, and her eyes ever on his, as if fascinated by the horror of what she saw. Thus until the extremity of the settle permitted her to go no farther. She started, then her glance flickered down, and she gave a sudden gasp of passion. Simultaneously the key rang on the boards at Caron's feet angrily flung there by Cecile.

"Go!" she exclaimed, in a suffocating voice, "and never let me see your face again."

For a second or two he sat quite still, his eyes observing her with a look of ineffable pity, which might have increased her disorder had she perceived it. Then slowly he stooped, and took up the key.

He rose from the settle, and without a word—for words he realised, could do no more than heighten the tragic banality of the situation—he went to the door, unlocked it, and passed out.

Huddled in her corner sat Cecile, listening until his steps had died away on the stairs. Then she cast herself prone upon the settle, and in a frenzy of sobs and tears she vented some of the rage and shame that were distracting her.

CHAPTER XX

THE GRATITUDE OF OMBREVAL

What La Boulaye may have lacked in knowledge of woman's ways he made up for by his knowledge of Cecile, and from this he apprehended that there was no time to be lost if he would carry out his purpose. Touching her dismissal of him, he permitted himself no illusions. He rated it at its true value. He saw in it no sign of relenting of generosity, but only a desire to put an end to the shame which his presence was occasioning her.

He could imagine the lengths to which the thirst of vengeance would urge a scorned woman, and of all women he felt that Cecile scorned was the most to be feared. She would not sit with folded hands. Once she overcame the first tempestuous outburst of her passion she would be up and doing, straining every sense to outwit and thwart him in his project, whose scope she must have more than guessed.

Reasoning thus, he clearly saw not only that every moment was of value, but that flight was the only thing remaining him if he would save himself as well as Ombreval. And so he hired him a cabriolet, and drove in all haste to the house of Billaud Varennes, the Deputy, from whom he sought to obtain one of the two signatures still needed by his order of release. He was disappointed at learning that Varennes was not at home—though, had he been able to peep an hour or so into the future, he would have offered up thanks to Heaven for that same Deputy's absence. His insistent and impatient questions elicited the information that probably Verennes would be found at Fevrier's. And so to Fevrier's famous restaurant in the old Palais Royal went La Boulaye, and there he had the good fortune to find not only Billaud Varennes, but also the Deputy Carnot. Nor did fortune end her favours there. She was smiling now upon Caron, as was proved by the fact that neither to Varennes nor Carnot did the name of Ombreval mean anything. Robespierre's subscription of the document was accepted by each as affording him a sufficient warrant to append his own signature, and although Carnot asked a question or two, it was done in an idle humour, and he paid little attention to such replies as Caron made him.

Within five minutes of entering the restaurant, La Boulaye was in the street again, driving, by way of the Pont Neuf, to the Luxembourg.

At the prison he encountered not the slightest difficulty. He was known personally to the officer, of whom he demanded the person of the ci-devant Vicomte, and his order of release was too correct to give rise to any hesitation on the part of the man to whom it was submitted. He was left waiting a few moments in a chamber that did duty as a guard-room, and presently the Vicomte, looking pale, and trembling with excitement at his sudden release, stood before him.

"You?" he muttered, upon beholding La Boulaye. But the Republican received him very coldly, and hurried him out of the prison with scant ceremony.

The officer attended the Deputy to the door of his cabriolet, and in his hearing Caron bade the coachman drive to the Porte St. Martin. This, however, was no more than a subterfuge to which he was resorting with a view to baffling the later possibility of their being traced. Ombreval naturally enough plied him with questions as they went, to which La Boulaye returned such curt answers that in the end, discouraged and offended, the nobleman became silent.

Arrived at the Porte St. Martin they alighted, and La Boulaye dismissed the carriage. On foot he now led his companion as far as the church of St. Nicholas des Champs, where he hired a second cabriolet, bidding the man drive him to the Quai de la Greve. Having reached the riverside they once more took a short walk, crossing by the Pont au Change, and thence making their way towards Notre Dame, in the neighbourhood of which La Boulaye ushered the Vicomte into a third carriage, and thinking that by now they had done all that was needed to efface their tracks, he ordered the man to proceed as quickly as possible to Choisy.

They arrived at that little village on the Seine an hour or so later, and having rid themselves of their conveyance, Caron inquired and discovered the way to the house of Citoyenne Godelliere.

Mademoiselle was within, and at sound of Caron's voice questioning the erstwhile servant who had befriended her, she made haste to show herself. And at a word from her, Henriette admitted the two men and ushered them into a modest parlour, where she left them with Mademoiselle.

La Boulaye was the first to speak.

"I trust that I have not kept you waiting overlong, Citoyenne," he said, by way of saying something.

"Monsieur," she answered him, with a look that was full of gratitude and kindliness "you have behaved nobly, and to my dying day I shall remember it."

This La Boulaye deprecated by a gesture, but uttered no word as the Vicomte now stepped forward and bore Suzanne's hand to his lips.

"Mademoiselle," said he, "Monsieur La Boulaye here was very reticent touching the manner in which my release has been gained. But I never doubted that I owed it to your good efforts, and that you had adopted the course suggested to you by my letter, and bought me from the Republic."

La Boulaye flushed slightly as much at the contemptuous tone as at the words in which Ombreval referred to the Republic.

"It is not to me but to our good friend, M. La Boulaye, that you should address your thanks, Monsieur."

"Ah? Vraiment?" exclaimed the Vicomte, turning a supercilious eye upon the Deputy, for with his freedom he seemed to have recovered his old habits.

"I have not sold you to the Citoyenne," said La Boulaye, the words being drawn from him by the other's manner. "I am making her a present of you—a sort of wedding gift." And his lips smiled, for all that his eyes remained hard.

Ombreval made him no answer, but stood looking from the Deputy to Suzanne in some hesitation. The expressions which his very lofty dignity prompted, his sense of fitness—feeble though it was—forbade him. And so there followed a pause, which, however, was but brief, for La Boulaye had yet something to say.

It had just come to him with a dismaying force that in the haste of his escape from Paris with the Vicomte he had forgotten to return to his lodging for a passport that he was fortunately possessed of. It was a laissez-passer, signed and left in blank, with which he had been equipped—against the possibility of the need for it arising—when he had started upon the Convention's errand to the Army of Dumouriez. Whilst on his way to Robespierre's house to secure the order of release, he had bethought him of filling in that passport for three persons, and thus, since to remain must entail his ruin and destruction, make his escape from France with Mademoiselle and the Vicomte. It was his only chance. Then in the hurry of the succeeding incidents, the excitement that had attended them, and the imperative need for haste in getting the Vicomte to Choisy, he had put the intended return to his lodging from his mind—overlooking until now the fact that not only must he go back for the valise which he had bidden Brutus pack, but also for that far more precious passport.

It now became necessary to explain the circumstances to his companions, and in explaining them the whole affair, from Robespierre's refusal to grant him the life of the Vicomte down to the means to which he had had recourse, could not be kept from transpiring. As she listened, Suzanne's expression changed into one of ineffable wonder.

148

"And you have done this for me?" she cried, when at last he paused, "you have ruined your career and endangered your life?"

La Boulaye shrugged his shoulders.

"I spoke over-confidently when I said that I could obtain you the Vicomte's pardon. There proved to be a factor on which I had not counted. Nevertheless, what I had promised I must fulfil. I was by honour bound to leave nothing undone that might result in the Vicomte's enlargement."

Ornbreval laughed softly, but with consummate amusement.

"A sans-culotte with a sense of honour is such an anomaly—" he began, when Mademoiselle interposed, a note of anger sounding in her voice.

"M. d'Ombreval means to pay you a compliment," she informed La Boulaye, "but he has such an odd way of choosing his expressions that I feared you might misunderstand him."

La Boulaye signified his indifference by a smile.

"I am afraid the ci-devant Vicomte has not yet learnt his lesson," said he; "or else he is like the sinner who upon recovering health forgot the penitence that had come to him in the days of sickness. But we have other matters to deal with, Citoyenne, and, in particular, the matter of the passport. Fool that I am!" he cried bitterly.

"I must return to Paris at once," he announced briskly. "There is no help for it. We will hope that as yet the way is open to me, and that I shall be permitted to go and to return unmolested. In such a case the rest is easy—except that you will have to suffer my company as far as the frontier."

It was Mademoiselle who accompanied him to the door.

"Monsieur," she said, in a voice that shook with the sincere intensity of her feelings, "think me not ungrateful that I have said so little. But your act has overwhelmed me. It is so truly noble, that to offer you thanks that are but words, seems tome little short of a banality."

"Tut!" he laughed. "I have not yet done half. It will be time to thank me when we are out of France."

"And you speak so lightly of leaving France?" she cried. "But what is to become of you? What of your career?"

"Other careers are possible in other countries," he answered, with a lightness he did not feel. "Who knows perhaps the English or the Prussians might be amenable to a change of government. I shall seek to induce one or the other of them to became a republic, and then I shall become once more a legislator."

With that, and vowing that every moment he remained their chances of leaving France grew more slender, he took his leave of her, expressing the hope that he might be back within a couple of hours. Mademoiselle watched him to the garden gate, then closing the door she returned within.

She discovered her betrothed—he whom La Boulaye had called her lover—standing with his back to the fire, his hands clasped behind him, the very picture of surliness. He made none of the advances that one might look for in a man placed as he was at that moment. He greeted her, instead, with a complaint.

"Will you permit me, Mademoiselle, to say that in this matter you have hardly chosen the wiser course?"

"In what matter?" quoth she, at a loss to understand him.

"In the matter of my release. I advised you in my letter to purchase my freedom. Had you done so, we should now be in a position to start for the frontier—for you would have made a passport a part of your bargain. Instead of this, not only are we obliged to run the risk of waiting, but even if this fellow should return, we shall be affronted by his company for some days to come." And the Vicomte sniffed the air in token of disgust.

Suzanne looked at him in an amazement that left her speechless for a moment. At last:

"And this is your gratitude?" she demanded. "This is all that you have to say in thanks for the discomfort and danger that I have suffered on your behalf? Your tone is oddly changed since you wrote me that piteous, pitiable letter from Belgium, M. le Vicomte."

He reddened slightly.

"I am afraid that I have been clumsy in my expressions," he apologised. "But never doubt my gratitude, Mademoiselle. I am more grateful to you than words can tell. You have done your duty to me as few women could."

The word "duty" offended her, yet she let it pass. In his monstrous vanity it was often hopeless to make him appreciate the importance of anything or anybody outside of himself. Of this the present occasion was an instance.

"You must forgive me my seeming thanklessness, Mademoiselle," he pursued. "It was the company of that sans-culotte rascal that soured me. I had enough of him a month ago, when he brought me to Paris. It offended me to have him stand here again in the same room with me, and insolently refer to his pledged word as though he were a gentleman born."

"To whom do you refer?" quoth she.

"Ma foi! How many of them are there? Why, to this fellow, La Boulaye?"

"So it seemed, and yet I could not believe it of you. Do you not realise that your ingratitude approaches the base?"

150

He vouchsafed her a long, cold stare of amazement.

"Mordieu!" he ejaculated at last. "I am afraid that your reason has been affected by your troubles. You seem, Mademoiselle, to be unmindful of the station into which you have had the honour to be born."

"If your bearing is to be accepted as a sign that you remember it, I will pray God that I may, indeed, forget it—completely and for all time."

And then the door opened to admit the good Henriette, who came to announce that she had contrived a hasty meal, and that it was served and awaiting them.

"Diable!" he laughed. "Those are the first words of true wit that I have heard these many days. I swear," he added, with a pleasantness that was oddly at variance with his sullen humour of a moment back, "that I have not tasted human food these four weeks, and as for my appetite—it is capable of consuming the whole patrimony of St. Peter. Lead the way, my good Henriette. Come, Mademoiselle."

CHAPTER XXI

THE ARREST

Facts proved how correct had been La Boulaye's anticipations of the course that Cecile would adopt, Within a half-hour of his having quitted the house of Billaud Varennes, she presented herself there, and demanded to see the Deputy. Upon being told that he was absent she determined to await his return.

And so, for the matter of an hour, she remained in the room where the porter had offered her accommodation, fretting at the delay, and only restrained from repairing to some other member of the Convention by the expectation that the next moment would see Varennes arrive. Arrive he did at last, when her patience was all but exhausted, and excitedly she told her tale of what had taken place. Varennes listened gravely, and cross-questioned her in his unbelief—for it seemed, indeed, monstrous that a man of La Boulaye's position should ruin so promising a future as was his by an act for which Varennes could not so much as divine a motive. But her story hung together so faithfully, and was so far borne out by the fact that Varennes himself had indeed signed such a document as she described, that in the end the Deputy determined to take some steps to neutralise the harm that might have been done.

Dismissing the girl with the assurance that the matter should have his attention, he began by despatching a courier to Robespierre at Chartres—where he knew the Incorruptible to be. That done, he resorted to measures for La Boulaye's detention. But this proved a grave matter. What if, after all, that half-hysterical girl's story should be inaccurate? In what case would he find himself if, acting upon it in the meantime, he should order Caron's arrest? The person of a Deputy was not one to be so lightly treated, and he might find himself constrained to answer a serious charge in consequence. Thus partly actuated by patriotism and the fear of Robespierre, and partly restrained by patriotism and the fear of La Boulaye, he decided upon a middle course: that of simply detaining La Boulaye at his lodging until Robespierre should either return or send an answer to his message. Thus, whilst leaving him perfect freedom of movement within his own apartments, he would yet ensure against his escape so that should Robespierre demand him he could without difficulty be produced.

To this end he repaired with a sous-lieutenant and six men to La Boulaye's house in the Rue Nationale, intending to station the soldiers there with orders not to allow the Deputy to go out, and to detain and question all who sought admittance to him. He nourished the hope that the ci-devant Vicomte might still be with La Boulaye. At the Rue Nationale, however, he was to discover that neither Deputy nor aristocrat was to be found. Brutus informed him that he was expecting the Citizen La Boulaye, but beyond that he would say nothing, and he wisely determined to hold his peace touching the valise that he had been ordered to pack and the fact that he knew the Deputy meditated leaving Paris. Brutus had learnt the value of silence, especially when those who sought information were members of the Convention.

Alarmed at this further corroboration of Cecile's story of treachery Varennes left the military at Caron's house, with orders not to allow the Deputy to again depart if in the meantime he should happen to return, whilst to every barrier of Paris he sent instructions to have La Boulaye detained if he should present himself. By these measures he hoped still to be able to provide against the possibility of Caron's seeking to leave Paris.

But Caron had been gone over an hour, and as a matter of fact, he was back again in Paris within a very little time of these orders having been issued. At the Barriere d'Enfer, although recognised, he was not molested, since the orders only, and distinctly, concerned his departure and nowise his arrival.

Thus, not until he had reached his lodgings did he realise that all was not as he had hoped. And even then it was only within doors that he made the discovery, when he found himself suddenly confronted by the sous-lieutenant, who was idling in the passage. The officer saluted him respectfully, and no less respectfully, though firmly, informed him that, by order of the Citizen-deputy Billaud Varennes, he must ask him to confine himself to his own apartments until further orders.

"But why, Citizen-officer?" La Boulaye demanded, striving to exclude from his voice any shade of the chagrin that was besetting him. "What do these orders mean?"

The officer was courtesy personified, but explanations he had none to give, for the excellent reason, he urged that he was possessed of none. He was a soldier, and he had received orders which he must obey, without questioning either their wisdom or their justice. Appreciating the futility of bearing himself otherwise, since his retreat was already blocked by a couple of gendarmes, Caron submitted to the inevitable.

He mounted leisurely to his study, and the ruin that stared him in the eyes was enough to have daunted the boldest of men. Yet, to do him justice, he was more concerned at the moment with the consequences this turn of affairs might have for Mademoiselle than with his own impending downfall. That he had Cecile to thank for his apprehension he never doubted. Yet it was a reflection that he readily dismissed from his mind. In such a pass as he now found himself none but a weakling could waste time and energy in bewailing the circumstances that had conspired to it. In a man of La Boulaye's calibre and mettle it was more befitting to seek a means to neutralise as much as possible the evil done.

He called Brutus and cross-questioned him regarding the attitude and behaviour of the soldiery since their coming. He learnt that nothing had been touched by them, and that they were acting with the utmost discreetness, taking scrupulous care not to exceed the orders they had received, which amounted to detaining La Boulaye and nothing more.

"You think, then, that you might come and go unmolested?" he asked.

"I think that I might certainly go. But whether they would permit me to return once I had left, I cannot say. So that they will let you pass out, that is all that signifies at the moment," said Caron. "Should they question you, you can tell them that you are going to dine and to fetch me my dinner from Berthon's. As a matter of fact, I shall want you to go to Choisy with a letter, which you must see does not fall into the hands of any of these people of the Convention."

"Give me the letter, Citizen, and trust me to do the rest," answered the faithful Brutus.

La Boulaye searched a drawer of his writing-table for the blank passport he required. Having found it, he hesitated for a moment how to fill it in. At last he decided, and set down three names—Pierre, Francois, and Julie Michael, players, going to Strasbourg—to which he added descriptions of himself, the Vicomte, and Mademoiselle. He reasoned that in case it should ultimately prove impossible for him to accompany them, the passport, thus indited, would still do duty for the other two. They could easily advance some excuse why the third person mentioned was not accompanying them. From this it will be seen that La Boulaye was far from having abandoned hope of effecting his escape, either by his own resourcefulness or by the favour of Robespierre himself, whose kindness for him, after all, was a factor worth reckoning upon.

To Mademoiselle he now wrote as follows:

I am sending you the laissez-passer filled in for the three of us. I am unfortunately unable to bring it myself as my abstraction of the order of release has already been discovered, and I am being detained pending the arrival of Robespierre. But I am at my own lodging, and I have every hope that, either by the use of my own wit, or else by the favour of my friend Robespierre, I shall shortly be able to join you. I would therefore ask you to wait a few days. But should I presently send you word not to do so any longer, or should you hear of events which will render it impossible for me to accompany you, you can then set out with Ombreval, travelling under the guise described in the passport, and informing any questioners that the other person mentioned has been forced by ill health to interrupt his journey. As I have said, I have every hope of winning through my present difficulties; but should I fail to do so, my most earnest prayer will be that you may make your way out of France in safety, and that lasting happiness may be your lot in whatever country you may elect to settle. You may trust the bearer implicitly, patriotic though he may appear.

He subscribed the letter with his initials, and, having enclosed the passport and sealed the package, he gave it to Brutus, with the most minute instructions touching its delivery.

These instructions Brutus carried out with speed and fidelity. He was allowed to quit the house without so much as a question, which left his plan for readmittance the greater likelihood of succeeding. In something less than an hour—for he hired himself a horse at the nearest post-house—he had delivered his letter to Mademoiselle at Choisy.

Its contents sowed in her heart the very deepest consternation—a consternation very fully shared by the Vicomte.

"Tenez!" he exclaimed, when he had read it. "Perhaps now you will admit the justice of my plaint that you did not make a simple purchase of my liberty, as I counselled you, instead of entering into this idiotic compact with that sans-culotte."

She looked at him a moment in silence. She was suffering as it was at the very thought that La Boulaye's life might be in danger in consequence of what he had done for her. With reluctance had she accepted the sacrifice of his career which he had made to serve her. Now that it became the question of a sacrifice of life as well she was dismayed. All the wrongs that she and hers had done that man seemed to rise up and reproach her now. And so, when presently she answered the Vicomte, it was no more than natural that she should answer him impatiently.

155

"I thought, Monsieur, that we had already discussed and settled that?"

"Settled it?" he echoed, with a sneer. "It seems none so easy to settle. Do you think that words will settle it."

"By no means," she answered, her voice quivering. "It seems as if a man's life will be required for that."

He shrugged his shoulders, and his face put on a look of annoyance.

"I hope, Mademoiselle, that you are not proposing to introduce sentimentality. I think you would be better advised to leave that vulgarity to the vulgar."

"I do not propose to pursue the discussion at all, Monsieur," was her chilly answer.

"The way of woman," he reflected aloud. "Let her find that she is being worsted in argument, and she calmly tells you that she has no mind to pursue it. But, Mademoiselle, will you tell me at least what you intend?"

"What do I intend?" she questioned. "What choice have we?"

"Whenever we are asked to follow a given course, we have always the choice between two alternatives," he theorised. "We can comply, or not comply."

"In the present instance I am afraid your rule is inapplicable. There is no room for any alternative. We can do nothing but wait."

She looked at him impatiently, and wearily she sank on to a chair.

"Monsieur," she said, as calmly as might be, "I am almost distracted by my thoughts as it is. I don't know whether you are seeking to complete the rout of my senses. Let me beg of you at least not to deal in riddles with me. The time is ill-chosen. Tell me bluntly what is in your mind, if, indeed, anything."

He turned from her peevishly, and crossed to the window. The twilight was descending, and the little garden was looking grey in the now pallid light. Her seeming obtuseness was irritating him.

"Surely, Mademoiselle," he exclaimed at last, "it is not necessary that I should tell you what other course is open to us? It is a matter for our choice whether we depart at once. We have a passport, and—and, enfin, every hour that we remain here our danger is increased, and our chances of escape are lessened."

"Ah!" She breathed the syllable contemptuously. "And what of La Boulaye?"

"Pooh! he says himself that he is in no great danger. He is among his fellows. Leave him to extricate himself. After all, it is his fault that we are here. Why should we endanger our necks by waiting his convenience?"

"But surely you forget what he has done for us. You are forgetting that he has rescued you from the guillotine, dragged you out of the very jaws of death. Do you think that to forsake him now would be a fair, an honest return?"

"But name of a name," rasped the Vicomte, "does he not say that he is far from despairing? His position is not half so dangerous as ours. If we are taken, there will be an end of us. With him matters are far from being so bad. He is one of the rabble himself, and the rabble will look after its own."

She rose impatiently.

"Monsieur, I am afraid the subject is not one that we may profitably discuss. I shall obey the voice of my conscience in the matter, and I shall wait until we hear again from La Boulaye. That is the message I am about to return him by his servant."

The Vicomte watched her fling out of the room, and his weak face was now white with anger. He rapped out an oath as he turned to the window again.

"Mad!" he muttered, through-set teeth. "Mad as a sun-struck dog. The troubles she has lately seen have turned her head—never a difficult matter with a woman. She talks as if she had been reading Rousseau on the 'Right of man'. To propose to endanger our lives for the sake of that scum, La Boulaye! Ciel! It passes belief."

But it was in vain that he was sullen and resentful. Suzanne's mind entertained no doubt of what she should do, and she had her way in the matter, sending back Brutus with the message that she would wait until La Boulaye communicated with her again.

That night Caron slept tranquilly. He had matured a plan of escape which he intended to carry out upon the morrow, and with confident hope to cradle him he had fallen asleep.

But the morrow—early in the forenoon—brought a factor with which he had not reckoned, in the person of the Incorruptible himself. Robespierre had returned in hot haste to Paris upon receiving Varennes' message, and he repaired straight to the house of La Boulaye.

Caron was in his dressing-gown when Robespierre was ushered into his study, and the sight of that greenish complexion and the small eyes, looking very angry and menacing, caused the song that the young man had been humming to fade on his lips.

"You, Maximilien!" he exclaimed.

"Your cordial welcome flatters me," sneered the Incorruptible, coming forward. Then with a sudden change of voice: "What is that they tell me you have done, miserable?" he growled.

It would have been a madness on Caron's part to have increased an anger that was already mounting to very passionate heights. Contritely, therefore, and humbly he acknowledged his fault, and cast himself upon the mercy of Robespierre.

But the Incorruptible was not so easily to be shaken.

"Traitor that you are!" he inveighed. "Do you imagine that because it is yours to make high sounding speeches in the Convention you are to conspire with impunity against the Nation? Your loyalty, it seems, is no more than a matter of words, and they that would keep their heads on their shoulders in France to-day will find the need for more than words as their claim to be let live. If you would save your miserable neck, tell me what you have done with this damned aristocrat."

"He is gone," answered La Boulaye quietly.

"Don't prevaricate, Caron! Don't seek to befool me, Citizen-deputy. You have him in hiding somewhere. You can have supplied him with no papers, and a man may not travel out of France without them in these times. Tell me—where is he?"

"Gone," repeated La Boulaye. "I have set him free, and he has availed himself of it to place himself beyond your reach. More than that I cannot tell you."

"Can you not?" snarled Robespierre, showing his teeth. "Of what are you dreaming fool? Do you think that I will so easily see myself cheated of this dog? Did I not tell you that rather would I grant you the lives of a dozen aristocrats than that of this single one? Do you think, then, that I am so lightly to be baulked? Name of God? Who are you, La Boulaye, what are you, that you dare thwart me in this?" He looked at the young man's impassive face to curb his anger. "Come, Caron," he added, in a wheedling tone. "Tell me what you have done with him?"

"I have already told you," answered the other quietly.

As swift and suddenly as it changed before did Robespierre's humour change again upon receiving that reply. With a snort of anger he strode to the door and threw it open.

"Citizen-lieutenant!" he called, in a rasping voice.

"Here, Citizen," came a voice from below.

"Give yourself the trouble of coming up with a couple of men. Now, Citizen La Boulaye," he said, more composedly, as he turned once more to the young man, "since you will not learn reason you may mount the guillotine in his place."

Caron paled slightly as he inclined his head in silent submission. At that moment the officer entered with his men at his heels.

"Arrest me that traitor," Maximilien commanded, pointing a shaking finger at Caron. "To the Luxembourg with him."

"If you will wait while I change my dressing-gown for a coat,

Citizen-officer," said La Boulaye composedly, "I shall be grateful."
Then, turning to his official, "Brutus," he called, "attend me."

He had an opportunity while Brutus was helping him into his coat to whisper in the fellow's ear:

"Let her know."

More he dared not say, but to his astute official that was enough, and with a sorrowful face he delivered to Suzanne, a few hours later, the news of La Boulaye's definite arrest and removal to the Luxembourg.

At Brutus's description of the scene there had been 'twixt Robespierre and Caron she sighed heavily, and her lashes grew wet.

"Poor, faithful La Boulaye!" she murmured. "God aid him now."

She bore the news to d'Ombreval, and upon hearing it he tossed aside the book that had been engrossing him and looked up, a sudden light of relief spreading on his weak face.

"It is the end," said he, as though no happier consummation could have attended matters, "and we have no more to wait for. Shall we set out to-day?" he asked, and urged the wisdom of making haste.

"I hope and I pray God that it may not be the end, as you so fondly deem it, Monsieur," she answered him. "But whether it is the end or not, I am resolved to wait until there is no room for any hope."

"As you will," he sighed wearily, "The issue of it all will probably be the loss of our heads. But even that might be more easily accomplished than to impart reason to a woman."

"Or unselfishness, it seems, to a man," she returned, as she swept angrily from the room.

CHAPTER XXII

THE TRIBUNAL

At the Bar of the Revolutionary Tribunal stood Deputy Caron La Boulaye upon his trial for treason to the Nation and contravention of the ends of justice. Fouquier-Tinville, the sleuth-hound Attorney-General, advanced his charges, and detailed the nature of the young revolutionist's crime. But there was in Fouquier-Tinville's prosecution a lack of virulence for once, just as among La Boulaye's fellows, sitting in judgment, there was a certain uneasiness, for the Revolution was still young, and it had not yet developed that Saturnian habit of devouring its own children which was later to become one of its main features.

The matter of La Boulaye's crime, however, was but too clear, and despite the hesitancy on the part of the jury, despite the unwonted tameness of Tinville's invective, the Tribunal's course was well-defined, and admitted of not the slightest doubt. And so, the production of evidence being dispensed with by Caron's ready concurrence and acknowledgment of the offence, the President was on the point of formally asking the jury for their finding, when suddenly there happened a commotion, and a small man in a blue coat and black-rimmed spectacles rose at Tinville's side, and began an impassioned speech for the defence.

This man was Robespierre, and the revolutionists sitting there listened to him in mute wonder, for they recalled that it was upon the Incorruptible's own charge their brother-deputy had been arrested. Ardently did Maximilien pour out his eloquence, enumerating the many virtues of the accused and dwelling at length upon his vast services to the Republic, his hitherto unfaltering fidelity to the nation and the people's cause, and lastly, deploring that in a moment of weakness he should have committed the indiscretion which had brought him where he stood. And against this thing of which he was now accused, Robespierre bade the Deputies of the jury balance the young man's past, and the much that he had done for the Revolution, and to offer him, in consideration of all that, a chance of making atonement and regaining the position of trust and of brotherly affection which for a moment he had forfeited.

The Court was stirred by the address. They knew the young sans-culotte's worth, and they were reluctant to pass sentence upon him and to send him to the death designed for aristocrats and traitors. And so they readily pronounced themselves willing to extend him the most generous measure of mercy, to open their arms and once more to clasp to their hearts the brother who had strayed and to reinstate him in their confidence and their councils. They pressed Robespierre to name the act of atonement by which he proposed La Boulaye should recover his prestige, and Robespierre in answer cried:

"Let him repair the evil he has done. Let him neutralise the treachery into which a moment of human weakness betrayed him. Let him return to us the aristocrat he has attempted to save, and we will forget his indiscretion and receive him back amongst us with open arms, as was the prodigal son received."

There was a salvo of applause. Men rose to their feet excitedly, and with arms outstretched in Caron's direction they vociferously implored him to listen to reason as uttered by the Incorruptible, to repent him and to atone while there was yet time. They loved him, they swore in voices of thunder, each seeking to be heard above his neighbour's din, and it would break their hearts to find him guilty, yet find him guilty they must unless he chose the course which this good patriot Maximilien pointed out to him.

La Boulaye stood pale but composed, his lips compressed, his keen eyes alert. Inwardly he was moved by this demonstration of goodwill, this very storm of fraternity, but his purpose remained adamant, and when at last the President's bell had tinkled his noisy judges into silence, his voice rose clear and steady as he thanked them for leaning to clemency on his behalf.

"Helas," he ended, "words cannot tell you how deeply I deplore that it is a clemency of which I may not avail myself. What I have done I may not undo. And so, Citizens, whilst I would still retain your love and your sympathy, you must suffer me to let justice take its course. To delay would be but to waste your time the Nation's time."

"But this is rank defiance," roared Tinvillle, roused at last into some semblance of his habitual bloodthirstiness. "He whose heart can be so insensible to our affections merits no clemency at this bar."

And so the President turned with a shrug to his colleagues, and the verdict was taken. The finding was "Guilty," and the President was on the point of passing sentence, when again Robespierre sprang to his feet. The Incorruptible's complexion looked sicklier than its wont, for mortification had turned him green outright. A gust of passion swept through his soul, such as would have made another man call for the death of this defiant youth who had withstood his entreaties. But such was Robespierre's wonderful command of self, such was his power of making his inclinations subservient to the ends he had in view that he had but risen to voice a fresh appeal.

He demanded that the sentence should be passed with the reservation that the accused should have twenty-four hours for reflection. Should he at the end of that time be disposed to tell them where the ci-devant Vicomte d'Ombreval was to be found, let them reconsider his case. On the other hand, should he still continue obdurate by the noon of to-morrow, then let the sentence be consummated.

There was some demur, but Robespierre swept it fiercely aside with patriotic arguments. La Boulaye was a stout servant of the Nation, whom it must profit France to let live that he might serve her; Ombreval was a base aristocrat, whose death all true Republicans should aim at encompassing. And so he won the day in the end, and when the sentence of death was passed, it was passed with the reservation that should the prisoner, upon reflection, be inclined to show himself more loyal to France and the interests of the Republic by telling them how Ornbreval might be recaptured, he would find them still inclined to mercy and forgiveness. Allowing his eyes to stray round the Court at that moment, La Boulaye started at sight of an unexpected face. It was Mademoiselle de Bellecour, deathly pale and with the strained, piteous look that haunts the eyes of the mad. He shivered at the thought of the peril to herself in coming into that assembly; then, recovering himself, he turned to his judges.

"Citizen-President, Citizens all, I thank you; but I should be unappreciative of your kindness did I permit you to entertain false hopes. My purpose is unalterable."

"Take him away," the President commanded impatiently, and as they removed him Mademoiselle crept from the Court, weeping softly in her poignant grief, and realising that not so much for the President's ear as for her own had La Boulaye uttered those words. They were meant to fortify her and to give her courage with the assurance that Ombreval would not be betrayed. To give her courage! Her lip was twisted into an oddly bitter smile at the reflection, as she stepped into her cabriolet, and bade the driver return to Choisy. Caron was doing this for her. He was casting away his young, vigorous life, with all its wealth of promise, to the end that her betrothed—the man whom he believed she loved—might be spared. The greatness, the nobility of the sacrifice overwhelmed her. She remembered the thoughts that in the past she had entertained concerning this young revolutionist. Never yet had she been able to regard him as belonging to the same order of beings as herself-not even when she had kissed his unconscious lips that evening on the

Ridge road. An immeasurable gulf had seemed to yawn between them—the gulf between her nobility and his base origin. And now, as her carriage trundled out of Paris and took the dusty high road, she shuddered, and her cheeks burned with shame at the memory of the wrong that by such thoughts she had done him. Was she, indeed, the nobler? By accident of birth, perhaps, but by nature proper he was assuredly the noblest man that ever woman bore.

In the Place de la Revolution a gruesome engine they called the guillotine was levelling all things, and fast establishing the reign of absolute equality. But with all the swift mowing of its bloody scythe, not half so fast did it level men as Mademoiselle de Bellecour's thoughts were doing that afternoon.

So marked was the disorder in her countenance when she reached Choisy that even unobservant Ombreval whom continuous years of self-complacency had rendered singularly obtuse—could not help but notice it, and—fearing, no doubt, that this agitation might in some way concern himself—he even went the length of questioning her, his voice sounding the note of his alarm.

"It is nothing," she answered, in a dejected voice. "At least, nothing that need cause you uneasiness. They have sentenced La Boulaye to death," she announced, a spasm crossing her averted face.

He took a deep breath of relief.

"God knows they've sentenced innocent men enough. It is high time they began upon one another. It augurs well-extremely well."

They were alone in Henriette's kitchen; the faithful woman was at market. Mademoiselle was warming herself before the fire. Ombreval stood by the window. He had spent the time of her absence in the care of his clothes, and he had contrived to dress himself with some semblance of his old-time elegance which enhanced his good looks and high-born air.

"You seem to utterly forget, Monsieur, the nature of the charge upon which he has been arraigned," she said, in a tired voice.

"Why, no," he answered, and he smiled airily; "he was sufficiently a fool to be lured by the brightest eyes in France into a service for their mistress. My faith! He's not the first by many a thousand whom a woman's soft glances have undone—"

"The degree in which you profit by the service he is doing those bright eyes, appears singularly beneath the dignity of your notice."

"What a jester you are becoming, ma mie," he laughed and at the sound she shuddered again and drew mechanically nearer to the fire as though her shuddering was the result of cold.

"It is yet possible that he may not die," she said almost as if speaking to herself. "They have offered him his liberty, and his reinstatement even—upon conditions."

"How interesting!" he murmured nonchalantly. "They have an odd way of dispensing justice."

"The conditions imposed are that he shall amend the wrong he has done, and deliver up to the Convention the person of one ci-devant Vicomte d'Ombreval."

"My God!"

It was a gasp of sudden dismay that broke from the young nobleman. The colour swept out of his face, and his eyes dilated with horror. Watching him Suzanne observed the sudden change, and took a fierce joy in having produced it.

"It interests you more closely now, Monsieur?" she asked.

"Suzanne," he cried, coming a step nearer, and speaking eagerly; "he knows my whereabouts. He brought me here himself. Are you mad, girl, that you can sit there so composedly and tell me this?"

"What else would you have me do?" she inquired.

"Do? Why, leave Choisy at once. Come; be stirring. In God's name, girl, bethink you that we have not a moment to lose. I know these Republicans, and how far they are to be trusted. This fellow would betray me to save his skin with as little compunction as—"

"You fool!" she broke in, an undercurrent of fierce indignation vibrating through her scorn. "What are you saying? He would betray you? He?" She tossed her arms to Heaven, and burst into a laugh of infinite derision. "Have no fear of that, M. le Vicomte, for you are dealing with a nature of a nobility that you cannot so much as surmise. If he were minded to betray you, why did he not do so to-day, when they offered him his liberty in exchange for information that would lead to your recapture?"

"But although he may have refused to-day," returned the Vicomte frenziedly, "he may think better of it to-morrow-perhaps even tonight. Ciel! Think of the risk we run; already it may be too late. Oh, why," he demanded reproachfully, "why didn't you listen to me when, days ago, I counselled flight?"

"Because it neither was, nor is, my intention to fly."

"What?" he cried, and, his jaw fallen and his eyes wide, he regarded her. Then suddenly he caught her by the arm and shook her roughly. "Are you mad?" he cried, in a frenzy of anger and fear. "Am I to die like a dog that a scum of a Republican may save his miserable neck? Is this canaille of a revolutionist to betray me to his rabble Tribunal?"

"Already have I told you that you need fear no betrayal."

"Need I not?" he sneered. "Ma foi! but I know these ruffians. There is not an ounce of honour in the whole National Convention."

"Fool!" she blazed, rising and confronting him with an anger before which he recoiled, appalled. "Do you dare to stand there and prate of honour—you? Do you forget why he stood his trial? Do you forget why he is dying, and can you not see the vile thing that you are doing in arguing flight, that you talk of honour thus, and deny his claim to it? Mon Dieu! Your effrontery stifles me! La Boulaye was right when he said that with us honour is but a word—just so much wind, and nothing more."

He stared at her in uncomprehending wonder. He drew away another step. He accounted her mad, and, that he might humour her, he put by his own fears for the moment—a wonderful unselfishness this in the most nobly-born Vicomte d'Ombreval.

"My poor Suzanne," he murmured. "Our trouble has demoralised your understanding. You take a false view of things. You do not apprehend the situation."

"In God's name, be silent!" she gasped.

"But the time is not one for silence," he returned.

"So I had thought," quoth she. "Yet since you can be silent and furtive in other matters, I beg that you will be silent in this also. You talk in vain, Monsieur, in any case. For I am not minded to leave Choisy. If you urge me further I shall burn our passport."

And with that she left him, to seek the solitude of her own room. In a passion of tears she flung herself upon the little bed, and there she lay, a prey to such an anguish as had never touched her life before.

And now, in that hour of her grief, it came to her—as the sun pierces the mist—that she loved La Boulaye; that she had loved him, indeed, since that night at Boisvert, although she had stifled the very thought, and hidden it even from herself, as being unworthy in one of her station to love a man so lowly-born as Caron. But now, on the eve of his death, the truth would no longer be denied. It cried, perchance, the louder by virtue of the pusillanimity of the craven below stairs in whose place Caron was to die; but anyhow, it cried so loudly that it overbore the stern voice of the blood that had hitherto urged her to exclude the sentiment from her heart. No account now did she take of any difference in station. Be she nobler a thousand times, be he simpler a thousand times, the fact remained that she was a woman, he a man, and beyond that she did not seek to go.

Low indeed were the Lilies of France when a daughter of the race of their upholders heeded them so little and the caste they symbolised.

Henriette came to her that afternoon, and, all ignorant of the sources of her grief, she essayed to soothe and comfort her, in which, at last, she succeeded.

In the evening Ombreval sent word that he wished to speak to her—and that his need was urgent. But she returned him the answer that she would see him in the morning. She was indisposed that evening, she added, in apology.

And in the morning they met, as she had promised him. Both pale, although from different causes, and both showing signs of having slept but little. They broke their fast together and in silence, which at last he ended by asking her whether the night had brought her reflection, and whether such reflection had made her appreciate their position and the need to set out at once.

"It needed no reflection to make me realise our position better than I did yesterday," she answered. "I had hoped that it would have brought you to a different frame of mind. But I am afraid that it has not done so."

"I fail to see what change my frame of mind admits of," he answered testily.

"Have you thought," she asked at last, and her voice was cold and concentrated, "that this man is giving his life for you?"

"I have feared," he answered, with incredible callousness, "that to save his craven skin he might elect to do differently at the last moment."

She looked at him in a mighty wonder, her dark eyes open to their widest, and looking black by the extreme dilation of the pupils. So vast was her amazement at this unbounded egotism that it almost overruled her disgust.

"You cast epithets about you and bestow titles with a magnificent unconsciousness of how well they might fit you."

"Ah? For example?"

"In calling this man a craven, you take no thought for the cowardice that actuates you into hiding while he dies for you?"

"Cowardice?" he ejaculated. Then a flush spread on his face. "Ma foi, Mademoiselle," said he, in a quivering voice, "your words betray thoughts that would be scarcely becoming in the Vicomtesse d'Ombreval."

"That, Monsieur, is a point that need give you little thought. I am not likely to become the Vicomtesse."

He bestowed her a look of mingling wonder and anger. Had he, indeed, heard her aright? Did her words imply that she disdained the honour?

"Surely," he gasped, voicing those doubts of his, "you do not mean that you would violate your betrothal contract? You do not—"

"I mean, Monsieur," she cut in, "that I will give myself to no man I do not love."

"Your immodesty," said he, "falls in nothing short of the extraordinary frame of mind that you appear to be developing in connection with other matters. We shall have you beating a drum and screeching the Ca ira in the streets of Paris presently, like Mademoiselle de Mericourt."

She rose from the table, her face very white, her hand pressing upon her corsage. A moment she looked at him. Then:

"Do not let us talk of ourselves," she exclaimed at last. "There is a man in the Conciergerie who dies at noon unless you are forthcoming before then to save him. He himself will not betray you because he—No matter why, he will not. Tell me, Monsieur, how do you, who account yourself a man of honour above everything, intend to deal with this situation?"

He shrugged his shoulders.

"Once he is dead and done with—provided that he does not first betray me—I trust that, no longer having this subject to harp upon, you will consent to avail yourself of our passport, and accompany me out of France."

"Honour does not for instance, suggest to you that you should repair to the Conciergerie and take the place that belongs to you, and which another is filling?"

A sudden light of comprehension swept now into his face.

"At last I understand what has been in your mind since yesterday, what has made you so odd in your words and manner. You have thought that it was perhaps my duty as a man of honour to go and effect the rescue of this fellow. But, my dear child, bethink you of what he is, and of what I am. Were he a gentleman—my equal—my course would stand clearly defined. I should not have hesitated a moment. But this canaille! Ma foi! let me beg of you to come to your senses. The very thought is unworthy in you."

"I understand you," she answered him, very coldly. "You use a coward's arguments, and you have the effrontery to consider yourself a man of honour—a nobleman. I no longer marvel that there is a revolution in France."

She stood surveying him for a moment, then she quietly left the room. He stared after her.

"Woman, woman!" he sighed, as he set down his napkin and rose in his turn.

His humour was one of pitying patience for a girl that had not the wit to see that to ask him—the most noble d'Ombreval—to die that La Boulaye might live was very much like asking him to sacrifice his life to save a dog's.

167

CHAPTER XXIII

THE CONCIERGERIE

It wanted but a few minutes to noon as the condemned of the day were being brought out of the Conciergerie to take their places in the waiting tumbrils. Fourteen they numbered, and there was a woman amongst them as composed as any of the men. She descended the prison steps in nonchalant conversation with a witty young man of some thirty years of age, who had been one of the ornaments of the prerevolutionary salons. Had the pair been on the point of mounting a wedding coach they could not have shown themselves in better spirits.

Aristocrats, too, were the remaining twelve, with one exception, and if they had not known how to live, at least they could set a very splendid example of how to die. They came mostly in pairs, and the majority of them emulating the first couple and treating the whole matter as a pleasantry that rather bored them by the element of coarseness introduced by the mob. One or two were pale, and their eyes wore a furtive, frightened look. But they valiantly fought down their fears, and for all that the hearts within them may have been sick with horror, they contrived to twist a smile on to their pale lips. They did not lack for stout patterns of high bearing, and in addition they had their own arrogant pride—the pride that had brought them at last to this pass—to sustain them in their extremity. Noblesse les obligeait. The rabble, the canaille of the new regime, might do what they would with their bodies, but their spirits they could not break, nor overcome their indomitable pride. By the brave manner of their death it remained for them to make amends for the atrocious manner of their lives, and such a glamour did they shed upon themselves by the same brave manner, that it compelled sympathy and admiration of those that beheld them, and made upon humanity an impression deep enough to erase the former impression left by their misdeeds.

Like heroes, like sainted martyrs, they died, these men who, through generation after generation, had ground and crushed the people 'neath the iron heel of tyranny and oppression, until the people had, of a sudden, risen and reversed the position, going to excesses, in their lately-awakened wrath, that were begotten of the excesses which for centuries they had endured.

Last of this gallant and spruce company (for every man had donned his best, and dressed himself with the utmost care) came

Caron La Boulaye. He walked alone, for although their comrade in death, he was their comrade in nothing else. Their heads might lie together in the sawdust of Sanson's basket, but while they lived, no contact would they permit themselves, of body or of soul, with this sans-culotte. Had they known why he died, perhaps, they had shown him fellowship. But in their nescience of the facts, it would need more than death to melt them into a kindness to a member of the Convention, for death was the only thing they had in common, and death, as we have seen, had not conquered them.

As he was about to pass out, a gaoler suddenly thrust forward a hand to detain him, and almost simultaneously the door, which had swung to behind the last of his death-fellows, re-opened to admit the dapper figure of the Incorruptible.

He eyed Caron narrowly as he advanced into the hall, and at the composure evident in the young man's bearing, his glance seemed to kindle with admiration, for all that his lips remained cruel in their tightened curves.

Caron gave him good-day with a friendly smile, and before Robespierre could utter a word the young man was expressing his polite regrets at having baulked him as he had done.

"I had a great object to serve, Maximilien," he concluded, "and my only regret is that it should have run counter to your wishes. I owe you so much—everything in fact—that I am filled with shame at the thought of how ill a return I am making you. My only hope is that by my death you will consider that I have sufficiently atoned for my ingratitude."

"Fool!" croaked Robespierre, "you are sacrificing yourself for some chimaera and the life you are saving is that of a very worthless and vicious individual. Of your ingratitude to me we will not speak. But even now, in the eleventh hour, I would have you bethink you of yourself."

He held out his hands to him, and entreaty was stamped upon Robespierre's countenance to a degree which perhaps no man had yet seen. "Bethink you, cher Caron—" he began again. But the young man shook his head.

"My friend, my best of friends," he exclaimed, "I beg that you will not make it harder for me. I am resolved, and your entreaties do but heighten my pain of thwarting your—the only pain that in this supreme hour I am experiencing. It is not a difficult thing to die, Maximilien. Were I to live, I must henceforth lead a life of unsatisfied desire. I must even hanker and sigh after a something that is unattainable. I die, and all this is extinguished with me. At the very prospect my desires fade immeasurably. Let me go in peace, and with your forgiveness."

169

Robespierre eyed him a moment or two in astonishment. Then he made an abrupt gesture of impatience.

"Fool that you are! It is suicide you are committing. And for what? For a dream a shadow. Is this like a man, Caron'? Is this— Will you be still, you animal?" he barked at a gaoler who had once before touched him upon the arm. "Do you not see that I am occupied?"

But the man leant forward, and said some words hurriedly into Robespierre's ear, which cast the petulance out of his face and mind, and caused him of a sudden to become very attentive.

"Ah?" he said at last. Then, with a sudden briskness: "Let the Citizen La Boulaye not go forth until I return," he bade the gaoler; and to Caron he said: "You will have the goodness to await my return."

With that he turned and stepped briskly across the hall and through the door, which the gaoler, all equality notwithstanding, hastened to open for him with as much servility as ever the haughtiest aristocrat had compelled.

Saving that single gaoler, La Boulaye was alone in the spacious hall of the Conciergerie. From without they heard the wild clamouring and Ca-iraing of the mob. Chafing at this fresh delay, which was as a prolongation of his death-agony, La Boulaye was pacing to and fro, the ring of his footsteps on the stone floor yielding a hollow, sepulchral echo.

"Is he never returning?" he cried at last; and as if in answer to his question, the drums suddenly began to roll, and the vociferations of the rabble swelled in volume and grew shriller. "What is that?" he inquired.

The gaoler, on whose dirty face some measure of surprise was manifested, approached the little grating that overlooked the yard and peered out.

"Sacrenom!" he swore. "The tumbrils are moving. They have left you behind, Citizen."

But La Boulaye gathered no encouragement, such as the gaoler thought he might, from that contingency. He but imagined that it was Robespierre's wish to put him back for another day in the hope that he might still loosen his tongue. An oath of vexation broke from him, and he stamped his foot impatiently upon the floor.

Then the door opened suddenly, and Robespierre held it whilst into the room came a woman, closely veiled, whose tall and shapely figure caused the young Deputy's breath to flutter. The Incorruptible followed her, and turning to the gaoler:

"Leave us," he commanded briskly.

And presently, when those three stood alone, the woman

raised her veil and disclosed the face he had expected—the beautiful face of Suzanne de Bellecour, but, alas! woefully pale and anguished of expression. She advanced a step towards Caron, and then stood still, encountering his steadfast, wonder-struck gaze, and seeming to falter. With a sob, at last she turned to Maximilien, who had remained a pace or two behind.

"Tell him, Monsieur," she begged.

Robespierre started out of his apparent abstraction. He peered at her with his short-sighted eyes, and from her to Caron. Then he came forward a step and cleared his throat, rather as a trick of oratory than to relieve any huskiness.

"To put it briefly, my clear Caron," said he, "the Citoyenne here has manifested a greater solicitude for your life than you did yourself, and she has done me the twofold service of setting it in my power to punish an enemy, and to preserve a friend from a death that was very imminent. In the eleventh hour she came to me to make terms for your pardon. She proposed to deliver up to me the person of the ci-devant Vicomte d'Ombreval provided that I should grant you an unconditional pardon. You can imagine, my good Caron, with what eagerness I agreed to her proposal, and with what pleasure I now announce to you that you are free."

"Free!" gasped La Boulaye, his eyes travelling fearfully from Robespierre to Mademoiselle, and remaining riveted upon the latter as though he were attempting to penetrate into the secrets of her very soul.

"Practically free," answered the Incorruptible. "You may leave the Conciergerie when you please, thought I shall ask you to remain at your lodging in the Rue Nationale until this Ombreval is actually taken. Once he has been brought to Paris, I shall send you your papers that you may leave France, for, much though I shall regret your absence, I think that it will be wiser for you to make your fortune elsewhere after what has passed."

La Boulaye took a step in Suzanne's direction.

"You have done this?" he cried, in a quivering voice. "You have betrayed the man to whom you were betrothed?"

"Do not use that word, Monsieur," she cried, with a shudder. "My action cannot be ranked among betrayals. He would have let you go to the guillotine in his stead. He had not the virtue to come forward, for all that he knew that you must die if he did not. On the contrary, such a condition of things afforded him amusement, matter to scorn and insult you with. He would have complacently allowed a dozen men to have gone to the guillotine that his own worthless life might have been spared.

"But he was your betrothed!" La Boulaye protested.

"True!" she made answer; "but I had to choose between the man it had been arranged I should marry and the man I loved." A flush crimsoned her cheek, and her voice sank almost to a whisper. "And to save the man I love I have delivered up Ombreval."

"Suzanne"

The name burst from his lips in a shout of wonder and of joy ineffable. In a stride he seemed to cover the distance between them, and he caught her to him as the door slammed on the discreetly departing Robespierre.

www.ingramcontent.com/pod-product-compliance
Lightning Source LLC
Chambersburg PA
CBHW052133170626
46812CB00004B/1391

* 9 7 8 1 6 3 6 3 7 5 3 0 4 *